The Bodyguards

Geraint Wyn Jones

The old, old story... as you've never heard it before.

PALESTINE

Mediterranean Sea
Sepphoris
Tiberias
Nazareth
Jezreel Valley
Jordan River
Jerusalem
Bethlehem
Judean Desert
(The Devastation)
Dead
Sea
Lisan Peninsula
(The Tongue)
0 10 20 30 40 mi
0 20 40 60 km

The Main Characters, in Order of Appearance

Gilchrist, captain of a select unit of warrior angels.
Cadman, his deputy.
Joram, a member of the unit.
Ebin, another member of the unit.
Caleb, the fifth member of the unit.
Abdallah, a merchant.
Mibsam, a captain in the Angel Armies.
Archangel Michael, leader of the Angel Armies.
Gabriel, the chief messenger angel.
Axa, conductor of the Angel Choir.
Tiras, his assistant.
Dylan, a member of the Angel Choir.
Sabta, Gether and Duma, Dylan's best friends.
Nathanael, captain of the guard at the gates of Bethlehem.
Shobal, his deputy.
Jedah, a beggar in Bethlehem.
Nidab, his friend, also a beggar.
Sandon, leader of the demons at Bethlehem's gates.
Mary, mother of Jesus.
Joseph, her betrothed and then, her husband.
Amos, an old bachelor who lives in Nazareth.
Ben, Mary's father.
Abigail, Mary's mother.
Antonin, a leading demon.
Lorcan, captain of a small unit of angel warriors.
Abida, his deputy.
Jonathon, a member of the unit.
Peleg, the fourth member of the unit.
Habilah, a demon, under Sandon's command.
Marzan, another demon under Sandon's command.
Seth, an old man, owner of a mule and cart.
Sabteka, an angel warrior.
Benaiah, an innkeeper in Bethlehem.

Ashtenaz, Riphthal, Tograman and Hazarm, four cruel demons.
Kandar, a leading demon.
Meshek, a captain in the Angel Armies.
Keenan, a captain in the Angel Armies.

Prologue

Gilchrist lay, deathly still on the arid ground. Though lying prone, he had a sweeping view of the surrounding land for he lay atop a huge rock escarpment. Far ahead, the sun slipped over the edge of the horizon. It had tried its best to prolong the day, throwing out finger-like rays in a vain attempt to hang on. As if furious yet again at its daily eviction, it turned the sky a raging red. It had had its day, but it would have others. Soon after, the sky changed into a twilight blue which deepened by degrees until it became black, accentuating the full white moon now playing the starring role, along with its accompanying cast of stars. Gilchrist felt a sultry breeze on his cheek blowing in from the vast Negev desert, to the south. Had the air been a freezing wind from the Siberian tundra it would have made no difference to him. Hot or cold, wet or dry, angels are immune to the vagaries of climate.

He looked towards where the breeze blew from. Although he could not see it from his vantage point, he knew that the barren, sandy landscape stretched southwards towards the terrible Sinai Desert that covered a large proportion of the peninsula that bore the same name. This was where the Hebrew nation, some 1,300 years earlier, had wandered for nigh on thirty-eight years, after escaping from Egypt. Who in their right minds, he wondered, would choose to live in the desolate environs of the Sinai Desert for so long when the proverbial land of milk and honey of Canaan was on offer?

The sparse, deserted landscape stretched before him. Escarpments and plateaus dominated the silhouetted scenery. Directly beneath him was the northern end of the infamous Scorpion's Pass, a treacherous descent in the middle part of the perfume route from Petra to Memphis, in southern Judah. It was a steep drop, along a series of sharp hairpin bends. These bends had to be negotiated with the utmost care or else one could easily topple over the edge. That would have meant almost certain death as one's body would be tossed and battered by the jagged rocks and sharp stones that clung to the sides. At certain junctures ugly rock faces protruded as if some giant had chiselled them with no regard for form or symmetry. In other places it seemed his huge hands had banked up massive mounds of sand against these ludicrously formed stony outcrops in a vain attempt to hide his embarrassing and dire attempts at rock sculpture. Then, in other places, rocky crags raced along the verges of the path, berating the travellers' insolence, for trespassing on the Scorpion's territory. It was as if they were angry that the rocky landscape had been disfigured merely to facilitate human travellers. The path was forbidding, yet its panorama left one breathless. It had a desolate, deserted beauty that stretched endlessly as far as the eye could see. Since hardly anyone lived here, the contours of the land had been left alone to develop of their own accord, free from the interference of man's indelicate and uncaring ways. Here and there, tussocks of coarse grass protruded from the ground, wafting to and fro in the warm breeze as if bending down and then standing tall for a respite from their mirth at anyone foolish enough to attempt to negotiate the pass. The only other vegetation was the occasional acacia tree, with its long narrow trunks sprouting forth short branches with thick green foliage, like small erupting geysers, standing forlornly, but defiantly in the parched ground.

Less than a foot from where Gilchrist lay a desert hedgehog scurried across the sand grateful that the blistering heat of the day had now abated somewhat. He was intrigued by its distinctive dark muzzle and wide, white band which stretched across its face and beyond, along both sides of its short torso. It was nature's war paint for the little hedgehog was a fearsome fighter. Then, a long-eared bat flitted hurriedly through the air. It was ironic that these two creatures had made an appearance so near to the Scorpion's Pass since both ate scorpions. Astonishingly, the flying mammal would bite the predatory arachnid's head off when fighting it. Accompanying sounds merely added to the intimidating and inhospitable nature of the environment. Loudest of all was the deranged chattering laugh of a striped hyena that could be heard in the far distance. These sounds were amplified tenfold and more by the stillness of the night. Such were the fearful, nocturnal killers of the desert night now keeping Gilchrist company. They were not the only lethal fighters present though.

Four other angels – Cadman, Joram, Ebin and Caleb – lay beside him. All five were soldiers in the Angel Armies of Heaven. Together, they formed an elite band of warrior angels that fought constant battles against Satan's spirit agents on behalf of God, the Lord of the Angel Armies. Lean and wiry, all five, except for Ebin, were shorter than the towering size one would expect of an angel. However, with rugged, grizzled faces, battle worn hands and arms and dishevelled clothing, they were a fearsome sight. They were also, utterly devoted in their service to their Lord.

Cadman and Ebin lay to Gilchrist's right. Cadman, Gilchrist's trusted lieutenant, had a sculpted face and golden brown, wavy hair that fell casually over his ears. His alert, blue eyes gave the impression of one who was perpetually ready for action. He was an angel of few words but his deeds were many. Two quivers full of arrows were slung across his back, but curiously, he had no bow. Bulkier and taller than the others, Ebin's thick forearms hinted at his immense strength. His hair was cut dangerously close to his scalp though his genial face and especially his button nose hinted at his benevolent nature. Joram lay the other side of Gilchrist. His rugged appearance and fierce eyes belied his caring temperament. He was a consummate disguiser so cool under pressure: even his eyes took an age to blink. He and Gilchrist both had long hair, but their manes were formidably tousled and knotted, like a horse's tail after a wild desert storm. Then, the other side of Joram lay Caleb.

They had been brought together as a fighting unit in the years before David had become king of Israel, some nine hundred years earlier. They had been assigned to protect him, especially during his troubled reign. However, they did not get to experience the glory years of his son and successor, Solomon. Once David had passed away they had immediately been tasked with protecting some other people on the other side of the world. Ever since, a close and intimate bond had grown between the five, all respectful and admiring of each other's particular talents and gifts.

Like all other angels, they were spirits, wingless wonders, created to serve God with the speed of an arrow and the intensity of fire. They had seen action all over the world and beyond. Selflessly dedicated to their Lord, withholding nothing in His service, every demon feared them. They were also admired by fellow warrior angels for their guile, ingenuity and creativity when on assignment. Consequently, they had often been hand-picked to perform particularly onerous tasks that required their especial skills. More often than not, those tasks involved protecting certain people. And that was precisely why they were lying on the bare ground at that moment.

They had been dispatched by the Archangel Michael, their commander, to protect Abdallah, a part-Idumean, part-Nabatean merchant from Petra, who was on his way to the aforementioned Memphis. He was by no means a work of art. Even his mother would have concurred. The most eye-catching part of his physique was his rather large belly. He was attached, both physically – obviously – and emotionally to it. Its size was a sign of his prosperity: over the years, as his worth had grown so had his girth. His wife also liked it, since it meant he could not get too close to her face when he was in his more amorous moods. Time had eroded much of his attraction. Other, younger men in her immediate vicinity in Petra appeared more enticing by the day: she was beginning to develop serious detachment issues. What little affection she had for her husband had been snuffed out a long time ago though his wealth still held her in its thrall. She found that irresistibly alluring! It was good now to have his stomach as a buffer between her and her husband.

Unbeknown to Abdallah, the five warrior angels had escorted him all the way from Petra. And while they were perched on the escarpment, he was making his way down the Scorpion's Trail with six other merchants. They were all grateful that the sun had disappeared and their eyes could relax after the blazing sunset had made their precarious descent that much more difficult. They travelled as a group since great comfort was derived from safety in numbers. However, they would have been unable to do much if bandits had set upon them. And that was what was on Gilchrist's mind as he observed the gang of around twenty brigands who were hiding behind the base of the escarpment, at the bottom of the trail. Abdallah and his co-travellers were still some fifteen minutes away, intent on getting to the bottom of the pass in order to set up camp on the flat plain that would take them to Memphis a few days later.

The angels had already decided how they would deal with the situation. The imminent threat of the outlaws was in itself, a trivial matter, easily dealt with. Gilchrist, Cadman and Joram would simply appear to them. By so doing they would frighten the living daylights out of them and they would flee the scene. Of more pressing concern was the small mob of ten renegade angels that had trailed along with the bandits. It was plain to see that these angels of Satan had the thieves in their grip and were mere playthings for them, much as a cat would toy with a mouse before devouring it. Frightening the thieves away would succeed only in postponing the inevitable, for they would still be the rebel angels' vassals. Abdallah and his fellow travellers had a few more days' travelling before they reached Memphis: plenty of opportunity for the thieves to strike again. The renegade angels had to be dealt with as well.

It was time for them to make their move. Gilchrist felt his being quickly tense. It was an involuntary reaction prior to any combat, which he welcomed. It reassured him that his senses were on heightened alert and that his reactions would be keen and sharp. He also knew the others would be experiencing the same emotions.

'Ready?' he whispered.

They all nodded, except for Caleb. He had been restlessly fidgeting and twitching for the last half hour – as he always did when on the verge of a violent encounter with any demons – eager to get at them. Gilchrist had never come across an angel with such a short distance between his brain and his mouth. He would often embarrass or irritate the other angels in the unit, in particular his long-suffering best friend, Ebin. Shorter than the others, due in no small part to his stupendously bowed legs, he always felt that he was at a disadvantage. Probably, as a consequence of this he always tied his long blonde hair back in a bun. Indeed, he would tie it back so tight shallow furrows would appear on his forehead. Along with the pallid colour of his face, this made him look like an anaemic melon. Hence, his nickname, Melon Head. However, Gilchrist, his commander, always called him by his proper name. He, himself was convinced his appearance made him look more threatening to the angels of the enemy. The other four angels indulged him with that misconception. They willingly conceded though, that he was a threat because of his fighting skills, rather than his intimidating face.

'Ebin! Caleb! You go.'

Caleb grunted, as if to say, 'About time an' all.'

They both left, careful not to show themselves to the enemy.

For years these two had worked together before coming under Gilchrist's command. During down time they would go off and hunt demons engaging them in violent skirmishes, habitually inflicting grievous demonic harm on them, to their immense satisfaction.

Seconds later, Gilchrist gave the order to fly down. Jumping off the escarpment, the three angels let themselves drop gracefully to the bottom where the bandits lay in wait. Just as they were about to land on the ground they made themselves visible. Most of the brigands were standing, talking quietly in small clusters, waiting patiently to jump on the approaching merchants. Consequently, most of them did not see Gilchrist, Cadman and Joram. But a handful of them did see them.

The blood drained from their faces. They moved their lips to speak, but generated no sound. They were like empty bellows, puffing vacant air. The only thing they could manage to do by way of communication was to raise their arms and point. The others turned to look. Their faces turned a shade of white. They froze. Their initial impulse was to run. They couldn't. It was as if they had each been lying on their backs for a whole year, their bodies cased in solidified mud. Their brains were active, aware of the situation, sending urgent messages to retreat. And although their muscles and joints were receiving these desperate despatches but were not responding to central command.

Gilchrist leant forward and poked one of them with his finger.

It was as if he had hit each one of them with a hammer. The caked mud cracked and fell to the ground in thousands of pieces. With one movement, they all turned and ran and ran as fast as they could, as far as they could.

The Satanic angels had been lounging on the ground a little distance away. Hideous in their appearance with a repugnant stench emanating from every pore in their beings, they had been looking forward to the sport that was about to happen as their band of thieves attacked the merchants. They were caught completely unawares. Seeing their pawns dispersing so quickly and panicky like hens skittering from a fox, they jumped to their feet. Only then did they see Gilchrist, Cadman and Joram standing before them, resplendent in their dazzling, angelic glory. Their initial thoughts were to fly away, before they realised that they were only three and there were ten of them. One by one, they were all emboldened and walked threateningly towards the warriors, their talons glinting in the stark moonlight. Surely, ten demons could defeat three warrior angels.

'Is this an exclusive party, or can anyone join in the fun?,' asked Caleb from behind.

The demons stopped in their tracks. They turned and saw two more warrior angels smiling benignly at them. They recognised one of them as Caleb, from his melon-like features. The confidence they felt just a few seconds earlier dissipated like a rain cloud in the scorching heat of the Negev Desert. They were trapped. There was nowhere to run, nowhere to hide, no choice but to stand and fight. They tensed themselves, ready for battle.

'Okay, everybody, fall back. Your turn, boss,' announced Joram to Gilchrist.

'You sure?' asked Caleb.

'Definite.'

'How come?' he persisted.

'The last time he got to fight was when he beat up those demons in Rome.'

'Yes, but what about the ones in the Judean Desert?' queried Ebin.

'That was a while after Rome and you did the honours then, and you know it,' replied Joram.

The demons looked on in confusion. Cadman was plainly irritated.

'We're always doing this. How many times have I said? We need to sort these things out before we pick a fight. It isn't fair on them,' he said, gesturing towards the demons.

'You're right,' conceded Gilchrist. 'Next time, we decide who does the fighting before we do anything.'

'So, let's get on with it,' said Cadman, stepping back. 'Your turn, Gilchrist.'

Up until now, Gilchrist had remained anonymous. Hearing his name, the demons trembled a little. They paid more attention and for the first time noticed how majestically powerful he looked. Even though he was no taller than the others, he was certainly the most imposing. His face exuded a self-possessed confidence, with its carved cheekbones and pronounced jaw; his bright, blue eyes piercing. As much as he was relaxed, they became tense. One or two, if not more, stole worried glances at each other.

'Oh, you didn't realise who he is,' said Joram in an affected voice. He had noticed a sudden apprehension in the demons' shifting eyes.

'We thought you knew it was Gilchrist,' added Ebin.

If this indeed was the legendary Gilchrist, then they were in deep trouble. They had heard stories about him. His fighting exploits on behalf of the Lord of the Angel Armies were both numerous and legendary. He was feared by all demons because he wielded his bright, dazzling sword with the accuracy and deftness of a practised surgeon, knowing precisely where to cut and slit to inflict the most damage to his assailants. Agile and nimble on his feet, even in the most restricted of spaces, he would glide effortlessly amongst his foes, all the while, inflicting the greatest injury. He would stand as a beacon in the heat of battle, never wavering, secure and confident in his abilities.

The other four angels walked to the rocks at the base of the escarpment, to sit down. The demons drew their swords and shouting obscenities, they flew at Gilchrist. To the warrior angel, whose senses and reflexes were so finely honed from numerous encounters with demon warriors in the past, everything happened in ultra-slow motion. Like a fly avoiding the swipe of a human hand, he easily evaded the sluggish thrusts and lunges of his pedestrian enemies, ducking and weaving in an elegant ballet of evasion. He let them continue their vain attempts to hurt him until he grew tired of the play fighting.

Then, he relaxed and let his shoulders drop. The other four warriors knew what that meant: evasion was about to turn into attack. It was as if he had expelled air, unburdening himself of any unnecessary weight thereby facilitating the utmost speed of movement. Gilchrist knew their weak points and sought to exploit these so as to bring things to an end. He was mindful that Abdallah and his co-travellers would be arriving soon.

Two demons flew directly at him at shoulder height, their swords aiming for his head. The one to his right was slightly in front of the other. He swiftly pulled his own sword from its sheath and parried the first demon's sword. Stepping to one side he delivered a short, sharp jab to his throat, with his fist. The demon's first thought was that he had been decapitated. As it was, he stopped mid-air clutching his throat, spluttering for breath. He slumped to his knees. In less than a heartbeat, Gilchrist brought his sword crashing down in a wide arc on the other demon's sword. Losing hold of his weapon the demon stopped in his tracks and turned to face Gilchrist. He couldn't believe how he had managed to move so easily from one point to the other. In that instant, the warrior stabbed his thumb hard into his eye. Blinded and incapacitated, he screamed in anguish.

Four more demons rushed at him. Again, Gilchrist used his weapon to parry the closest adversary's sword to one side before dancing a quick one-two step on the ball of his foot. As he did so, he sharply lifted the other. He waited barely a perceptible split-second for the demon to breathe in. He hit him hard with the heel of his foot in the solar plexus. Such a hit usually left the afflicted gasping for air, but this was even more intense since it was delivered as he breathed in. He should have been howling with pain: he couldn't for he could not breathe. The next demon in line came hurtling towards him. Gilchrist sped at him, parried his sword to one side and swung his right fist, striking him on his temple, leaving him totally disorientated. The last two of the gang of four demons were upon him, swords outstretched. Gilchrist suddenly took off and did a swift backward somersault. As he swung his feet upwards he simultaneously kicked either demon sharply under the chin. Their whole beings catapulted backwards, uprooting their feet and smashing the backs of their heads against the ground.

Only four left.

Caleb, unable to resist the temptation, left the other three warriors. He crept up behind one of the demons standing in the shadows, a little away from the others. He was getting more and more worried seeing Gilchrist getting the better of his colleagues. Tapping him on the shoulder Caleb greeted him.

'You're an ugly brute. Let's see if we can make you look more presentable.'

The last three demons attacked Gilchrist all at once, in triangular formation. He quickly sheathed his weapon. Cadman, Joram and Ebin lifted their heads wondering what on earth he was doing. Effortlessly, Gilchrist took off and flew at his adversaries. In one sweeping move, he smashed the sole of his foot in one demon's face. As he did he bounced off his head and launched himself at the next one. As he got near to him, he jerked his left knee back and cracked the sole of his foot against his head, snapping it backwards. Rebounding off the second demon's head, he then swung his right foot round to hit the last one's temple hard with his instep. Three shuddering blows had been meted out in the bat of an eyelid. The three angels sitting on the rocks winced at the damage inflicted on the demons. They had not seen this particular move before and were astounded at their captain's combat skills.

Gilchrist landed on his feet again. He realised there had been ten demons and he had only dealt with nine. He looked around.

'Where's the tenth...?' he asked himself.

It was then that he saw Caleb.

'Sorry, boss, you looked like you needed some help.'

With his right hand, Caleb was holding the last demon's fist and with a whip of his own hand propelled him away, but only as far as his arm's length, before pulling him back suddenly towards him. He then struck the demon's fist against his own face. He was powerless to stop the painful self-pummelling. This strange kind of three-part movement continued with the demon involuntarily rearranging his own face.

'That's enough, Caleb,' Gilchrist said quietly.

Caleb stopped immediately and let the demon drop to the ground.

The whole episode had only lasted three or four seconds at most.

Cadman, Joram and Ebin uttered admiring 'Bravos', and clapped their hands.

'Thank you, thank you, thank you,' responded Caleb, bowing in front of them, like a seasoned actor, milking the applause.

'Not you,' retorted Joram. 'It was for the boss.'

'Why should we applaud you?' added Ebin. 'This was the boss' turn.'

Caleb shrugged his shoulders sheepishly.

'I couldn't help myself.'

'Always want to be in on the action,' chided Ebin.

Gilchrist heard Abdallah and the other merchants approaching.

'Ebin, chuck 'em,' he said, pointing at the prostrate demons, 'but don't throw them too far.'

Ebin stepped forward to pick up the rebel angels and one by one, threw them up in the air far into space. Where they landed only they would know, but neither Ebin nor the other angels were concerned.

No sooner had he cleared the battlefield than Abdallah and the other traders appeared from behind the escarpment, having safely navigated the final stretch of the Scorpion's Trail. They set up camp in the exact spot where the skirmish had just occurred. Makeshift tents were erected, food was prepared and the weary travellers spent the rest of the night trying to outbid each other as regards who had made the greatest profit on their last journey together.

Everyone, that is, except for Abdallah. He was pensive, keeping his thoughts to himself. He was convinced that should they have this debate on their next journey together, then he would easily lay claim to the most amount of money made from this particular trip. He was the first to retire and the others soon followed. They needed to be up and gone at the crack of dawn.

Days later, the small party arrived at Memphis. Memphis was an important caravan stop on the incense route from southern Arabia to Mediterranean ports, such as Gaza. However, for many years, Ishmael, Abdallah's contact in Memphis, had shunned those routes, preferring to trade with merchants in the East. The risks may have been greater, but the profits he could make were stupendous. As it happened, Ishmael intended leaving for the East in a matter of days, and wouldn't return for another year at least. The timing was perfect. They struck a deal and Abdallah secured a handsome price for the goods he had brought. He couldn't have been happier. As he left Ishmael's house, Gilchrist and his warriors, made way for him to walk over to his lodgings.

'Right, another job done,' declared Ebin.

'What's next?' Joram asked Gilchrist.

'We go back...'

Before he could finish his sentence he paused and watched, as a small unit of warrior angels descend from the sky. The others turned to look. Mibsam, who, like Gilchrist, was a captain in the Angel Armies landed next to them with his warriors. Neither unit had seen each other for some time and were pleased to reacquaint themselves. There was a lot of leg-pulling, mainly at Caleb's expense. Then, Gilchrist asked Mibsam what he and his warriors were doing there.

'We've been sent by Michael to escort Ishmael to the East.'

'Why didn't he get us to do that?'

'Dunno,' answered Mibsam. 'But you're all to return to heaven immediately. He has another mission for you.'

The five warriors looked at each other.

'We'd better get going then,' said Gilchrist.

'You know, I've been thinking,' Caleb started.

'Hold on, now. You need at least two brain cells to do that,' Ebin reasoned.

'Two more than you've got,' was his friend's ready retort.

The other angels grinned, all except his commander.

'What's bothering you, Caleb?'

Caleb crinkled his nose, ignoring his friend.

'Well, if Abdallah's a merchant, he didn't have much stuff to sell, other than those two bags made of goat's hair slung across his donkey's back. I saw what was inside 'em the other night when he opened 'em for the others to see.'

'And?' asked Gilchrist.

'They were full of nick knacks. Some of it was more like tat, if you ask me.'

'Well, whatever,' said Gilchrist, 'our job was to make sure he arrived safely in Memphis.'

Caleb ignored him.

'So, why were we guarding him?'

Gilchrist didn't bother trying answering his question, for the simple reason, he didn't know.

'Right, come on, we'd better get going.'

They bid their farewells and the five warriors took off and sped back to heaven, with Caleb still muttering to himself,

'I'd have liked to have known why we had to look after him.'

The truth of the matter was, they had not been sent to ensure Abdallah's safety, but rather the safety of what he was carrying.

A few weeks earlier Abdallah, which meant servant of God in Arabic – although he considered himself to be no servant of God or any man, other than himself – had met up with Hasib. Hasib was his contact from the narrow coastal strip of land far to the south, beyond the Arabian Desert. When Hasib had arrived at his house in Petra, he delicately placed a small crystal in the palm of his hand. The perfume was exquisite. In all his years of trading this crystal Abdallah had never come across such a sweet, citrusy fragrance. He knew enough about the process of collecting the resin from the trees, that tapping was performed no more than three times a year and that the final taps yielded the best tears. For some reason, unknown to Abdallah, the cloudier and more opaque the resin the better the quality. The resin this crystal had come from must have been as murky as mud. He looked at Hasib who had smiled back at him triumphantly. He knew Abdallah was hooked. He'd have to have it. Abdallah was even more delighted when Hasib informed him that the two bags of produce this sample had come from, were the only ones available, and at that very moment, they were slung across the back of his camel, that was standing outside Abdallah's front door.

That night, after the transaction had been completed, Abdallah lay in his bed, his wife snoring gently beside him. He pondered how to get the best price for this astounding piece of merchandise. He would take it along the secondary perfume route to Memphis in southern Judah. He had a contact there – Ishmael – who had long done business with men in Persia, whose wealth was beyond his imagining. Abdallah knew this fine product was highly desirable to them. Travelling to Memphis would mean having to traverse the notorious Scorpion's Pass, but the prospect of high returns far outweighed the risks. Although it was another muggy night, he soon fell sound asleep, cushioned by the mounds of money he was to make from this venture.

When, eventually he arrived in Memphis, under angel escort, he had immediately sought out Ishmael. Once inside his house he produced the small jar from the secret pocket of his tunic, containing the sample Hasib had brought. Ishmael was as struck as he had been: he simply had to have it! Then, Abdallah went to fetch the two sacks from the back of his donkey. Once he returned, without uttering a word, he opened one of them. On seeing the cheap gems, Ishmael felt frustrated.

'Abdallah!' he started to protest.

He, merely lifted his finger bidding him be quiet.

Carefully, he shifted the cheap goods to one side to reveal the crystals beneath. With a wide smile he repeated the very same words Hasib had spoken to him, back in Petra.

'These are the only crystals from this resin.'

Ishmael nodded his head in satisfaction. He knew of a number of wealthy men who would bid large sums of money for what was in the sacks. Abdallah named his price, and Ishmael gladly paid it, knowing in his heart that when he arrived in any of the eastern courts he could demand a much higher price for it.

And so, having sold the merchandise to Ishmael, Abdallah had unwittingly lived up to, and honoured his name as a worthy servant of God. For what he had bought from Hasib was nothing less than the finest frankincense he had ever come across. The southern rim of the Arabian Peninsula was renowned throughout the known world for the frankincense trees that grew there. Their produce had been solely responsible for the development of the Silk Road to China and the trade routes between southern Arabia and the Mediterranean and India. Now taken by Ishmael and guarded by Mibsam and his warriors, it would end its journey in the courts of a certain wise man in the East. That would not be the end of its journey, though. Frankincense spoke of divinity and in around two years' time, that same wise man would return the crystals westwards as a precious gift for Jesus, the Infant Priest.

Chapter 1

'Well, what was her reaction?'

Gabriel, God's chief messenger angel, had just returned to heaven from earth. He had conveyed the startling news to Mary that she had been chosen by God to carry Jesus in her womb. He had proceeded directly to Michael's Hall to report to the archangel, who had been on the edge of his seat – literally – waiting for Gabriel's return.

'She hardly flinched. She queried me on a few things, in particular the biological improbability of her becoming pregnant, she being a virgin.'

Gabriel stole a glance at Michael, and noticed a smidgen of discomfort in his manner. He was taller than most other warriors in the Lord's Angel Army and had been invested with outrageous might and power, by God, as befitted the archangel of the heavenly host. Every part of his being radiated strength and authority. Nothing unnerved him. However, his usual calm exterior highlighted by his smooth, even complexion, creased a little at the edges. He appeared flustered and ruffled. Obviously, he was taken aback by her plain speaking.

'I see,' he said. 'No beating about the bush then.'

'No.'

'What did you say?'

Gabriel shrugged his shoulders.

'I told her that the Holy Spirit would come on her and the power of the Most High would overshadow her.'

'Best to keep it simple, aye?' offered Michael.

'Yes.'

There were a few seconds of silence. The archangel brushed away a wisp of his thick, wavy hair that had strayed onto his face.

'I'm glad you took this message to her and not me.'

'I'm glad as well,' smiled Gabriel in response. 'She's an incredible young woman. She just accepted what I said, and that was that.'

'Do you think she'd not understood the enormity of what's about to happen to her?'

'Yes, she knew full well – I'm convinced'

'People are going to talk.'

'Probably.'

'Wasn't she concerned?'

'It seemed to me she was more concerned about what God thought of her.'

Michael was impressed.

'What did she say when you told her that her cousin was six months pregnant?'

'She was a little shocked, because she knew as well as everybody else that Elizabeth had been unable to conceive, but...'

'But?'

'She accepted it. When I told her that nothing was impossible for God, it was obvious she already knew and believed that. Do you want to know the last thing she said to me?'

Michael looked at Gabriel expectantly.

' "I am the Lord's servant. May it happen just as you say".'

'Remarkable girl.'

The archangel suddenly thought of something.

'What about her fiancé, Joseph, the carpenter?'

'She'll tell him at the right time. She has a wise head on young shoulders.'

'I wonder what his reaction will be,' pondered Michael.

'Could be awkward.'

'Are you ready for that?'

'Yes, but Gilchrist and his warriors need to be in place.'

'We have a week of earth time before Jesus leaves. Remind me, when did we call them back to heaven?'

'Two weeks ago.'

'And they've been here ever since – confined to barracks – shall we say,' Michael said, with a wry smile on his face. 'I'm sure they're chomping at the bit, and wondering why they've been kicking their heels for so long.'

'They're a little restless, to say the least.'

'Right, the time has come to tell them. We have a week to go,' Michael said purposefully, before lowering his tone to say, 'and I think it's time to have a word with Axa as well, don't you think?'

'Certainly,' agreed Gabriel, with a knowing smile.

'Reu! Elum!' called Michael.

Two angels, who had been standing by the doorway to Michael's Hall strode towards him.

‘Elum, go fetch Axa. Tell him I want to see him immediately. Turning to Reu he said, ‘Stay outside, but once Axa leaves after our meeting fetch Gilchrist and his angels.’

Reu returned to his post, but Elum didn’t move. Michael stared at him inquiringly.

‘You know choir practice is to start soon. He’s resting in preparation. He won’t like being disturbed,’ explained Elum.

Michael looked at Gabriel.

‘He’ll want to hear what I’ve got to say to him, rest or no rest. Now, go, quickly!’

No sooner was the word said than Elum raced along the corridors of heaven to Axa’s rooms.

Chapter 2

Elum did indeed find Axa resting on his bed in readiness for choir rehearsal.

'Axa! Archangel Michael sends an invitation for you to join him in his hall.'

Axa turned to look at Elum.

'Why?'

'He didn't say.'

'On my way!' he responded, subtly managing to hide his irritation, as he got up from his bed. He wondered why Michael wanted to see him, especially since choir practice was about to start in a few minutes.

Axa was an exceptionally tall, slim, almost skeletal angel. His angular face, especially his long, slightly sharp nose emphasized his pointed appearance. He had never liked the idea of being 'invited' to see Michael, for he always knew that whenever he had been 'invited' by the archangel, it really meant that he was being summoned. And he felt that he deserved to be treated with more respect as behoved an angel of his standing, the conductor and musical director of the Angel Choir. After all, when there was cause for celebration in heaven, or anywhere else in God's endless cosmos, Michael always came knocking at his door. Not that he begrudged serving God: far from it. His greatest desire was to serve his Lord in any way possible, but Axa believed he should be appreciated more, that's all. He entered Michael's Hall, and as he had done on these occasions before, was struck by how simple and unpretentious the room was, considering this was an archangel's operational hub. He was greeted warmly by Michael. Gabriel was standing beside him.

'Axa! Come in and sit down.'

He noticed there were five chairs before Michael and Gabriel. They must be expecting more.

'Thank you, archangel. Gabriel.'

The chief messenger angel nodded his acknowledgement.

'Strangely quiet,' thought Axa.

'How is the choir sounding these days?' asked Michael, once Axa was seated in the chair opposite.

'Very good,' he replied.

'From what I'm hearing, I'd say they are more than "very good". You should be extremely proud of them.'

Axa bent his head to the side in humble acknowledgement.

'That's very kind of you.'

'I'd say it hasn't sounded better.'

'Thank you, Michael,' he replied, accepting the archangel's praise. He decided it prudent not to speak of the fly in the ointment.

'Now, you must be wondering why I asked you here?'

'Well... yes.'

Michael stood in front of him.

'As you know, long before earth was created God had a plan in mind to Right the Wrong that would be committed soon after creation.'

Axa nodded his head. It was nothing new that Jesus would go to earth to rectify the wickedness visited on the world when Adam had eaten the forbidden fruit in the Garden of Eden, but no one knew when this was going to happen. However, Axa had already been informed that the Angel Choir would have the great honour of heralding Jesus's arrival on earth. His brief was to produce a grand spectacle to announce His arrival.

'Well,' and at this Michael lowered his voice, 'the time has come.'

Axa was suddenly interested and listened attentively.

'In just over nine months of their time, our Lord will appear on earth, specifically in Bethlehem, Palestine, and you and the Angel Choir will go there too.'

It was plain to see that the Archangel was so thrilled he could hardly contain himself. The sense of excitement transferred to Axa.

'And what's more,' continued Michael, 'God wants you to be the one to announce His arrival!'

Michael sat down, as if he had expended a considerable amount of energy informing Axa.

Slowly, the magnitude of what Michael had just said seeped through Axa's mind. His choir, was to go to earth, and under his direction, it was to bear the good news that the Saviour had come. More than that, he, Axa, was to make the pronouncement. He could not quite believe it. He envisioned all eyes being on him as he announced Jesus's arrival on earth. For half a second, he thought to ask Michael why nine months' time. He let it pass. He could bring it up some other time. There were important matters to consider, such as, was he allowed to tell the choir, and if so when?

'I see no reason why you can't tell them now.'

'You mean during this rehearsal?'

'Yes,' Michael answered.

Axa shot to his feet. He couldn't get to the rehearsal quickly enough.
'May I leave, Michael, the choir will be thrilled.'
'I'm sure they will be. You've probably got a lot of things to do.'
He bid them both farewell, and rushed back to his room.

Chapter 3

Soon after he left five fearsome warrior angels appeared in the doorway.

'Come in! Come in,' said Michael, as he and Gabriel rose to greet them.

As the five strode towards him, Michael looked at them admiringly. He regarded them the most valiant and faithful comrades he had ever fought with in the many battles against Satan and his rebel angels. Their commander, Gilchrist was loved by those under his command, for he constantly displayed that rare and precious quality of a true leader: that of having less regard for himself than for those he led. He honoured them and held them in the highest esteem, and always displayed unflinching loyalty towards them. Consequently, they accepted his authority unquestioningly. In numerous cosmic conflagrations, Michael had stood shoulder to shoulder with Gilchrist and the others, and not once had Satan's murderous hordes prevailed against them. All the same, their general appearance bore witness to centuries of violent encounters with Satan's agents. How different they all looked from Gabriel, with his long, flowing curls, winsome features and sparkling tunic.

Gilchrist, never the most patient of angels decided that enough time had been spent looking at Michael musing dreamily to himself.

'You called for us, archangel,' he said.

The archangel stirred himself.

'Take a seat, all of you,' he instructed.

He, himself sat down, with Gabriel beside him.

'We have... or should I say, our Lord has a special assignment for you, an assignment like no other.'

All five listened intently. The last two weeks had been prolonged agony.

'As you all know, God has always had a redemptive plan for the world.'

They nodded their heads.

'Well, the time has come to activate that plan.'

The warriors looked at each other expectantly.

'God's Son will leave heaven and go and live on earth,' Michael continued. 'Now, even though the scriptures have foretold the coming of the Messiah and that He be born a baby – and you all know this – it still hasn't sunk in with every angel.'

'How do they think our Lord's coming to earth is going to happen then?' asked Gilchrist.

'They think that He is going to invade earth with a host of angels. Let's be clear: this is invasion earth, but not in the way they expect.'

'Well, no,' said Joram. 'We've all known that He'll be born a baby.'

'And that means a woman will have to be made pregnant. I know that much,' added Caleb, ever eager to display his understanding of complex matters, though he stopped short of asking the next obvious question.

Joram was more than willing to pick up the baton.

'So... how's that going to happen?' he asked.

Michael gazed ahead, looking at no one in particular.

'Gabriel,' he said, eventually, 'I think you might have the answer to that one.'

The chief messenger angel sat up straight as he spluttered a cough.

'Err... the Holy Spirit will come on a young woman, and the power of the Most High will overshadow her,' he replied, trying his utmost to sound knowledgeable and informed.

Gilchrist, Joram, Cadman and Ebin screwed their faces slightly in confusion. Caleb stared at him in splendid vacancy.

'What does that mean?' he asked.

'Exactly what I said,' Gabriel answered coolly.

'Yes, but how?' he persisted.

'Ours is not to ask how,' responded Michael, trying to find some way out of this interrogative quagmire.

'You don't know, do you,' stated Caleb.

'No, I don't,' admitted Michael irritably. 'Will anyone ever know or understand? Think about it. The Son made flesh – something more amazing than Creation itself. How will it happen? I have no idea. One thing I know, the eternal Godhead, the Three in One can do it.'

Thus far, Cadman had not contributed to the conversation, but now, he broke his silence.

'The fact that we don't know doesn't mean it's not going to happen, does it?'

'Quite!' said Michael, thankful for the respite from the cross examination. 'Now, I must stress that what I am about to tell you, go no further than these four walls.'

The others looked around. The cosmos was the ceiling, the walls and the floor. Gabriel stuttered another strangled cough.

'Yes, okay,' Michael responded, 'just, don't tell anyone, right?'

He leant forward a little and lowered his voice.

'This is why you've all been summoned here. In order for God's redemptive plan to be fully operational, the Saviour must experience life as a human being in all its fullness, from beginning to end, so that He can fully identify with them. So, He must be born as a baby. Therefore, He will be delivered into the womb of a young woman – Mary, who lives in Nazareth, in Galilee. In her womb, He will grow and develop as a baby. This miracle will be performed by the Godhead. Gabriel has not long returned from telling her the good news.'

'How did she take it?' asked Gilchrist.

'Amazingly calmly,' replied Gabriel.

'In nine months of their time, He will be born in Bethlehem,' continued Michael.

'But that's nearly a hundred miles away, to the south of Nazareth,' said Ebin. 'Why Bethlehem?'

'King David's city. It's been foretold that the Messiah will be born there,' answered Gilchrist.

'Precisely,' said Michael. 'Thank you, Gilchrist.'

'But what reason has she got to go to Bethlehem? Surely, she won't want to travel a hundred miles during the last few days of her pregnancy?' queried Ebin, looking at the other angels.

'And will she be travelling down there on her own?' asked Joram.

'Questions, questions, questions,' Michael thought to himself.

'No, her husband – Joseph – a carpenter from Nazareth will be with her. To answer your question Ebin, she'll have no choice in the matter. In a few months' time, the present Caesar, Augustus, will announce a census and every man will have to return to his ancestral town or city. Joseph is of the house of King David, who came from...' with this Michael spread his arms out, and said triumphantly, '... Bethlehem.'

'And as his wife, she'll have to go with him,' mused Ebin.

'Neat, very neat,' said Joram.

Silence fell on the small band of angels. There was something inexorable, irresistible even about it all, thought Gilchrist. He was not surprised though, since God's redemptive plan to save the world had been worked out to the last detail. Even the mighty Roman Empire's Caesar would be an unwitting bit player. If only he knew that he was facilitating the birth of Jesus, the King of Kings, in David's city.

Something was bothering Ebin.

'Err... what's this got to do with us? I mean, we don't belong to the maternity wing of the angelic host, not that there is one. And babies have nightmares about Caleb's face.'

Caleb smiled broadly, although he appealed to Michael for some succour.

'Tell him, Michael. He's pickin' on me. And, me such a sensitive soul.'

'You're an angel Caleb: you don't have a soul. Getta grip!' he responded.

The other warriors grinned.

'And another thing, since when have you been sensitive?'

Gabriel sat quietly unable to partake in the hilarity. How could they say such things to each other? Weren't they considerate of one another's feelings? Did they have feelings? What he didn't understand was that the deep, mutual respect and affection within the group allowed for such inanities and insults. What shocked him the most was that Michael had contributed to the amusement. And then Caleb seemed to be enjoying the fun, even though it was at his expense!

The Archangel Michael looked at them in earnest. He was getting to the nub of the meeting. Gilchrist and his warriors became more alert.

'Shortly, our Lord will leave heaven. There will be no fanfare or farewell ceremony. He will leave quietly. Your job is to protect Mary as she carries our Lord. Make sure no harm comes to her. Go with her: everywhere she goes, you go. Before long she will travel to the hill country in Judah to see her cousin, Elizabeth. You go with her. When she goes to Bethlehem with Joseph, again, you go with her. She will give birth to Him in a cave in the city. You must watch over her, and protect her. In doing so you safeguard Him, for she is His shelter, His home for the next nine months. He is completely dependent on her. Be especially aware of any enemy angels. They could hurt her, even kill her, by using the influence they have on certain men and women, and so kill Him. But, and I must emphasize this, they must not get wind of what's happening.'

'Why not send a legion of angels to protect her?' asked Joram.

Michael shook his head.

'Can you imagine what would happen? Satan and his generals would know there was something up and would send a vast army to engage our warriors. There would be an almighty battle. Bethlehem would be laid waste and who knows how many people would die as a consequence. We can't let that happen.'

The five angels agreed.

'It has to be done this way, without their knowing, or at least until He is born. Once He is born, Mary will be safe and so will Jesus, since they won't be able to touch Him. She is key here: protect her, and we protect our Lord. But I must emphasize that you engage with the demons only as a very last resort. However, use your wits and guile in any way you can. Every angelic resource is at your disposal. Understand, this is the most important assignment given to any angels.'

The five looked at each other in silence, as they digested what Michael had just told them. They thought of their Lord, a baby, inside Mary's womb, entirely reliant on her for oxygen and sustenance. However and whatever way God had created women's bodies to carry their babies, it had better work properly in Mary's case.

Caleb piped up.

'One last thing, when Mary tells Joseph – assuming she's the one who tells him...'

'Yes, she will tell him,' confirmed Gabriel.

'That could be awkward.'

Michael heard an echo of what Gabriel had said earlier.

'We're expecting her to tell him. You will need to keep an eye on them. If needs be, Gabriel will go down to reassure him. Am I right?' he asked, looking at Gabriel.

'Ready to leave at a moment's notice.'

'May I remind you,' emphasized Michael, 'no-one is to know. We do not want enemy angels finding out. They probably know that Jesus is to be born of a virgin – that's been foretold by Isaiah the prophet – and they know for definite that the Saviour is to be born in Bethlehem, so they've already posted a demon guard at the gates to the city. They've been there for a number of centuries, in fact, changing the personnel regularly. Sandon's unit's there now, and Kandar as well.'

'Interesting,' observed Joram.

'I know. I needn't tell you to be wary of him.'

Gilchrist nodded his head slowly.

'That will be your one big problem: how to get Mary and Joseph into Bethlehem past the demons, without them knowing.'

The five warrior angels pondered the matter.

'There'll be thousands of people on the move from all over the Roman Empire, thanks to the planned census,' Joram pointed out.

'We could make use of that,' suggested Cadman.

'Yes,' said Gilchrist, 'and even if they know where He is to appear, they won't know that He'll be brought down from Nazareth, by an inconsequential young woman and her carpenter husband.'

'Quite!' agreed Michael.

'We have things to do,' announced Gilchrist, getting up from his chair. The other four followed his lead.

'There's one other thing you need to know. Antonin has been put in charge of the demons' operations to find the woman carrying Jesus.'

If Michael had looked at Gilchrist more than the others when he said this it was hardly noticeable. Cadman, Joram, Ebin and Caleb shifted their feet uncomfortably and one or two stole their captain a quick glance. For his part, Gilchrist simply stared ahead at Michael.

'Fine,' said Michael, 'I won't delay you, but I will see you before you leave for earth.'

Once they were out of earshot Gabriel turned to him.

'Well?'

'They're the best at what they do. She's in the safest hands and because of that, He's in the safest hands possible.'

'I agree, but I don't understand one thing.'

'What's that?'

'Why have they never questioned us?'

'About what?'

'Why they didn't get to join the other warrior angels when God orders a show of force, as we did when Elisha prayed that his servant's eyes be opened centuries ago. I mean, virtually all of the other captains were there, along with their units. There were thousands of us. Where were they? Away on the other side of the world, escorting some war refugees through a bandit infested mountain range in the middle of winter.'

'That's how it had to be, all in preparation for this one task. That's why they've been on hundreds of such missions.'

'Have they ever brought the matter up with you?'

'They were none too happy with their first assignment: looking after David, an ordinary shepherd boy. That is, until they found out that someday, he would be king of Israel.'

'You could have told them.'

Michael smiled.

'I know – it was all part of their training. But since then? No, never. Not once have they questioned their orders – didn't even ask me now, why they'd been looking after Abdallah from Petra to Memphis. I'll tell them when we meet up with them in Bethlehem.'

'If they arrive safely – with Mary and Joseph.'

'You're right.'

'They asked a lot of questions this time.'

'To be expected,' reassured Michael. 'It was a huge thing to take in all at once.'

Conversation stalled for a second or two, both angels considering what lay ahead of Gilchrist and his troop of warriors.

'One thing I'm glad of,' Michael said.

'What's that?'

Turning to look at Gabriel, he replied,

'When I said that our Lord would have to experience life as a human from beginning to end, they were so concerned about the beginning, they forgot about… the "end" bit. I don't know how they would have reacted. Best leave that for another day.'

Chapter 4

Whilst Gilchrist and his warrior angels started to plan how they were to fulfil their crucial mission, Axa was telling Tiras of the incredible honour that had been given to him.

Tiras was Axa's assistant, his sidekick, and much more than that. He was his confidante, his comfort blanket. Many a time it has been said that a musical director is only as good as his assistant, and this was true of Axa's relationship with Tiras. He was Axa's scaffold when his edifice felt weak and about to collapse. As musical director, Axa was abundantly – some might say excessively – creative, but along with that came a significant amount of emotional baggage. Others, who are not creatively inclined find it difficult to relate to this excitable sensitivity, but it is a constant travelling companion of the artistically literate. Furthermore, we could go so far as to say that Tiras was Axa's punch-bag, not in the physical sense, but in the emotional sense. Quite often, the latter's passion would boil over into animated verbal utterances. Tiras took it all. Thus, Axa had a ready outlet to vent his tensions and stresses. In simple terms, Tiras took the strain, giving Axa free rein. As such, Tiras was looked upon with affection by God, for he who was servant was considered the greatest in the kingdom of heaven. Everyone is loved by God, but those who facilitate others are held in high regard by Him.

'So, there you have it, Tiras. I have been chosen by God to make the announcement, not any of the messenger angels mind, not even Gabriel, but me,' he said proudly.

Tiras was genuinely thrilled for him.

'What a tremendous honour.'

'I know. Right,' he said excitedly, getting up from his seat. 'Choir practice starts soon. Michael said I could tell the choir angels of their special role when Jesus arrives on earth. Come, Tiras, we have work to do.'

Tiras could hardly keep up with Axa as he raced along to the huge rehearsal room where most of the choir angels had arrived ready for their practice. Standing in front of them now, Axa could hardly contain himself, such was his excitement at what he was about to announce. He called on the assembled throng to be quiet. This they did relatively quickly, considering there were literally thousands of them there.

'Thank you, thank you. Before we start to sing, I have one or two things to say to you, that you will all find very interesting, I'm sure.'

Axa normally kept any announcements until the end of rehearsal, so they all leaned forward a little, like a vast forest of trees, swayed by a strong breeze.

'I have not long come from a meeting with the Archangel Michael and Gabriel.'

The breeze seemed to change and blow in all sorts of directions as the angels looked at their neighbours, or turned back to speak to those standing behind. Axa raised his voice a little louder.

'My dear choral angels, you all know we have been preparing for the triumphal appearance of Jesus on earth. Well, I can tell you, we will be going to earth in nine months of their time.'

A swell of emotion spread throughout the gathered multitude. Before it reached a crescendo Axa managed to add,

'When that time comes, we will be there to welcome our Lord, to celebrate His coming.'

Ripples of applause broke out amongst the angels, which gave way to prolonged whistling and cheering. Many embraced, their eyes glistening with expectation. This was the news they had all been waiting for.

Axa let them enjoy the moment and then called for silence once again, before proudly announcing,

'And I have been invited to announce His victorious arrival.'

If Axa had been expecting shouts of approval and support for this particular announcement he was sorely disappointed. Instead, it was met with a stony silence, and the awkwardness which he and the rest of the angels felt was only broken when Tiras, sensing the difficulty of the situation, started clapping, thereby leading everyone in applause. Axa accepted the stiff, somewhat halting congratulations. He looked at Tiras disconsolately. Simultaneously, Tiras managed to look at him comfortingly whilst encouraging him to start the practice. Axa, not for the first time, drew comfort from the fact that his assistant knew how to console and embolden him as he turned to face the choir. He called on them to calm themselves once more.

'I know this is stirring news,' he said, his voice booming effortlessly so that the furthest angel could hear him clearly. 'You will play an essential part in the appearance of our Lord, but we must try to contain ourselves. We have a lot of work to do so that we can give Him of our best.'

The angels sensing a slight admonishment in his voice reined in their emotions and prepared to sing. Axa raised his hands.

'After four,' he invited them. His right hand counted four beats and with a slight turn of his head Axa signalled that the choir start singing.

Not unlike heaven's division of warrior angels, who had an elite group, such as Gilchrist and his fighters, the Angel Choir had what Axa described as the elite of the vocalists. This was a hand-picked group of twelve singers – three base, tenor, alto and soprano voices – who stood in the front of the choir, and led the other angel choristers. Axa often called on them to sing intricate melodies whilst the rest were silent. Their harmonious sounds were a joy to the ear and Axa simply called them, 'The Twelve'. He was particularly fond of the three sopranos – Sabta, Gether and Dumah – recently elevated to this exalted position in the choir. Their voices rang true and as clear as a bell on a crisp winter's morning.

The four parts of the Angel Choir sang their dulcet notes independently, dovetailing via Axa's skilful conducting into one dynamic whole.

'Lovely! We will be ready,' Axa reassured himself, 'and the choir will sing a sound the like of which will not have been heard before or since.'

His arms swayed rhythmically, keeping time. All four voices were singing in seamless harmony, each part contributing to what could only be described as – and he knew this was a cliché – a heavenly sound. For a few blissful moments, Axa closed his eyes and felt himself relaxing under a cloudless blue sky, lying in complete surrender to the exquisite sound the choir was producing. Then, in his mind's eye, he saw a small grey cloud, no more than the size of a small fist approaching from afar. At first, he thought nothing of it, surmising that it would pass, and would not intrude on his enjoyment. To his deep displeasure, the little grey cloud soon developed in size as it came nearer and turned a darker shade of grey. As it did, it seemed to taint the once blue laden, sun drenched sky. Axa suddenly realised what it was. He opened his eyes.

Dylan!

He was late again.

Axa didn't know where Dylan had come from. He was renowned in heaven for going off on his own to no one knew where. Very few of the angels, were bothered where he went, least of all Axa, and if these mysterious journeys happened to coincide with choir rehearsals then all the better. In Axa's opinion he was musically ignorant, a vocal vandal. The root of the problem was that Dylan was tone deaf. In all the centuries he had conducted the Angel Choir he had never come across such a destructive choral phenomenon. Sometimes he was flat, sometimes sharp, and at other times he was in completely the wrong key. Sometimes, because he was so all over the place, random notes he sang would harmonise with the rest of the choir. That didn't happen very often though.

And he was like a little spark of fire in a dry and parched forest. Once he started singing, the other angels standing nearest to him would start singing out of tune, and it spread like wildfire. Soon the whole choir was completely tuneless, and the angels would look dejectedly at Axa, their eyes pleading for him to do something. As for Dylan, he was oblivious to the other angels' attitude towards him, for worshipping and praising God was his utmost joy. He loved God.

Axa looked at him now.

Strangely, he was as bald as a peeled onion save for a short wisp of hair that grew slightly off-centre at the top of his forehead. His rotund face was dominated by two flaming red cheeks that often turned a deep, shiny red when he exerted himself either physically or emotionally. His eyes were close together and he had huge nostrils. When he was happy, these would flare wide open, like a roused bull. Unfortunately for Dylan, this happened often since he was a jolly little angel. The cheeks stood guard over a jovial mouth that fathered an infectious smile reminiscent of a crescent moon lying on its back. This particular lunar outline of the lips was replicated to perfection on the lower side of his belly. His generous constitution was admirably supported by two short, stubby legs.

Irritated that he had been stirred from his dreamy interlude, Axa shouted at him.

'Dylan!'

Abruptly, the choir stopped singing. Everyone looked at the subject of Axa's ire. Knowing he was late for choir practice, he had crept in quietly at the back of the massed ranks of choristers, intending not to draw attention to himself. This was a forlorn task, like a lion hoping to sneak in amongst wildebeests on the Serengeti. As soon as he had arrived, the singing angels nearest to him had begun to move away, giving him a wide berth. It was all to no avail though, as discordant notes clashed with melodic intonations of the most delicate kind. What had been a celestial melodic sound soon deteriorated into a chaos of jarring cries.

Axa was distraught, verging on the hysterical. What was he going to do? There were only nine months to go before his choir's command performance, announcing Jesus's arrival on earth, and they sounded shambolic. He would have to speak to Michael and Gabriel. He decided to cut his losses for this particular session. Trying to sound unconcerned and reassuring, although he didn't convince anyone, he said,

'We've done enough for now. We have plenty of time to prepare. I'll see you next rehearsal.'

The choir trooped off, with many shaking their heads, whilst others muttered under their breaths how well they had been singing until Dylan appeared on the scene.

Once they had all left, Axa turned forlornly to Tiras.

'What are we going to do about Dylan?'

Tiras was bereft of ideas. Axa sat down and stared into the distance.

'We've tried everything: putting him at the back and when that failed we placed him amongst The Twelve and that was a disaster. And those three sopranos are his best friends, for goodness' sake! Remember when we told him to mime the words: he looked like a goldfish asphyxiating. And anyway, he just can't be quiet. What are we going to do, Tiras? We've been given a definite date now. These nine months will fly by.'

'You'll have to speak to Michael.'

'You know, I think you're right.'

Chapter 5

Meanwhile Dylan had caught up with his friends, Sabta, Gether and Dumah, the three sopranos so adored by Axa, for their singing prowess. They were all great friends and had been for many centuries. They decided to mess around in space. After the constraints of choir practice, it was always good to fly freely, leaving a trail of patterns in their wake on the blank canvass of the cosmos.

Dylan was in awe of Dumah, in this respect, as were the other two angels in the gang. He flew so swiftly and so nimbly, he could trail the shape of an elephant, a large centipede or even a tyrannosaurus rex. Dylan and the other two hung in space now and watched as Dumah fluttered and deftly drew with intricate detail a butterfly, down to the smallest veins on its wings even. Dylan felt so inadequate. He wished he could draw like Dumah. He had no problem visualising whatever he had in mind to draw, but the execution always let him down. Nothing was ever in proportion and the lines he drew were so shaky, whatever animal he sketched, always seemed to be petrified or had been struck by lightning.

They then decided to go for a jaunt around a few stars. Bombing around space always proved a challenge to Dylan, since Sabta, Gether and Dumah could fly swiftly and effortlessly, their sleek forms gliding smoothly through the dark expanse. They would fly at variable speeds, darting here and there, whereas Dylan's speed was constantly set at, 'leisurely', never wavering from that. Consequently, he had trouble keeping up with them. More often than not, they would wait patiently for him, but there were times when they got lost in their own velocity and would forget about him. On such occasions he would stop and hang in space, his short legs swinging sadly in the vacuum, trying to comfort himself by running his fingers along his wisp of hair, not knowing where they'd got to. Then, he would fly back to heaven on his own, feeling a little aggrieved. Thankfully, that did not happen this time and soon they were back in heaven.

They quickly made their way to the garden and lounged beside a brook glistening in the sun's rays. Rich green pastures stretched into the distance leading to rolling emerald hills, which, in turn led to snow topped craggy mountains, majestic in the hazy sunshine. For a while nothing could be heard other than the lazy trickling of the stream. Then, Sabta, eyes closed, lying on his back with his hands cradling the back of his head, spoke to Dylan.

'Well, you messed up good and proper today again.'

Dylan lowered his head.

'I know,' he said quietly.

Even when he talked, his voice sounded like it had been strained through a colander.

'So, what is the problem?' asked Dumah. 'I mean, why can't you sing in tune?'

'I don't know,' answered Dylan, raising his voice a little in irritation. They had had this conversation before, more than once. 'I don't try to sing out of tune.'

'But don't you hear yourself singing out of tune?' asked Gether.

Dylan shook his head.

'No. I hear my voice singing in perfect tune. I guess that's what tone deaf is. Maybe, the problem isn't with my voice, but with my ears. Thing is, I know I *can* sing.'

The others looked at him pitifully. They said nothing, not wishing to hurt him. Dylan was really well liked by all the angels in heaven – maybe not so much by Axa – and his infectious enthusiasm and genuine love for God was matchless amongst the whole celestial host.

Ignoring Dylan's assertion, Gether made him an offer.

'Do you want us to give you singing lessons?'

Dylan shook his head again.

'No, we've done that before: it didn't work.'

'Well, we've got to do something,' announced Dumah. 'We've only got nine months.'

Dylan lifted his head smartly.

'What do you mean, "nine months"?'

'Of course, you missed the beginning of the practice. You were on one of your travels.'

'Tell me, what's going to happen in nine months?'

Sabta had a query of his own

'Where do you go to on your escapades, Dylan?'

Dylan was getting impatient.

'What's going to happen in nine months?'

'Axa made a very important announcement at the beginning of re-hearsal,' stated Gether.

'Which was?' responded Dylan, bursting to know.

'You know the Angel Choir is to sing to herald the Saviour's arrival on earth? Well, we've been given a date: nine months from now.'

Dylan stood on his feet. He could hardly contain himself. He began to pace back and forth alongside the brook. The arrival of the Son of God on earth! This was going to be a stunning celebration of His, and God's love for the whole world. He was going to be a part of it, singing as one of the Angel Choir, doing what he enjoyed best, worshipping and glorifying his Lord. He was overcome with a deep joy and elation: he couldn't wait. The same thoughts raced through Sabta, Gether and Dumah's minds, but they, felt a certain foreboding as well.

Chapter 6

It had been a busy day. A constant stream of traders and visitors had either come, or left Bethlehem. Nathanael, the officer in charge of the guard at the city gates was tired and he could feel the evening chill of winter permeating through his skin. A heavy cloud hung overhead. His body gave an involuntary shudder. He was ready for food and an early night, next to his wife. The men under his command started to close the gates. As they did, two vagrants were slouching their way up the hill towards them.

'Shift yourselves, if you want to come in before we close these gates,' shouted Nathanael impatiently.

Dressed as they were in clothes slightly better than rags and labouring under some physical impediment or other, the two tried to hasten their step. It was not fast enough for Nathanael's liking. With each faltering footstep, his irritation grew.

'Get a move on, quick!' he shouted louder.

Still the two made little or no effort to quicken their pace, or so it seemed to him.

The gates were being swung shut when the two slipped slowly inside, but not before Nathanael gave them each a painful kick up the backside for wasting his precious seconds.

'What are your names?'

'Jedah and Nidab, sir,' replied Jedah.

'Just keep out of my way if you intend staying here,' he warned.

Shobal, Nathanael's deputy and the other soldiers in attendance laughed their derision and the demon guards, unseen by all the humans, grinned with satisfaction as some more of the unfortunates of life were mis-treated by those with power. Neither itinerant could do anything about his physical abuse. They merely accepted it as part and parcel of their lowly lives. They approached the city well that was just inside the gates and took their fill of its water. Then, they stumbled their way into the depths of Beth-lehem, getting as far away from the soldiers as possible. As they wandered the labyrinthine streets, they begged for food, but were either refused or ig-nored. Hours later, they reached the west side of the city and did their best to find a deserted spot and lay down to sleep for the night, gorging their stomachs on dreams of tables full of sumptuous meals.

Not far above them, Gilchrist glided through the night air, thankful that the thick cloud afforded him some cover. Three nights had passed since the five warriors' initial meeting with Michael and Gabriel. He circled round the western edge of the city and landed on a clearing beside an old, slightly neglected inn, on the south side. The night was still; the place void of human life. He looked around. A hoopoe bird, unaware of his presence, strode confidently past him, its crown of feathers wafting regally in the gentle breeze. It suddenly stopped and bore its long beak into the ground in search of any insects, but especially some tasty mole crickets. Gilchrist looked up at the massive rock that threw its dark shadow over the open space. He saw the cleft at its base and stood a while, lost in his thoughts.

He took off, this time, slowly following the line of the city wall on the western side. He was looking for something. It wasn't long before he thought he'd found it.

He landed elegantly on the ground in front of a small derelict house. It seemed ideal, save for one thing: there were too many people about. A husband and wife were quarrelling loudly and a few women were chatting with each other on the doorstep of a nearby house, totally unconcerned with the marital strife. He was looking for something more out of the way. He took to the air again. Twice he landed thinking he had found the perfect building. However, like the first one, one of them was situated in a busy part of the city, whilst the other just looked too good for what he had in mind. On and on he went, until he eventually came across a small house set against the periphery wall on the north side of town. It was more of a lean-to than a house. Windowless, its one door was situated in front. To his right he saw a narrow, dank and damp ally that ran along the city wall. To his left and behind him there were other small decrepit buildings that didn't show many signs of habitation. There was no light in any of them, and it was obvious they had been left derelict. Sad remnants of habitats that had housed no doubt the poorer elements of the town in days gone by.

'Perfect,' he said to himself.

He took off again, this time for the city gates. This was the most dangerous part of his mission. If he was seen by one of the demon guards on duty there, it would do irreparable harm to the plan he and the other four warrior angels had in mind. Keeping close, and parallel to the ground he flew towards the inside of the gates, that had not long been closed. Veering upwards, he landed gracefully on the walkway directly above the gates. Carefully, he looked down at the demons that were standing outside the city walls. He recognised one of them as Sandon, the leader of the small contingent. He was unfamiliar with the others. He looked out on the ground that sloped gently away from the city, to a narrow valley and beyond to the hill that rose the other side. On that hillside, he could see shepherds looking after some sheep as they grazed the lush pasture. Everything seemed so peaceful. They were as oblivious as the inhabitants of the city as to what was to happen here in nine months' time. He brought his gaze back to his immediate surroundings and studied in particular the area to the right and left of the gates. It wasn't long before he saw a small hollow about ten paces to the left of where the demons were now standing, and importantly, within earshot of them. Conveniently situated it had the added bonus of thick tussocks growing along the edge nearest the demons.

Satisfied that he had seen everything he jumped back off the wall. He flew to the other side of the city and quickly made his way back to heaven.

Chapter 7

Gilchrist, Cadman, Joram, Ebin and Caleb spent the time before Jesus left for earth devising and formalising their plan to look after Mary. Nothing was left to chance. Other warrior angel units were summoned to facilitate the scheme. One of these units, numbering around seven angels, was highly skilled in undercover work and had already left for earth. Another, smaller unit, amounting to no more than four, under the leadership of Lorcan, trained and vastly experienced in forward observation of enemy forces had already left for Bethlehem. Every heavenly resource was to be utilized.

They had endless meetings with Michael, and some with Gabriel. The archangel's main concern was how they were going to get Mary into Bethlehem, unseen, or at least unnoticed by the demon guards. During one of the latter meetings with Michael Gilchrist told him that they wanted Sabteka's help, though the archangel wasn't convinced even after Gilchrist explained why.

'What if he gets caught? It'll mess up your plan.'

'Sabteka get caught? Along with Joram, they're the best at what they do.'

'Why not have Joram do it, then?' asked Michael.

'He could be otherwise engaged,' Gilchrist pointed out.

'But if, as you say, Gilchrist – and I tend to agree with you – the demons will be looking for, and expecting a woman on her own, won't that be enough?'

Gilchrist shook his head. He was adamant.

'This will make doubly sure that Mary gets in to Bethlehem unnoticed and unseen.'

Michael succumbed to Gilchrist's arguments and acceded to his request.

'Where is he now?' asked Gilchrist. He hadn't seen Sabteka in heaven for a while.

'As it happens, he's in Palestine himself, embedding some of our agent angels, ready for Jesus's ministry. You'll have left before he returns. I'll explain to him what he needs to do.'

When, finally, the time came for them to leave for earth, they met with Michael and Gabriel in the archangel's hall for the last time. They could sense the tension and excitement as they spoke to the five warriors, although outwardly, they displayed total calm.

'Everything in order?' Michael asked Gilchrist.

'Yes,' he answered, slowly nodding his head, looking at the archangel with his sharp, alert eyes.

Not for the first time, Michael felt at ease that Gilchrist, of all the angels in the Angel Armies had been entrusted with this mission. He was no more loyal and faithful to God than any of the other warrior, choral or messenger angels in heaven, but he was certainly the most attuned to, and understanding of God's will. As such, there was none better to lead this most critical of missions to protect this most important of cargoes.

'Now then,' Michael continued, 'may I remind you that as part of the coming of Jesus, the Angel Choir, under Axa's direction will announce His arrival to some shepherds in the hillside above Bethlehem.'

'Erm, could I ask something?' ventured Ebin. 'Will the whole choir be there?'

'Certainly.'

'Even Dylan?' chortled Ebin.

'Even Dylan,' Michael affirmed.

Rarely did the warrior angels cross paths with the Angel Choir, but all of them had heard of the infamous Dylan, and had literally heard him as well. However, they also knew that he adored God: an attribute the five hardened warriors appreciated immensely.

'Wouldn't mind hearing that,' said Caleb.

'Maybe, but I doubt you will, since you'll have more than enough to do guarding Jesus.'

Gilchrist was getting impatient.

'We'd better get going, boss.'

'Yes,' agreed Michael, 'we don't want to leave Mary and Jesus unprotected any longer than needs be.'

Gilchrist nodded his head.

The five turned to leave, but Michael had one last reminder, one last urging.

'The five of you,' he called.

They turned to look at him.

'Remember, you look after her, you look after Him.'

All five angels stared at him. They were about to embark on the most precious mission any of them could have imagined. Its gravity and seriousness struck home. A certain nervousness percolated through their beings: it was a sensation they had never experienced before. Standing together, they silently contemplated the great honour that had been bestowed on them: to guard and protect their Lord, a helpless babe in the womb of a young woman.

Gilchrist gave the order to leave. They made their way to heaven's perimeter, took off and raced towards Nazareth, to their Lord, and to the woman chosen by God to carry Him for the next nine months.

Chapter 8

She knew something had happened to her body. Although, only ten days had passed since the visitation, she knew. In the eyes of those around her she was still considered young, an age at which she was still familiarising herself with the physical attributes of a young woman, inexperienced in the ways of the world. She looked down at her stomach and marvelled at the fact that the Son of God – her Son – was in there, in her womb. She hadn't dared tell anyone. Not that she doubted what she had been told, but she was finding it difficult to get her head round the idea that she, Mary, an insignificant girl had been chosen to carry God's Messiah.

She sat on the doorstep, leaning against the limestone wall of her parents' house that her father had built. It was late afternoon, and it had been another hot day. However, she was now enjoying the shade afforded by the steep cliff on the western side of the village. The high hills of the lower Lebanon Range flanked the northern and eastern edges of Nazareth. Even from her present lowly position, she could just about manage to see the tops of the olive and fig trees growing on the southern slopes that rolled down to the Valley of Jezreel far below. She could also see that the almond trees would soon be flowering, magnificent in their brilliant white colour. From afar, they would look like misshapen clouds that had fallen from the sky, floating, lost and limp just above the green and fertile Galilean countryside. It was indeed a beauteous place to live, she thought.

She acknowledged many of the people sauntering about their business: many she had known since childhood, and familiarity made her feel safe and secure. How would they respond to her though, if they knew that she was pregnant? More than that, how would they react to the fact that she was carrying God's own Son. Would they still greet her? Or would they ridicule her as being out of her mind for having the temerity to claim that she was pregnant with the Messiah? Besides, why on earth would God choose a woman from Nazareth to bear His Son? Had she forgotten that the village was an object of derision? Didn't she know that Jews everywhere questioned whether any good ever came from Nazareth?

There was one person she needed to tell: Joseph, her intended. He deserved to know before anyone else. And he had to be told today or tomorrow, at the latest, since she intended leaving in two days' time to go and see her cousin Elizabeth and stay with her and her husband Zechariah until their baby was born. Elizabeth was quite old and she would probably welcome the help. There was no way she could leave without first telling Joseph. She simply had to speak to him. That morning, Mary had got up from her bed, determined to grasp the nettle. But it was already late afternoon, and she had put it off, always managing to find an excuse, any excuse. She couldn't postpone the moment much longer though.

How would he would react? Would he reject her? It pained her to think of that prospect. What if he were to terminate the betrothal? According to Jewish law he was perfectly entitled to have her stoned to death for adultery. He would know that he was not the father. Throughout their relationship he had been respectful of her body and had not presumed on her, even after they had become engaged. When and how to tell him though, those were the questions.

Then, there were her mother and father. They would have to be told, too. Mary felt a cold sweat rise from inside. She sighed, dropping her shoulders. They didn't even know Elizabeth was pregnant. Neither did they know of her intention to go and stay with her. So many things to say, yet so little time.

How *was* she going to tell her father? He was a very religious man, who would read the ancient scriptures avidly and could recite large chunks from memory. He was only a simple stonemason, but rabbis would be astounded at his knowledge of the old manuscripts. To him, the commandment to love the Lord your God with all your heart and all your mind was paramount and his utmost desire was to please Him. Then there was her mother, so concerned about what others thought. It seemed to Mary that the most important regulation for those who lived in her mother's house was not to bring shame on the family.

Despite these portents, ever since the angel had told her of her blessed role in the coming of the longed-for Messiah, Mary's heart had been brimful of joy. She felt herself aglow, and the night before, her father smiled at her as he remarked how radiant and happy she looked of late.

And Mary was nothing but feisty. Boys feared her, girls admired her. Older people loved her since she unfailingly brought a smile to their faces when she talked to them and the sheer joy she displayed at the simplest things of life was contagious.

Suddenly, she pulled her shawl around her shoulders and got to her feet, as if she had been given an astounding revelation. She had to tell Joseph – now! Though it filled her with dread, she loathed even more the idea that he would find out from someone else. She walked the first few steps, full of intent, but then, she stopped abruptly, struck by the enormity of what she had to tell him. An angel had appeared to her! What's more, he had told her that she was to become pregnant of the Holy Spirit and the baby in her womb would be none other than the Messiah! Why should he believe her? She didn't want to hurt him either. In the deepest recesses of her heart she knew that he loved her. How on earth was she to tell him?

She very nearly turned back. She would tell him tomorrow. She took another deep breath and sighed. No, it would be better to see him today. She started on her way again, but still felt her insides churning.

He would be in his workshop, making a table of cedar wood for a local merchant. It was the first time that he had had such a lucrative order, and he had told her that if he could manage to make a good job of it, then he could expect more such orders to follow.

Mary walked slowly along the dusty streets. She arrived at his workshop, with its roughly hewn stonework and layers of branches on wooden rafters, much like any other workshop and house in the village. Owing to the lightness of her step, and the fact that he had his back to her, she had time to look at him without his knowing. She leant her shoulder on the post and folded her arms

She admired his broad powerful shoulders, and sinewy, yet muscular arms: all evidence of a life spent in hard labour carrying heavy pieces of wood. More than that, she noticed the delicate fingers that skilfully crafted the most detailed toys for the children of the village. She smiled at him, as he took great care and time to wipe the dust of the day's labours from the cedar table. He was so meticulous, to the point of being fastidious.

She broke the silence.

'I can't decide whether you look better from the back or the front.'

Recognising her voice, he replied,

'And I can't decide whether you look better from the back, front or side.'

He turned to look at her. Mary flashed her gleaming teeth, which seemed to sparkle all the more surrounded as they were by her olive tinged face. Her high cheek-bones and – to him – a perfectly shaped forehead that framed gleaming hazel eyes, completed his own personal vision of beauty.

'What's more,' he continued, 'I'm caught between a deep desire just to look at you and a longing to hold you in my arms.'

Her nose crinkled a little, and small dimples appeared on her cheeks. She tossed her long brunette hair behind her shoulders. Mary was enjoying herself.

'Please, don't to that,' he pleaded. 'You know it drives me crazy.

She giggled quietly.

'Right, let me finish wiping this table down, and then we'll go for a walk up to the hills.'

There was nothing they enjoyed more than to make their way to the hilltops overlooking Nazareth and once there, gaze to the east at the Sea of Galilee, all the while sharing their dreams and hopes for the future; a future entwined since Joseph had asked for her hand in marriage.

He worked on the other side of the table, affording her a chance to admire his handsome face. His dark brown hair hung straight either side of his face, but on his high forehead – she imagined to be as hard as stone – two thick wisps curled, like the horns of a bull. She giggled quietly to herself, as she always did when she saw them. His bushy beard and dark glistening eyes, completed the vision of him that she would carry in her heart, if she were never to see him again. She heard the birds tweeting and chattering in the early evening, and people outside walking and talking, doing the things that the inhabitants of Nazareth usually did at that time of day. It seemed a crime to shatter the tranquillity of ordinary village life. She felt she was about to take a heavy hammer to a pool of clear frozen water, or about to open floodgates releasing torrents of raging water that she would not be able to stop, ever again. But it was something she had to do though.

'Joseph, I have something to say to you.'

She had tried her best to sound calm. She failed, miserably. He stopped wiping and looked at her, his face a study in worry. His smooth forehead furrowed a little.

'You'd better sit down.'

As soon as those words had left her lips, she regretted them: she had only succeeded in compounding his fears. He did as she said though, setting himself gingerly on the stool beside his workbench. Mary could hear his deep, nervous breaths and she wondered whether he could hear hers.

'I know this is going to sound crazy, but... ten days ago, an angel... an angel appeared to me.'

Joseph cocked his head to one side, narrowing his eyes a little at this incredulous news. He said nothing.

'I was scared stiff, but he told me not to be afraid.'

Still, no response. Mary continued.

'What he had to say... was unbelievable... mind blowing.'

She stopped. She had to be careful, delicate even.

'He told me... he told me that I would become pregnant...'

'What?'

Joseph shot to his feet.

'I know, I know. Please let me finish, Joseph... I can hardly take it in myself.'

'Well... who's the father? Do I know him?'

'Yes, Joseph, you know Him, but He's not from Nazareth.'

'Have you been seeing someone outside the village?'

Joseph was flabbergasted. She breathed deeply and said gently,

'It's Yahweh, Joseph.'

He sat back on his stool and looked at her with confused, stern eyes. She took advantage of his silence.

'When he told me I was to become pregnant, I asked him, "How? I've never slept with a man".'

Joseph looked at her in disbelief.

'You have to believe me, Joseph!'

Then, looking him in the eye, she said slowly,

'I have not slept with any man, Joseph.'

He stared at her with stern eyes.

'What did he say to that?'

'He said that the Holy Spirit would come upon me and the power of God would hover over me, and so the child would be Holy, the Son of God.'

'W... wait a minute. So, you're telling me that Yahweh's the father?'

'Yes,' she replied, an insistent tone to her voice that temporarily took Joseph aback.

'And when will this happen?'

'It already has. I'm pregnant; am with child.'

'And this child is the Son of God, the Messiah? The One the nation of Israel has been waiting for... for centuries?'

She nodded.

'The One foretold by all the prophets?'

She nodded her head again.

He fell silent, gazing reflectively at the table he had been wiping. The outside world was silent too: birds had stopped singing; people stopped talking. It was as if the whole world was agog at what she had just told him. The silence was unbearable, but Mary thought better than to say any more. She had said what needed to be said. Inside, she was frantic though, wanting him to say something. Talking meant lines of communication were open; conversation was the bridge that spanned the gap between them. Thankfully, he started again. At last, a reaction.

'But why you, Mary?'

'I... don't know,' her voice by now trembling, as the magnitude of what Joseph had just asked hit her as it had done a number of times since the angelic visitation.

'Do you expect me to believe all of this?'

'Well, yes... I do. Please... I beg you... it's the truth.'

He looked at her, unsettled by her answer.

'I'm scared, Joseph. I feel all alone. I want you to be with me, to come with me.'

'What if I don't?'

Her heart froze. She quickly gathered herself. Whispering, she said,

'Then I must do it all on my own.'

It was his turn to be silent, as he contemplated what she had just said. He gathered his thoughts again.

'What about your father and mother? It'll bring great shame on them.'

In the months they had been engaged, Joseph and her father had become firm friends, probably because they were both master craftsmen in their chosen trade and so there was a mutual admiration for the other's skills. She knew her father would not be able to look him in the eye, besides the rest of the community, once her pregnancy was made public.

'Do you think I haven't thought of that? He loves you, Joseph, like you were his own.'

Silence descended again. Joseph knew this to be true. It was something he appreciated since both his parents had died years earlier, leaving him on his own. Mary heard the birds singing outside once more, and normal life resumed on the streets, as if they had finally managed to get over the shock of what they had just heard.

He got to his feet and began to pace back and fore. She could see that he was struggling with his thoughts. She imagined his mind to be a jumble of woollen strands. It was obvious that he was trying to work out what to do. What he would determine in the next few seconds would decide her fate. She said nothing; he had to come to this decision on his own.

He looked out of the window at the hills silhouetted by the setting sun, and in his mind's eye he saw the deep blue of the Great Sea that lay beyond them. He remembered, as a child he had always wanted to see the Mediterranean. It wouldn't be that difficult to get there. He had heard stories of the great trading ships of Tyre and thought to himself he would probably be able to get work there building the ships that traversed the world's seas. It would be a good way to escape the shame of being let down by the one woman, the only woman, he had ever loved. Bachelorhood beckoned, for he could not see himself marrying anyone else. No other woman came close to her. Once one had tasted the finest wine, everything else was bland and insipid. He contemplated his predicament for what seemed like an age to her. Mary was in agonies of despair, waiting impatiently for his decision. Presently, he turned to look at her.

'Our betrothal is at an end,' he said, in a flat voice.

Not only was Mary stunned by what he said, but also by his manner, as cold and impassive as an incontestable legal document. She let her head drop to one side. Just as she did, a few strands of hair loosened and fell over her smooth, silken forehead. She looked sorrowfully at him, holding back a great reservoir of tears that had suddenly collected behind her eyes.

'Joseph...' she began to plead, her voice hoarse with hurt. She looked at him reproachfully. How could he think that she had been with another man? Did he not believe her?

'You'd better go now. I'll call to see your father early in the morning to explain to him.'

'But Joseph...'

'Like I said, it's best if you were to leave,' he interrupted, staring past her.

A deep sadness gripped her. She suddenly found it difficult to breathe. What was he doing? Didn't he know the hurt he was causing her and himself? And it was all so unnecessary. What could she do? The evidence was stacked against her; irrefutable even. There was no way she could disprove his misconception. Even though the shock rendered her whole body weak, she surprised herself by how well she coped. Looking at what would have been, until ten minutes ago, her future husband, she hid the picture of him deep in her heart and turned to make her way quietly out into the lane. Then, and only then, did Joseph sit down and let profuse tears of sadness run down his cheeks.

Outside the back wall of Joseph's workshop, Gilchrist turned to look at the other four warriors. They had all bowed their heads feeling aggrieved and disappointed; aggrieved because, in their eyes, Mary had been treated unfairly. From the moment they had arrived in Nazareth they had taken an instant shine to her, and during the next few days, nothing had happened to diminish the affection they had for her. They could see why God had chosen her as mother for His Son. She was loving and caring, but at the same time she possessed a sparky, spirited character, with a strong streak of independence. They were disappointed, because they had hoped for, and even expected better from Joseph.

As they walked out from behind the workshop to follow Mary home and ensure, as best they could, that she was okay, Caleb volunteered his services.

'Do you want me to sort him out, G.?'

His captain stopped, irritated with his subordinate.

'You said that when King Saul threw a spear at David, remember? So, tell me, Caleb, what exactly do you mean by, "sort him out"?'

He shrugged his shoulders.

'Well, you know...'

'No, I do not know. Whatever it is, I do not want you to do it,' Gilchrist replied, sharply. 'We don't do that sort of thing. Demons, yes, humans, no, and anyway we haven't got the authority to do that. Besides, Michael told me that if something like this were to happen, I was to report back to him, immediately. So, that's what we'll do. I'll go back to heaven while you four stay here and carry out our main mission, which is to look after her,' he said, pointing at the forlorn figure walking faltering steps some fifty paces in front of them. 'Is that too much to ask?'

'No, boss. He shouldn't have turned her away, though,' Caleb persisted, disconsolately.

'Maybe, but put yourself in his situation. Right, Cadman, you're in charge until I get back.'

With that, he took off, leaving the others to follow Mary, each one of them consumed with an insatiable desire to put their arms around her, but feeling the frustration of not being able to do so.

Chapter 9

While Gilchrist was on his way back, Archangel Michael and Gabriel were both called to meet with God. Their steps were light as they made their way along the corridors of heaven to the Hall of the Eternal Throne. It was always a delight to see Him.

As they approached the Throne, they beheld the seraphim that hovered around God, rendering Him timeless and perpetual worship. Once again, they were struck by His matchless beauty. They bowed their heads and raised their hands in joyous worship. A gentle, thunderous voice spoke.

'Michael, Gabriel, good to see you.'

They both raised their heads and in a loud voice, said,

'My Lord.'

'Is everything in place for the birth of My Son?'

'Yes, my Lord,' answered Gabriel.

'Good. Now then, I have one other charge for you.'

Michael and Gabriel listened carefully.

'Dylan,' He announced, 'I have a very special mission in mind for him the night my Son is born.'

Both angels looked in bewilderment at each other.

'Anything wrong?'

Michael and Gabriel knew their Lord well enough by now to know that He liked to do the unexpected. Too many people thought they could control Him, manipulate and regulate, even domesticate Him. He was no more than a servant, at their beck and call, available whenever and wherever, so that His services could be engaged to accomplish their agenda, as if He was obligated. He was not a conforming God. He loved doing the unpredicted, and nothing pleased Him more than giving people who thought themselves worthless very important jobs. Elevation not degradation was a big part of His game plan. But Dylan, a member of the Angel Choir who was tone deaf? What special mission could God possibly have in mind for him?

They both looked at God,

'Dylan?' queried Gabriel.

'But he can't sing,' said Michael.

'Axa wants to get rid of him from the choir. He says he can't get him to sing one note in tune,' added Gabriel.

'I know.'

God was smiling broadly. He pondered a while, and then continued.

'No doubt, you've both noticed that he leaves heaven quite often. Have you ever wondered where he goes to, or what he does?'

Both angels slowly shook their heads.

'Or maybe, like Axa, everybody's secretly glad when he's not here? He can't upset the choir practice then. Have you seen him when the choir worships Me? He is so happy to see Me. I know he sounds out of tune, but I see what's inside. He loves Me very much.'

God waited before continuing.

'It's time for you to find out where he goes. Tell Gilchrist to follow him the next time he leaves heaven. Dylan must not know that he is being followed. Have Gilchrist report back to you as soon as he returns. You'll know then what Dylan's special mission will be. Remember, he must not know about this.'

'But Gilchrist's in Nazareth, looking after Mary,' said Michael.

'Gilchrist is on his way here, to see you. Gabriel, you have work to do: you need to go and reassure Joseph.'

Once again, the two angels looked at each other, mirror images of their own astonishment. They stirred themselves, bowed their heads and returned smartly to Michael's Hall.

Chapter 10

Thus, neither Michael nor Gabriel were surprised when Gilchrist arrived breathless, having made the return journey to heaven in what he would argue was the quickest time ever. He concluded the retelling of what had happened in Joseph's workshop, by warning,

'He's going to divorce her!'

Michael took immediate charge.

'You must go now, Gabriel. No time to lose.'

Gabriel nodded, and began to leave the hall. Gilchrist turned to accompany him.

'Gilchrist,' said Michael.

The warrior angel turned back to look at him.

'We have another task for you.'

'What?!'

'What mission was more important than looking after Mary and his Lord?' Gilchrist thought to himself.

'You remember Dylan?'

'The angel who can't sing?'

'Well, he can sing, it's just he's out of tune.'

'Same difference,' Gilchrist thought to himself.

'He often leaves heaven, of his own accord. You're to follow him next time he leaves. No one knows where, or why he goes.' Then, he said, reflectively, more to himself than to Gilchrist, 'No one has ever been that bothered to find out. You are to tail him, but under no circumstances is he to know.'

'So, when does he leave next?'

'I simply don't know. He leaves on a whim, it seems, and he comes back... when it pleases him,' answered the archangel, lifting his arms in ignorance.

'This means I've got to stay here, until he goes...'

'Yes.'

'Wherever he goes...'

'Yes. The one thing I can tell you is that he leaves heaven quite often. So, you shouldn't have long to wait.'

'But what about Mary?'

Michael could understand how Gilchrist felt. Protecting Mary was much more important than following an insignificant angel on what was probably a pointless journey, to no one knew where.

'I know, but this has come directly from God, Gilchrist. He has a special mission in mind for Dylan the night our Lord is born. I have no idea what that could be. All I know is, God knows better than you or I.'

Gilchrist had no answer to that. If God desired it, he couldn't refuse.

'Where is he now?'

'In the Eternal Throne Room,' Michael replied a little apprehensively. Surely Gilchrist wasn't going to remonstrate with God?

'I know where God is. Dylan, where's he?'

Michael relaxed.

'Right. Elum!' he called, and the angel standing guard at the doorway to his hall approached.

'I asked you to locate Dylan for me.'

'He's in the garden, with his friends, Sabta, Gether and Dumah. They've been diving in the Pool of Tears. Well, his friends have been diving,' Elum corrected himself. 'Dylan has been... well I don't know what you'd call it, more... bombing, I suppose.'

'Thank you. You may leave. You remember where the garden is?' Michael asked Gilchrist.

The warrior nodded.

'Oh, and one thing, there's choir practice before long, so they'll all be going there.'

'And after he returns from wherever he goes, I'm to report back to you?'

'The sooner you do that, the sooner you can go back to Nazareth.'

With that, Gilchrist took his leave.

Chapter 11

Gilchrist stepped out into the garden of heaven. He couldn't remember the last time he had been here and he'd forgotten how spectacular it was. He looked around in awe, as if he was seeing the place for the first time. Wherever he looked, various flowers proliferated in a sea of vibrant colour. He could not have named one of them: after all, he was a warrior, not a gardener. However, there was no need of a gardener for there were no choking thorns or weeds and the flowers danced in delight. His eyes feasted on their sumptuous colours: there were flowers of white and crimson, yellow and blue, but as they swayed in the gentle breeze, so they changed subtly into a shade of their original hue; alabaster, ruby, gold and azure. Then, a stronger breeze blew, and they changed to rich shades of colours that he had never seen before. He ran his fingers through the nearer ones. They gave out intoxicating aromas. Beyond the flora, vast meadows of lush grass stretched far into the distance fringed by snow covered mountains, riven by gently flowing rivers, and streams and waterfalls that glistened as they cascaded down the steep slopes.

What he saw saddened and grieved him, for it offered more than a glimpse of what the Garden of Eden had looked like before Adam partook of the forbidden fruit. He saw what could have been. He deplored the betrayal of God's love, especially since he had witnessed the devastation and depredation wrought by that singular event. It was as if a drop of pervasive poison had fallen into an ocean of pure, clean water, and it had spread its lethal venom far and wide to every part of God's creation. He could think of nothing more insidious. And Adam had traded that for this!

Gilchrist made his way to the Pool of Tears. It was a deep pool of soft water. At the water's edge a large rock stood sentinel. It had a small hole in its flat top, and out of this hole sizeable droplets of water would occasionally shoot in the air to float and land gently in the pool below. Hence the name, Pool of Tears. Even though Gilchrist was still a distance away, he could hear the four angels shouting and yelping with delight. Then, he saw them, diving from the top of the rock into the emerald water: all except Dylan. Gilchrist walked silently through the dense green foliage and colossal leaves that stretched around the perimeter of the pool. He found a conveniently situated stone, well hidden, and sat down to watch the four.

Sabta and Gether flew up to the top of the rock. Dumah was already there, preparing to dive. Gilchrist was impressed by his agility as he plummeted through the air towards the water, hardly causing a ripple as he cut through the surface. He strained his eyes, for he couldn't see Dylan anywhere. Suddenly, Dylan flew out of the water and landed not far from Gilchrist's hiding place. He straightened his tunic, that had become wedged in his bottom, briskly shook himself, and in an instant, he was completely dry. Gilchrist was astonished. How could he have forgotten? He remembered how he and his one-time best friend, Antonin, had spent hours diving in this very same pool, unable to comprehend how they could dry so quickly after coming out of the water. Recalling his friend stung, as Antonin was one of the angels who had sided with Satan against God in the Great Rebellion.

Sabta and Gether had dived into the water in perfect unison and Dylan was thrilled, applauding his friends vigorously. Then he flew up to the top of the rock. As he stood on top of it, Gilchrist's curiosity was piqued when he saw the little angel rubbing either side of his belly with his hands very hard. Dylan watched carefully as a teardrop of water shot out of the hole atop the rock, high into the air. Once it had reached its highest point, it floated serenely down to the pool. The warrior angel was taken aback when he saw Dylan thrust his head and shoulders firmly into the hole. With his bottom in the air and his legs flailing wildly, he stood on his head for a few seconds. Gilchrist was about to shout to his friends, who were all watching from the poolside to go and help him, when he saw a teardrop doing its utmost to squeeze itself out of the cavity that was now jammed by Dylan's head. Eventually, it managed to burst forth in a loud explosion – more of a bubble than a teardrop – with Dylan encased inside. Gilchrist couldn't believe his eyes. He looked at Dylan's three friends, who were watching the teardrop as it shot into the air with the little angel inside. Once it reached its apex, the teardrop plunged downwards, at an alarming speed owing to its unexpected load. His friends weren't in the least bit worried. They had obviously seen him do this before. Dylan's face turned a slight tinge of orange because of the exertion of trying and failing to get a grip on the smooth wet surface of the teardrop. He slipped and slid clumsily before hitting the water, the teardrop exploding into a burst of nothingness. A spray shower engulfed the three angels who were standing at the side of the pool. Even Gilchrist, sitting a good ten paces away felt a few droplets of the far-flung wetness.

Dylan appeared from under the surface and his head bobbed sharp staccato movements as he swam to the side of the pool to the applause of his friends.

'That was the best one yet,' one of them remarked.

They continued to jump and dive into the pool for a while, Gilchrist witnessing a few more remarkable bubble acts from Dylan, before one of them informed the others that the next dive would have to be their last because choir practice would be starting soon. The other three flew to the top of the rock one last time. Dylan began to follow them, when Gilchrist noticed a sudden change in his demeanour. Something had drawn his attention and he was looking skywards. The other three angels took off and dived towards the water.

Gilchrist kept his eye on Dylan.

As they disappeared under the water, Dylan turned to look at them, seeming to bid them farewell. Then he did a strange hop, skip and a jump and took off. Without looking back at his friends, he flew high in the sky and headed for space. The three angels came out of the water. They watched him fly away. Gilchrist understood from their reaction that they were used to this. He thought he heard one of them say, 'Gone again,' but that was all. They sauntered off to choir practice. Gilchrist came out of his hiding place, anxious that he not lose Dylan. He needn't have concerned himself, for as he looked in the direction Dylan had taken off, he could see him not so far away.

Gilchrist took off and sped after him. By the time he was in outer space, he had caught up, but kept his distance, remembering Michael's stipulation that on no account was Dylan to know that he was being followed.

Chapter 12

Joseph lifted his weary legs, and shifted them on to the thin mattress stuffed with wool. He lay back, thankful that he could rest his head after the trauma of the day. He was so tired. The thin edges of skin that encircled his eyes stung. He was in dire need of some sleep, but he couldn't foresee having a restful night.

He went over things in his mind for the umpteenth time, and every time he came to the same conclusion. If Mary was pregnant, she must have been with another man, since he had acted respectfully throughout their betrothal.

'How could she?' Joseph asked out loud, banging the back of his head on the pillow in frustration. She had promised herself to him, as he had to her; pledged their hearts to each other. Had she been unfaithful to him? Deep in his heart he knew the answer: that wasn't the Mary he recognized. From the very beginning and throughout their relationship he was convinced she was as committed and devoted to him, as he was to her. He just knew! Pretence was alien to her and he trusted her. But now, this! Joseph was both confused and bewildered.

A myriad questions swirled around inside his head and one in particular. If he, Joseph, wasn't the father, then who was? Yet, he didn't want to pursue that question, for to know would hurt him even more.

She had given him the answer, though. She had told him that she had been made pregnant by the Holy Spirit: Yahweh was the Father. But that was preposterous; insane, even. How on earth could she expect him to believe that? And if he were to believe her everyone in the village would think him out of his mind. Even so, as he lay in his bed, trying his utmost to convince himself that he had done the right thing there was this nagging thought in his mind that made him feel uncomfortable, like having a thorn in his side: what if it were true? What if an angel had appeared to her and she had indeed been made pregnant by the Holy Spirit?

'No, no, no' he said, shaking his head.

He couldn't entertain the thought. How was it possible for a woman to become pregnant without a man's donation, contribution, intervention, call it what you will. It was beyond the bounds of human understanding.

'No, I've done the right thing,' he comforted himself, as if speaking the words into the darkness fed the conviction of his belief.

Termination of the marriage contract was the only option. He was entitled to have her stoned. He dared not think of that for it was cruel and barbaric. He had seen it once. A young woman, who had not long been married had been caught in adultery with an older man. Yes, she had done wrong, she knew she had done wrong. Joseph though, had seen how alone and fearful she looked, facing her accusers – all male, of course – with a quiet dignity in the face of such brutality. He could still hear her piercing screams as the first stones pounded her fragile body until she fell on her knees in a carpet of jagged rocks, and the relief he felt when at last, a heavy stone hit her on the temple rendering her unconscious and thankfully, free of pain.

He rubbed his eyes, trying in vain to ease the irritation.

He let his mind wander to when they first started going out together. He had fallen in love with her even before they had started their relationship. He loved everything about her. Indeed, everyone in the village loved her for her energy and ebullience and her humour and compassion. Joseph could hardly contain his pride whenever they walked side by side, through the streets of Nazareth.

He stared at the roof.

'Have I done the right thing?'

He remembered what she said when he had asked her what she would do if he left her.

'I'll do it all on my own.'

Her answer had unnerved him then, and still did. He knew that she was a determined woman, maybe a little stubborn, but he had not realised until then, the depth of her resolve. She was ready to run the gauntlet of old women's gossips and old men's incriminations, with or without him.

He closed his eyes, still trying to convince himself.

'I've done the right thing. I've done the right thing. There was no other way. I've done the...'

His mind was a battlefield. Arguments and counter arguments attacked each other from all angles, with neither side gaining the ascendancy. He tossed and turned. Eventually though, sleep overtook him, and it proved to be a more restful sleep than he had anticipated, since other powers – powers beyond this world – were at work.

A few minutes earlier, Gabriel had met up with Ebin and Caleb in the centre of Nazareth. Cadman and Joram had stayed in Ben and Abigail's house to watch over Mary.

'Where's Gilchrist?' asked Ebin.

'He's on a mission from God.'

Ebin and Caleb looked at each other.

'Nothing to be concerned about. He'll be back soon and he'll tell you all about it. Right, we got his message about Joseph and I came immediately. Take me to his house. We've got to sort this out... tonight.'

The three proceeded to the carpenter's house, and walked in through one of the walls. They looked at Joseph as he lay on his bed, evidently deep in thought.

'What are you going to do?' asked Caleb.

'I'll wait until he's asleep, and then appear to him in a dream. Poor man, he's had a rough day. You can see that by the way he's tossing and turning in his bed, and even though his eyes are red with tiredness, sleep is a long way off. I don't want to alarm him even more by appearing out of the blue.'

'He needs to be with Mary these next nine months as well,' said Ebin. 'He's integral if we're to get her past those demon guards and into Bethlehem safely.'

Caleb looked at the walls adjacent to the bed and at the rest of the sparsely decorated house, adjoining the workshop.

'I'd say he definitely needs a woman's touch in here, whatever.'

They turned to look at Joseph as he rubbed his eyes. After a while, he slowly closed them and they heard him say,

'I've done the right thing. I've done the right thing. There was no other way. I've done the...', over and over.

They waited a few more minutes. Soon, he was snoring gently, exhausted by the day's emotional and physical exertions. Then, Gabriel sat down by Joseph's feet, leant back and rested his head against the wall. Caleb stared at him.

'What?' inquired Gabriel.

'Well, aren't you going to do something?'

'Yes,' he replied nonchalantly.

'Well, do it.'

'Do what?'

'I dunno, your thing.'

'I will do my "*thing*", as you call it, but not yet.'

'Why?' Caleb was getting a little frustrated.

'I'm waiting.'

'Waiting for what?'

Ebin was just as intrigued and could empathise with Caleb's edginess.

Gabriel pushed himself from the wall to sit up and started to explain to them.

'I'm waiting for his body to relax and his mind to become more active. That is when dreams occur, and that will be the time to enter the doorway into his mind and communicate with him through his dreams.'

'But you showed yourself to Mary,' responded Ebin.

'I know, but you must remember that it was daytime. This is the dead of night. My appearing to him before his eyes would probably overwhelm him, especially after the day he's had. Anyway, just maybe, women can handle angelic visitations better than men. So, we wait.'

'When will you know he's dreaming?' asked Caleb.

'You'll see.'

Outside, the nocturnal world was colonising the darkness. They heard night owls cooing in the stillness, rabbits flitting about and hedgehogs scratching the ground.

Then Gabriel got to his feet. He had been watching Joseph.

'See his eyes?'

'No, they're closed,' answered Caleb.

Gabriel looked at him despairingly.

'His eyes are flickering quickly under his eyelids. That's a sure sign that dreams are on their way.'

Ebin and Caleb looked closer. Gabriel was right.

Gabriel walked to stand beside Joseph's head. He looked down at him for a while. The two warriors held their breath. They were about to witness something they had never seen before. Gabriel stretched down and placed his hand on Joseph's head. He reminded Ebin of a doctor standing above a sick patient, but with the remedy already at hand. Then, in a gentle but authoritative voice he said,

'Joseph, son of David, don't think twice about taking Mary as your wife. God's Holy Spirit has made her pregnant. She will give birth to a son, and you will call him Jesus – God saves – because he will save his people from their sins.'

That was it! Ebin and Caleb were impressed with how everything had been done with the minimum of fuss, but with the maximum effect. They looked at Gabriel in a new light.

'His muscles will soon relax,' he said presently. 'His blood pressure and breathing rate will drop, and he'll then enter a deep sleep. When he wakes up in the morning, he'll feel refreshed, and dare I say, reinvigorated. Right, my work here is done. I'll let you be witnesses to the great reconciliation.'

They responded warmly, appreciative of his talents.

'Nice one, Gabe,' said Caleb.

An awkward silence descended. Ebin gave him a cold hard stare. What on earth did he think he was doing calling God's chief messenger, 'Gabe'?

Gabriel decided not to respond.

'I probably won't see you until Jesus is born in Bethlehem. Do your best.'

'We will,' Ebin answered.

'A lot depends on you,' he reminded them.

They escorted him out through the wall of the house and watched as he took off, sweeping majestically through the night air. Then they made their way over to Mary's parents' house to continue their vigil with Cadman and Joram.

Chapter 13

Even though Gilchrist kept a safe distance, Dylan wouldn't have noticed that he was on his tail. Numerous angels flew past him, yet Dylan would not even look at them. Gilchrist could see that he was headed for earth. Having cut through the atmosphere, the little angel flew towards the Mediterranean, and for a moment Gilchrist thought that he was going towards Palestine, but he veered south, leaving that land behind him, far to the north-east. Gilchrist took one last glance at Palestine, and wondered what was happening in Nazareth, now that Gabriel had gone down there to see to Joseph. He shook his head and sighed to himself as he recalled Caleb suggest that he knock some sense into him.

Eventually, Dylan began to slow down and stopped above a small village in what Gilchrist knew to be Egypt. He remembered centuries earlier when he had been on many missions here when the Jewish nation had been enslaved. Those were dark times and he had not enjoyed the sight of so many Jewish baby boys being slaughtered at the behest of the Pharaoh. He was also overwhelmed with sadness on seeing the first born of the Egyptian nation killed prior to the Jews' escape. The village was situated amidst lush fields to the west of the Nile, in the southern part of the country, not far from the river. The sun had long gone down and lights flickered in most people's homes.

Gilchrist slowed down too. Dylan dropped himself and landed outside a house. He walked in through the back wall: nothing strange in that. Every angel was intangible and could phase through walls and inanimate objects at will. Gilchrist looked round. It was very much a nondescript village, not unlike any other in Egypt. Although the house was quite large, it was evidently a poor family's home probably built with a single wall.

Gilchrist landed smoothly at the back of the house, near to where Dylan had phased through. He resisted the temptation to lean in to the wall to see what was inside for fear of being seen by Dylan. At head height, there was a small, square hole, just big enough for a child to crawl through, in the wall. Its wooden shutters were slightly ajar. Carefully, Gilchrist peered inside.

Instantly, he saw Dylan, facing him. Quickly, he pulled away, thinking that he had surely seen him. Nothing happened. Gilchrist realised that thankfully, Dylan had been looking down at what seemed to be a bed below the window.

Taking great care, he looked inside again. Dylan was still standing in the same place. Gilchrist took his time, and had a proper look. Dylan was standing by the side of a bed, looking down at a small boy who was curled up tightly, crying to himself. He noticed there were tears streaming down Dylan's face as well and that he was shaking with emotion. A thick curtain was hanging from a big beam of wood that was holding the roof up, and so this little space was almost completely dark.

Gilchrist drew back from the window again, and leaned against the wall of the house. What was Dylan doing? What reason did he have to come to this village and to this little boy who was lying, crying in his bed? Gilchrist was at a complete loss. He looked around, as if that would help him solve the mystery.

Then, he heard a most beautiful voice singing a sweet lullaby. He had never heard such a divine sound before. He looked around, and above him, thinking that The Twelve, from Axa's Angel Choir had come to earth on a mission that he didn't know of. No, there was no other angel in sight, and besides, he would have sensed the presence of another angel, as he sensed now that Dylan was the other side of the wall. Where could the singing be coming from? Then, to his consternation he understood.

Dylan!

The angel everybody in heaven knew couldn't sing because he was always out of tune! It couldn't be anyone else.

Gilchrist turned to look through the shutters again. He couldn't believe his ears. Dylan was still standing by the side of the bed, but was now singing a song of such beauty, Gilchrist felt as if he was soaring high above in the sky. At the same time, a comforting peace flowed through him. He sat on his haunches and pressed his back against the wall. Staring ahead of him, he realised how much he missed heaven when he was away from there. Dylan's song was caressing him. He felt himself luxuriating in a lake of the warmest, softest water imaginable. His voice was crystal clear and every note sung seemed like a drop of honey. Tears started running down Gilchrist's face and his powerful shoulders heaved under the emotional weight of Dylan's singing. He even had to use the bottom of his tunic to dry the flow of tears.

Gilchrist understood that Dylan had come to sing a lullaby to the little boy. But why? He could not say. Neither did he know how Dylan knew about him. It could only be a gift that had been given him by the Lord of the Angel Armies.

Then, the singing stopped.

Soon, Dylan appeared from inside the house and wiped his last tears away. He tripped over a rock and as he fell he hit his knee hard against it. He let out a sudden cry of pain. He didn't remember seeing this rock on the way in. Slowly, he got up and limped a few paces before he hobbled his customary hop, skip and a jump as he took off, this time headed back for heaven. Gilchrist quickly transformed himself back from the rock, and rubbed his head.

'How did he get such a hard knee?' he asked.

He could see Dylan gaining height in the distance. He turned and went into the house through the brick wall. The child was sleeping peacefully, no longer crying. Gilchrist looked around, wondering where his mother and father were. He poked his head through the heavy curtain and there he saw them sitting on the floor. The mother looked back at him sorrowfully. Momentarily he was fazed by the thought that she had seen him. The father's sullen face, on the other hand, stared into space. Gilchrist had no idea what was happening and why Dylan should have come down here to sing the boy a lullaby. One thing he did know: he needed to get back to heaven.

Soon he was flying through the night sky, to report back to Michael and Gabriel.

On his return, he immediately made his way to the Archangel Michael's hall. He could hear the choir practising in the great rehearsal hall. Dylan was late after his singing errand on earth and had tried to slip in at the back hoping that Axa would not see him.

'Dylan!' he bellowed.

All the angels turned to look back at Dylan as the singing quickly petered out.

'What have you been doing that is more important than this rehearsal?' asked Axa.

'If only you knew,' thought Gilchrist, smiling to himself.

When Gilchrist reached Michael's Hall, there were a lot of angels receiving orders from the archangel. He knew many of them since he had been on a number of joint missions with them over the centuries. Watching them now, listening keenly before they left on their different errands, Gilchrist felt great pride in knowing that he was a cog – maybe an insignificant one – but still a cog in the great host of angels who worked tirelessly for the Lord of the Angel Armies.

Finally, the great hall was empty.

'Gilchrist,' greeted Michael. 'Come in.'

As he walked in, Gabriel followed, not long having returned from earth himself. He was eager to hear what Gilchrist had to report. The warrior, sensing someone behind him turned and saw the messenger angel. Before Gilchrist could say anything, Michael asked Gabriel how it had gone with Joseph.

'Let's just say the marriage is back on track. When you get back to Nazareth Gilchrist, your troops will fill in the det...'

He stopped short for as he looked at Gilchrist he could see the unmistakable evidence of streaks of tears on his cheeks. In the ensuing silence, first Gabriel, and then Michael turned to look at Gilchrist.

The archangel saw what Gabriel had noticed. He looked quizzically at Gilchrist.

'Have you been crying?' he asked, disbelievingly.

'Yes.'

Michael was shocked. He couldn't quite believe. What made it more difficult to comprehend was that Gilchrist had given him such a straight answer: no embarrassment, no sheepishness. What's more, Michael and Gabriel had the distinct feeling he was daring them, and anyone else to taunt or ridicule him for crying. What had made Gilchrist, the great warrior of heaven cry?

'Why?'

'Dylan.'

'Dylan?!'

'Dylan,' he confirmed flatly.

Michael and Gabriel were intrigued.

'That bad, was he?' asked Michael, the slightest trace of a smile tickling his lips.

'No!'

The manner in which he uttered that short, monosyllabic answer, with a hint of defiance, his hand on the hilt of his sword made them think he was ready to defend the little angel's honour and good name. The archangel was unsettled.

'You'd better sit down and tell us all about it.'

Gilchrist related everything that had happened, in detail. When he came to the part where Dylan had sung so beautiful a lullaby to the child, he told them he felt a deep river of peace flow through him. He was not ashamed to tell them that elation overwhelmed him and that he cried tears of uncontrollable joy.

'So, where is he now?' asked Michael.

'The last I saw of him, Axa was asking him why he was so late for choir practice.'

Michael turned to Gabriel.

'We need to speak to him.'

'Yes.'

'Gilchrist, go and fetch him.'

'What? Now?'

'This very minute.'

'But he's in choir practice.'

'Fetch him.'

Gilchrist left immediately. He soon arrived at the rehearsal room.

Gilchrist marvelled at the sound. This celebration to present their Lord to the world was going to be very special. He waited until they had finished the song, and Axa, who was aware of his presence, turned to him.

'Gilchrist, a pleasure to see you.'

'Axa,' nodded Gilchrist.

'Have you come to join the choir?'

Gilchrist's reply was emphatic.

'No, thank you. I think it would be better if I didn't – for your sake. You haven't heard me sing, obviously,' he replied, smiling.

'Yes, of course,' Axa agreed.

Every angel in the choir listened with great curiosity.

'What can I do for you?' asked Axa.

'Archangel Michael and Gabriel: they want to see Dylan, immediately.'

A murmur swept through the host of angels, as they turned to speak to a neighbour.

'What's Dylan done?'

'It must be serious.'

'Yes, for Michael and Gabriel to want to see him.'

Those angels standing nearest to Dylan at the very back of the choir turned to look at him. Dylan himself had not been paying much attention, lost in his own thoughts.

'Dylan!' he heard Axa call from the front.

It was only then that he realised that all the angels were looking at him.

'Gilchrist says that Archangel Michael and Gabriel want to see you.'

Slowly, and nervously, Dylan made his way down to the front, where Gilchrist was waiting. All the angels were silent, wondering what on earth had he done. Had he disobeyed them in some way? Maybe, it was all those times he was away from heaven.

'Come with me,' said Gilchrist, curtly.

With head bowed, Dylan followed Gilchrist in silence. Then, he stopped, and as if pleading his case, and in a pitiful voice, he said,

'I *can* sing you know.'

Axa, as did a number of the angels, especially The Twelve, had to restrain themselves from laughing. Others looked down, embarrassed for the angel, who was so liked by many of them.

'But I can,' he protested.

No one except Axa saw Gilchrist nod his head in agreement.

'You had better go now, Dylan,' said Axa.

With heavy feet, Dylan turned and was led away by the warrior angel.

Axa was relieved that the awkward scene was over, and returned to his choir practice. Now, they could really get down to work, and prepare properly.

Gilchrist and Dylan walked the short distance to Michael's Hall in silence.

By now Dylan was very worried. What could he have done that both Michael and Gabriel wanted to see him? And why had Gilchrist been sent to fetch him, one of Michael's most trusted warrior angels? Maybe they were going to tell him that he would not be allowed to sing in the choir ever again, and that Axa had finally got his way. Panic shot through Dylan's whole being as he realised that if he wasn't allowed to sing in the choir, he probably would not be allowed to go to the celebration.

With short, hesitant steps, Dylan followed Gilchrist as he strode ahead of him to Michael's Hall. Once there he saw Michael and Gabriel sitting, waiting for him. Gilchrist showed him to a chair in front of the two mighty angels and without a word bid him sit on it. Gilchrist's silence discomforted him. In fact, the whole experience got the better of him.

'I really can sing you know,' he pleaded again.

'We know,' said Michael. 'We know.'

Dylan thought he was only trying to comfort him.

'Yes, but I can!'

'We do know that Dylan, I can assure you,' Michael answered with a quiet, strangely comforting authority that made Dylan relax a little.

Michael looked at him intently.

'Dylan, you often leave heaven for earth. Tell me, where do you go and what do you do?'

Dylan shifted nervously on the chair. He looked at Michael and Gabriel, towering over him, before slowly turning his head to look behind him. There was Gilchrist, standing tall, his left hand resting on the hilt of his sword shining in its sheath. He felt afraid.

Sensing his fear, Michael calmed him.

'You have absolutely nothing to worry about,' he assured him. 'We just want to know what happens when you leave heaven. You have done nothing wrong.'

Relieved, Dylan decided to tell them everything. He took a deep breath and slowly started his confession.

'Well... I go to certain people on earth. Babies, children, married couples and old people, well, old women mainly. There are more old women than old men on earth,' he laughed nervously.

'To do what?'

Dylan didn't answer him. He breathed heavily. He felt he was standing on a high cliff edge, with no option but to jump.

'I... I sing to them!'

He lowered his head, fully expecting Michael, Gabriel and Gilchrist to burst out laughing. But no-one laughed; didn't even snigger. Emboldened, he raised his head. He was surprised to see Michael nod his head. He asked him another question.

'Yes, but why these people? What's so special about them?

'Well, because they're sad of course!' he replied, a little indignantly.

Michael sat back in his chair.

'How do you know they're sad? Who lets you know?' asked Gabriel.

'No one. I just get this feeling inside me that tells me that I'm needed: a sadness fills me. I'm drawn to people who are sad: two magnets attracting each other, I suppose.'

'Are you sad?' asked Michael.

'No, only when they are.'

A second or two elapsed.

'So, you don't know where you're going. You're just, shall we say, pulled by the need,' said Michael.

'Yes.'

'And it could be anywhere in the world.'

Dylan nodded in reply. Then a thought struck him.

'Why, do you want to come with me? Is that what this is all about?' he asked enthusiastically.

Gilchrist felt a laugh jump out of his stomach. By the time it arrived in his mouth he had managed to disguise it as a cough.

Michael gave him a puzzled look.

Gilchrist had just imagined Michael – the Archangel Michael – his mighty general, flying down to earth, following Dylan, not knowing where he was going and ending up singing with him. A faint smile raced across Gabriel's lips too.

'No, but thanks. Tell me about your last journey.'

'It was a five year old boy, called Kamal. I go to see him often. His father isn't very nice to him. For some reason, once the sun goes down, he's sent to bed, with no light. He'd like to spend more time with his mother, but his father won't hear of it. Thing is, Kamal is petrified of the dark – scared stiff of it. He lies there crying quietly to himself, because he knows if he cries out loud then his dad will get angry and start shouting at him – sometimes he even beats him – and then his mother will take his side and then his father will start shouting and swearing at her. Then Kamal blames himself for causing the upset.'

'So, you sing to him, you say.'

'Yes.'

There was short silence in the great hall. The stars and moon above and below them twinkled brightly. Michael was thinking how to say what he had to say next. He didn't want to hurt the angel's feelings. He ran his hand across his brow.

'Pardon me for saying, but when you sing in the choir you're always out of tune.'

'When I sing in the choir,' Dylan stated. 'When I sing to Kamal and the other sad people I visit, a beautiful voice comes from inside.'

Through the corner of his eye, Michael saw Gilchrist nod his head.

'How do you mean?' asked Gabriel.

The three great angels pricked up their ears to hear Dylan's answer.

Dylan let out another sigh. He didn't know how to explain this.

'I really don't know.'

He thought a little more.

'When I'm there with them, a deep sadness fills me. They shouldn't be like this. Our Lord didn't create them to be like that. And I want to help them in any way I can. It's very difficult for me to explain, but I open my mouth and from this deep sorrow a beautiful voice comes out. I sing soaring melodies and tunes that ease their pain, and their tears are dried from within. I even harmonise with myself, and they're comforted.'

'You take away their pain then,' reasoned Michael.

Dylan shot his answer back.

'No, no, no. I couldn't do that. That's impossible for me or any other angel to do. I can only comfort them for a short time. I can't take away their pain. Only our Lord would be able to do that. I wish He would, but I don't know how He can.'

At this, Michael and Gabriel looked hurriedly at each other, their eyes wide with astonishment. They were amazed at how perceptive this little angel was.

Dylan continued.

'I sing a song of comfort to them.' Then he raised his voice and spoke defiantly. 'I don't care what age you are, everybody loves a song sung to them.'

Michael and Gabriel looked at each other again, and it dawned on them what Dylan's great mission was to be the night baby Jesus would be born.

'Thank you, Dylan,' said Michael.

'Am I to stop doing what I'm doing?' he asked nervously.

'Not at all.'

Dylan breathed a sigh of relief.

'You carry on. Don't let us stop you.'

'Well, what shall I tell the others when I go back to the choir? I'd like to keep this a secret. No one will believe me if I told them and they'd all probably laugh. They'll all want to know why I was brought here.'

Gabriel volunteered an answer for him.

'Tell them we talked about your singing in the choir, that we are very pleased with what you're doing, and would like you to carry on being part of the choir.'

'Axa won't be too happy with that. He can't wait to get rid of me.'

Michael smiled and looked intently into Dylan's eyes.

'Don't you worry about him. You just keep on singing your heart out worshipping and serving our Lord in your own special way.'

Dylan couldn't believe what Michael had said. For the first time since he had been brought into his hall a broad smile stretched across his worried face. He shrugged his shoulders.

'Worship is the same as service and service is much the same as worship.'

'Quite! Gilchrist!'

'Boss.'

'Take Dylan back to the choir practice.'

The warrior stepped forward.

Dylan got up off the chair and walked towards him. As he neared the doorway he turned back to look at the two senior angels.

'All I want to do is sing to them and make them happy.'

They both smiled as Dylan and Gilchrist left.

Gabriel stood up.

'A remarkable angel.'

'Yes, I agree.'

'I was amazed when he said only our Lord can take away their pain.'

'He must live his life close to Him.'

'Well, at least we now know what our Lord wants him to do,' declared Gabriel.

'Yes. He won't be able to sing during the announcement with the choir, though.'

'He'll be very disappointed.

'Axa won't be.'

'Yes, but Dylan will have much more important work to do.'

'It will be quite a shock to him. Do you think he'll be able to handle it all?'

'Yes. Gilchrist will be nearby, as will the other four,' replied Gabriel. 'They'll look after him.'

'And anyway,' added Michael, 'our Lord wants him to be there.'

Chapter 14

Joseph slowly stirred from his slumbers. He felt he'd been in a deep sleep. He hadn't expected that after the stresses of the previous day. He stretched himself from head to toe. Then he shot up in his bed at the sudden recollection of his dream. An angel had come to him, and he could remember every word it had said to him. He said them out loud to himself.

'Joseph, son of David, don't think twice about taking Mary as your wife. God's Holy Spirit has made her pregnant. She will give birth to a son, and you will call him Jesus – God saves – because he will save his people from their sins.'

The angel reiterated what Mary had told him, that God's Holy Spirit had made her pregnant, and that she would have a Son, and would call Him Jesus. Joseph then recalled the very first thing the angel had said: it was aimed at him. He was not to hesitate: he was to take her as his wife.

He thought of Mary. What had he done? She had been telling the truth all the while. She had been made pregnant by the Holy Spirit. What came next to Joseph made him jump to his feet. If that were true, it followed that she had not been made pregnant by man. She had not been having an affair! What's more, as the angel told him, he was to take her as his wife!

He was dressed in no time and he walked briskly over to her parents' house. Such was his desire to see Mary, he didn't hear Amos, an old bachelor man who daily sat by one of the town's wells, greet him. He was so old no one in Nazareth knew his age, not even he himself. Amos remarked loud enough for Joseph to hear,

'Youth of today.'

The object of his scorn ploughed on, his face set like flint. He walked purposefully up to the house, and knocked excitedly on the door, his whole body was shaking with nervousness. He was concerned that she would have told her parents what had happened between them the night before. The door opened, and Ben, Mary's father stood there.

He was a man approaching early middle age with receding hair line. For as long as Joseph knew him Ben had walked with a slightly stooped back. Some of the less charitable of the villagers attributed this to the burden of being married to Abigail for so long. However, his bright, vibrant eyes and youthful face spoke of a man in love with life, and with his wife.

'Joseph! You're early today. Come in, come in.'

Joseph breathed a sigh of relief. It was obvious from the way Ben greeted him that he knew nothing of the previous day's events.

'No, I won't come in, Ben, but could you call Mary, and could you do me a great favour and not tell her it's me: I want to surprise her.'

Ben looked at him, a wry smile on his face, recalling the days when young love was thrilling before the pressures of everyday life and over-famili-arity had blunted the novelty and dulled the lustre.

'Mary!' he shouted out, smiling at Joseph. 'Someone to see you.'

He turned to walk away, not wanting to intrude. Joseph stepped out of sight and waited. Less than a minute later, he sensed that Mary had come to the door. He stepped back into view, and confronted her with as big and as endearing a smile as he could muster through the dark, small curls of his beard. The smile soon disappeared as he noticed her swollen eyes and streaks of dried tears on her cheeks.

On her way home the previous evening, Mary too, had cried stinging tears. She had hardly walked a quarter of the way home than she stopped, feeling physically weak. She couldn't walk a step further and had to rest a while. Pulling her shawl tightly over her bent head she had leant against the side of a house. She couldn't go home, not like that. Her parents would want to know what had happened to upset her so. She couldn't be dealing with that just then. Besides, she wanted to be alone, needed time to compose herself before she faced them. After a few minutes she had walked, with heavy heart, to the village well to wash away her tears.

When, eventually, she arrived home, dusk had already descended on the village. She went indoors, her shawl still wrapped around her head. She went straight to her bed, telling her mother, without looking at her, that she didn't want any supper. Her parents were mystified at her demeanour. This was very unlike their daughter, who usually had plenty to say, always making her presence felt whenever she was in the house. She looked like a withered autumn leaf. They let her be, but would have been deeply troubled had they known that she had cried silently throughout the long dark hours of that night.

Standing before Joseph now, desolate and dispirited, made him want to take her in his arms and tell her that everything was going to be okay. He would stand by her; she was not on her own; they would be together, forever. The one small problem was he had dismissed her unceremoniously the previous evening; terminated their betrothal, forthwith. He had work to do and he didn't know whether she would have him back.

'Mary, I'm sorry. I've been a fool. Could you please come with me?'

She looked at the ground, letting her long hair fall haphazardly around her face. There followed a long silence. Joseph was very nearly at the end of his tether. At last, she raised her head and looked at him. He breathed again, as he felt her open the door to her heart a little.

'Why should I?'

'I have something very urgent to tell you, and I can't say it here.'

'But I thought...'

'Mary, if I could, I would carry you away with me, but I can't touch you. So, please, come. We need to speak.'

Not knowing or understanding what was happening, nevertheless sensing the urgency in his voice, she followed him. They passed Amos. He wasn't one to hold a grudge for too long and seeing Mary – who always stopped to speak to him – accompanying Joseph, he ventured another greeting. Joseph was so concerned about how he was going to tell Mary about the night visitation he did not hear him. Likewise Mary, for she was at a loss as to what Joseph was doing. The old man lifted both hands in the air in despair, and let them fall, slapping either knee. Presently, Joseph and Mary arrived at his workshop. He went inside and stood by the cedar wood desk, whilst she stayed in the doorway. Mary looked at him with troubled eyes. Had he brought her back to berate her for her perceived unfaithfulness to him? And yet his face was beaming like the sun on the fourth morning of Creation. He looked at her excitedly, like a little boy who had an announcement to make regarding some success of his.

'He came to see me last night.'

Mary was bewildered.

'Who did?'

'The angel! Probably the one who spoke to you.'

'What? He came to see you?'

Mary shivered. She was wide eyed with excitement and curiosity.

'Well, in my dreams.'

'Did he say anything?'

Joseph couldn't hide the shame he felt as he answered sheepishly.

'He told me that the Holy Spirit had made you pregnant...' He stopped to take a deep breath before uttering what he had to say next, '...and that I wasn't to think twice about taking you as my wife.'

She looked at him, unmoved by what he had just said. After a few seconds of silence, she responded.

'So, what are you going to do'? she asked, her face impassive.

In less than a heartbeat, he answered her.

'I want to marry you Mary. I love you. I'm in love with you. Always have been, always will be.'

He walked up to her, and got down on one knee.

'Forgive me for doubting you. Will you please marry me, Mary?'

She looked into his dark eyes. For what seemed like an eternity to Joseph she was lost in her thoughts. Eventually, she said,

'Let me think about it.'

She looked out of the window as he had done the night before, whilst Joseph held his breath. Instantly, she turned her eyes back and engaged his.

'I've thought about it... yes! 'Yes! Yes! Yes! Joseph,' she answered enthusiastically.

Cadman, Joram, Ebin and Caleb let out loud, triumphant hollers.

Thrilled beyond his wildest dreams, Joseph stood in front of her, and looked at her radiant face.

'I'm sorry, Mary. I should have believed you. I didn't. It took an angel to come from heaven to convince me of the truth.'

'Well, what I had to tell you *was* quite incredible,' she confessed.

He smiled.

'It certainly was.'

They looked lovingly into each other's eyes.

'I still can't believe that God should have chosen me to do this.'

'I can understand why,' replied Joseph.

'Do you? I can't.'

'He knows you, Mary.'

'Yes, but there are thousands of girls my age in Israel. Why me?'

'Mary. He knows you,' he reassured her. 'And anyway, I could ask the same thing.

She looked at him a little puzzled.

'The angel told me to marry you, Mary. That means I will be Jesus's father, here on earth. Can you imagine how much responsibility that will be for me, and for you as His mother?'

Mary blew through her lips, amazed at the privilege given them and the trust that God had in them.

She looked into his eyes.

'Are you sure about this, Joseph?'

He answered in a soft but fervent voice, which reverberated to her core.

'Don't ever ask me that again. You are mine, and I am yours.'

She breathed easier on hearing that confirmation.

'It could be awkward though,' she said.

'I know. Women are going to talk.'

'Mostly behind my back... let them.'

'Let them,' agreed Joseph.

'Men are going to talk about you.'

'I know.'

'Whatever we say about the way I've become pregnant, they'll still think that you had your way with me.'

'Yes, but this is from God, Mary. And you said yourself that, with or without me, you were going to go through with it.'

'And I also said I'd prefer to have you with me.'

'Well, that's good, because you're stuck with me now.'

They looked into each other's eyes once again, and in the silence that ensued, a wordless contract was exchanged, whereby they agreed to stand by each other for the rest of their lives, come what may.

'We will have to tell your parents.'

Mary pondered a while.

'That could be awkward, especially the way my mother is, and my father won't be happy.'

'When are you going to tell them?'

Mary sighed, and shook her head,

'I don't know, but I've got to... '

'Let's go tell them now! We can start arranging the wedding then.'

Of course, the wedding! Last night, she had put all thoughts of a wedding out of her mind. Now, it was back on; they'd been re-betrothed!

'Well, the angel did tell me not to hesitate taking you as my wife. I take that to mean that we are to marry before Jesus, the Messiah, is born. And anyway, the sooner we tell them, the sooner we can get married, and the sooner I can bring you home here to look after you.'

Mary smiled.

'Your house is in dire need of a woman's touch.'

Caleb looked at her quizzically. This woman was poaching his words.

'Are you ready, then?' he asked.

She was lost in her thoughts for a few seconds, worried about how her parents would respond to the news. She sighed aloud.

'Fine, let's do it.'

Another potential confrontation was in the offing. The second of many probably: she would have to get used to them.

Together, they walked to her house. They came upon Amos, still sitting by the well, musing about the inconsistencies of human nature.

'Morning, Amos. Haven't seen you for a long time,' remarked Joseph cheerily.

'Nice to see you,' added Mary.

The old man was dumbfounded.

'What's wrong with you today? The cat got your tongue?' asked Joseph, as they left him by the well. He continued his reflections on the fickleness of people.

'Where are you lot going?' asked Gilchrist, as he landed behind the four angels.

Caught unawares, they all jumped. They turned to face him.

'G!' rebuked Ebin. 'Don't do that.'

'Where have you been?' asked Cadman.

'We were expecting you back much sooner,' stated Joram.

'I had to go on a special mission for our Lord. I'll tell you about it...'

'No time, G. You'll have to tell us later on,' said Ebin.

'Things could well be kicking off here,' warned Caleb.

Gilchrist was confused.

'Gabriel did the job last night. Joseph and Mary are back together again, but now, they're going to tell her parents, and if her father doesn't like it, then...' explained Joram.

'...we could be back to square one,' said Caleb, breathless, 'and you may need to go back to heaven to fetch Gabriel again.'

'Surely not,' thought Gilchrist, as he fell in with the others behind Joseph and Mary.

Chapter 15

As they approached Mary's home she turned to Joseph.

'I'm dreading this more than having to tell you.'

'Well, I'm with you. You're not on your own. We'll do it together,' he reassured her.

For the second time, in less than half an hour, Joseph knocked the door to Mary's house. When Ben opened it and saw his daughter with Joseph, he thought it strange that she hadn't just walked into her own house. It pained him. For the very first time in her life she had shown that she did not consider his house to be her home any more. Then, when Joseph inquired, 'May we come in?' his heart bled. It was as much as he could do to muster enough energy to hide the pain from his face. It felt like an ocean had just appeared between him and his daughter.

He stepped back, holding his hand out to make way.

'Of course,' he said, lightly. 'Come in.'

They walked in and Ben called his wife, who was outside at the back of the house.

'Abigail! Mary and Joseph are here.'

Joseph and Mary sat beside each other on the cushions that lay on the floor by one side wall of the house. Abigail came in through the door, brushing some dirt from just inside the house with her sweeping brush. Although only a few years younger than her husband, she had already begun to display the features of middle age. Her lined face – especially the thick furrows on her forehead – made her look older than him. Mary was convinced her natural propensity to fret about what other people thought of her manifested itself in her worried brow. Then again, maybe it was because she felt aggrieved that she had only given birth to one child and the sore had not healed and was still sensitive. She didn't see the young couple, behind the open door. Nevertheless, seeing the pensive look on her husband's face she knew something was wrong.

'What's the matter?' she asked, closing the door. It was then that she saw Joseph and Mary on the cushions. She sensed the awkward silence and tension that pervaded the room and a cold shudder ran down her body from head to toe.

'They have something to tell us, Abigail.'

She carefully leant the sweeping-brush against the wall and sat on the cushions adjacent to the young couple. Her husband joined her. Despite Joseph's earlier bravado, facing his prospective parents-in-law, in the confines of their home, he was struck dumb. Mary looked expectantly at him. Seeing his reticence, she decided to take up the cudgels.

'Eema, Abba,' she said, using the Hebrew terms for mum and dad. 'I have something to say to you.'

'Your father just told me that,' her mother informed her, curtly.

Things had not begun well. She gathered her courage.

'I know this is going to sound crazy, but... just over a week ago, an angel appeared to me,' she heard herself say for the second time in less than twenty-four hours.

Her father and mother looked at her wide-eyed. Once again, Mary decided the best course of action was to tell them exactly what the angel had said to her. She could think of no other way and she knew she had to be mindful of them. This was beyond their wildest imaginings.

'He greeted me, and told me I was highly favoured.'

She stopped, to take a deep breath.

'He said that I was going to conceive, and give birth to a Son, and I was to call him Jesus.'

Her mother's hand shot up to her open mouth. This was what she had always feared. She looked despairingly at her daughter and then at Joseph. She was surprised to see them returning her gaze with determined faces.

'Joseph isn't the father.'

Slowly, and deliberately, Mary continued.

'He said he would be called the Son of the Highest, and the throne of his father David would be his, and he would rule the house of Jacob forever.'

She saw her mother wringing her hands.

'Here we go,' she thought to herself. This was her usual reaction on hearing some shameful news. However, it was her father's reaction that concerned her more, as his face turned deathly pale. He stared at the wall behind them, lost in his own thoughts.

'Don't look at Joseph like that, Eema. Like I said, he had nothing whatsoever to do with it.'

'You mean to tell me that you've been with another man?'

Abigail felt a slight nausea inside. This would be more shame than she could bear. How would she be able to face anyone in Nazareth ever again?

'No, Eema. Listen to me. This is of God.'

Her mother ignored her protestations; her father was dumbstruck.

'If Joseph isn't the father, then it's pretty obvious to me what's happened.'

Mary remained calm, patiently explaining to her.

'I asked the angel, "How? I've never slept with a man".'

Her mother looked disdainfully at her. Mary persevered.

'He said, "The Holy Spirit will come upon you, and the child you bring forth will be called the Son of God".'

'You can't expect me to believe that,' her mother said scornfully.

At last, Joseph found his tongue. Mary was thankful.

'It's true. I can empathise with you, Abigail. When Mary told me this yesterday, I didn't believe her. I even broke the betrothal. Then, last night, the angel – I presume it was the same one – appeared to me in a dream and told me not to hesitate as regards taking Mary as my wife, for she had indeed been made pregnant by the Holy Spirit.'

'Do you know how preposterous that is?' she asked, raising her voice. 'I'm a woman, and a mother, Joseph. I was made pregnant, but I couldn't have done that without my husband's help – her father. Benjamin! Say something.'

Mary was getting increasingly concerned about her father, as, by now, the blood had completely drained from his face, and his hands were shaking. He seemed to be bubbling inside and sooner or later he was going to erupt like some long forgotten, dormant volcano, and she would be in the path of the lava. By way of response to his wife's injunction, he slid from the cushion he was on and slowly got to his feet, all the while looking at his daughter as if he had seen a ghost. Mary looked at him tremulously. She hadn't seen him like this before. Poor man, she thought. He was only a humble stonemason and now he was confronted with this.

'Benjamin! Say something!' Abigail repeated.

Her husband said nothing. Instead, he walked over to the other side of the house, and looked out the window, to the hills surrounding Nazareth. As Mary watched him, she was reminded of the way Joseph reacted the night before and then told her that the betrothal was over. She shuddered as she remembered. Why didn't he say something? In that moment – some would say, moment of madness – Mary decided to tell them something else that the angel had told her she had not even told Joseph. Mary felt she had nothing to lose now.

'The angel told me one other thing,' she started.

Abigail stared at her.

'He said that cousin Elizabeth is pregnant.'

'Elizabeth! Pregnant!?' She gave a sneering laugh.

Mary continued undeterred.

'She's conceived a son.'

'At her age!'

'Despite her old age.'

Mary repeated the angel's message word for word.

'But she's barren!'

Abigail was throwing darts of absurdity at what her daughter was saying. Mary remained steadfast in the face of the onslaught of scepticism.

'Despite her barrenness,' she said, slowly nodding her head.

Joseph sitting quietly beside her admired her doggedness and gentle persistence. Mary hadn't finished.

'And what's more, the angel said, "She is six months pregnant! Nothing, you see is impossible with God," and I'll be leaving tomorrow to go and see her,' she announced.

'Will you?' Joseph blurted out.

'Yes.'

'You never told me.'

Abigail looked over at her husband, still standing at the window, holding on tightly to the small table that was in front of him, his whole body shaking. He was still lost in his thoughts, although, now and again, his eyes would stray to look disbelievingly at his daughter.

'See what you've done to your father. He can't speak from the shock and the shame you've brought on us.'

Mary was adamant however.

'This is none of my doing, Eema. This is from God,' she repeated, looking at her mother in all seriousness.

The five angels looked on, concerned. This was not going at all well. Gilchrist began to think that he might well have to return to heaven to fetch Gabriel again. Mary's mother was being unreasonable, while Ben, it seemed, was winding himself up to do something regrettable to Mary. Thus far, Cadman had been leaning back against the wall near to where Ben was standing, his arms folded across his chest, seemingly half asleep. Now, he pushed himself away from the wall as his eyes narrowed signalling his intent to react to any danger to Mary. The other four surrounded her father, also ready to defend his daughter at the slightest sign of peril to her. Abigail broke the silence.

'Am I the only one who thinks there's something wrong here? Or am I missing...?'

' "The seed of a woman".'

All eyes in the house, both human and angel, turned to look at her husband.

'What?' Abigail asked.

He looked at them intently.

' "The seed of a woman",' he repeated, but this time in a more logical and reasoned voice, as if he was providing the answer to a profound mathematical problem that had confounded the best minds for generations. The five angels relaxed. Joram looked at Caleb and Ebin who were standing between the old man and Mary.

'Make way: hero coming through, hero coming through,' he announced joyfully.

Both angels gave way as he walked towards Abigail, Mary and Joseph, to resume his seat. Then, he gently took hold of his wife's hand. Looking so intensely into her eyes that he frightened her, he recited,

' "I will put enmity between you and the woman, between your seed and her seed".'

With that, he looked at Mary, with the same intensity.

'What are you babbling about?' asked Abigail. She was beginning to think he'd lost his mind.

Still looking at Mary, he continued.

'The Torah, Abigail,' he said excitedly. 'The first five books of our scriptures. Right at the beginning, just after Satan had tempted Adam and Eve to eat the forbidden fruit, Yahweh spoke to him and said that he would forever crawl on his stomach and that from henceforth...' and here he spoke slowly, in hushed tones '... He declares war between his seed and her seed.'

Abigail was even more confused. Mary and Joseph were not far behind. The five warrior angels began to warm to the stonemason.

Squeezing her hand tighter, he chose his words carefully to explain to her.

'You were right, Abigail.'

'I know I was! Don't tell me! Tell her... and him!' she responded, pointing her finger at Joseph.

'No, no! You were right about needing my help to conceive Mary. Remember, my seed was impregnated in you. Do you remember?'

Despite her confusion, the faintest of smiles appeared in the corners of her mouth. Then she remembered that Mary and Joseph were sitting next to them. She suddenly went red with embarrassment. Her husband had never been so forthright with her about such things, and now he was having a full and frank airing of views on the matter, not only in front of their daughter, but her future husband as well.

'Right at the beginning, immediately after sin entered the world, God said that he would send someone to Right the Wrong. That One, would come from the seed of a woman. Abigail, that short sentence has perplexed our scholars for centuries. How could a man be born of a woman's seed, since every man, woman and child on this earth has been conceived from the physical union of a man and a woman? A man has supplied the seed and a woman the fertile soil for the seed to grow. And so, the sin that came into the world, was perpetuated, passed on by men; every child's desecrated inheritance. However many heirs were born, that inheritance was never diluted, never exhausted: a never ending legacy; an unbroken chain... until now. For this One, who was to come, would not be born of a man's seed, but would be of God, an immaculate conception...' and at this he turned to look at Mary again, this time in wonderment, '... through a virgin, the seed of a woman.'

They fell silent and stared at Mary. They were all stunned by what Ben had just said, even the angels. For too long, sin had had its own way on earth, keeping people enslaved in its dark and insidious kingdom. But this was the beginning of the end and before long there would be an escape. For her part, Mary felt a great desire to give her father a kiss for she could see that her mother was succumbing to his persuasion. Nevertheless, she was not about to give up without a fight.

'But why our Mary?

'Why not? I wouldn't be surprised that God wanted a woman who's as tough as she is, who isn't afraid to go against the grain, because she will have to be strong, with or without us.'

'But she's just an ordinary girl.'

'Doesn't God have a track record of using ordinary people in these circumstances? Who would have chosen David, the youngest of Jesse's sons to be king of Israel after Saul? But God did.'

At this, Ben gave Joseph a knowing smile.

Abigail tried another tack.

'What about Elizabeth? How can she be pregnant, Ben? She and Zechariah have been trying for years. They're both past it now.'

Ben shrugged his shoulders.

'I don't know. But what about Abraham and Sarah, Rebecca, Isaac's wife, and Hannah, the mother of Samuel, the prophet? They were all barren, and Sarah was way past it, as you say, but they all gave birth to boys.'

'That was centuries ago.'

'Are you telling me that God can't make it happen now? No, Abigail, He is the same yesterday, today and tomorrow.'

'I know,' she conceded, 'but a virgin birth, Ben. It's beyond belief. How's it possible.'

Ben caressed his wife's cheek lovingly.

'I don't know the answer to that either, Abbie.'

She took a sharp intake of breath. He hadn't called her that in years.

'One thing I do know is that we are fearfully and wonderfully made. And if God made the human body, then He knows how to make a woman – our Mary, Abbie – pregnant, without the intervention and assistance of any man. Mary and Joseph have not slept together, and neither has she been with another man. I believe her.'

Mary felt a sudden lump in her throat.

At last, Abigail succumbed to her husband's reasoning. They stared into each other's eyes. For them, there was no one else in the room. And much as Joseph and Mary had looked into each other's eyes less than an hour earlier and signed a wordless contract, so Ben and Abigail did the same, to stand by their daughter, come what may, at whatever cost, during the next few months.

'I like him,' said Joram.

'Yeah, so do I,' agreed Gilchrist.

The others grunted their approval.

Ben jumped to his feet, startling everyone, including the watching angels.

'Joseph!' he announced. 'Are you willing to marry our daughter, in spite of what's happened to her, and what's going to happen to her?'

'You mean... her pregnancy?'

'I most definitely do.'

'I most definitely am.'

They smiled at each other. He looked at his daughter.

'Mary, stand up.'

She did as she was told. He put his arms around her and held her tightly.

'You are my daughter,' he whispered in her ear, 'and you are indeed highly blessed and favoured by our Lord. I am proud to be your father.'

She lay her head on her father's shoulder – a four year old little girl once again – blissful tears of acceptance on her cheeks. The ocean Ben felt between them earlier had all but evaporated in an instant. With one arm still round her shoulders, he held his other arm out to his wife.

'Abbie.'

Once on her feet, he gently pulled her into the embrace with their daughter. Silent for a while, they were locked together. Joseph felt himself an awkward intruder on intimate, familial terrain. Ben looked over the women's heads at him.

'Joseph,' he announced. 'You are a big bear of a man, but I have heard that even bears embrace their own family.'

'But Ben, you know I'm not allowed to touch my prospective wife until we are married.'

'I know. But you know as well as I do that that rule is for when you two are on your own. Abigail and I are here. Besides, this is no ordinary situation. So, come.'

With that, he shot up and wrapped his powerful arms around them all.

'We'll need to arrange the wedding,' said Ben. 'After all, we're only three months away from the end of your twelve month betrothal.'

He had taken complete control of the situation.

'That's why we came to see you,' explained Joseph.

'As soon as I get back from seeing Elizabeth,' added Mary.

All three looked inquiringly at Abigail.

She simply nodded and smiled through her tears.

Caleb was overcome. Standing behind the other angels, he stepped forward to put his arm around Ebin and rested his head on his shoulder.

'Stop it! Now!' he ordered, in a flat, slightly threatening voice.

Caleb quickly lifted his head and took his arm away.

Chapter 16

Next day, Mary left Nazareth, heading south for the hills of Judah, and unbeknown to her, with five warrior angels in tow. She stayed with Zechariah and Elizabeth for three months, until the birth of John, their son. Having witnessed these events, full of joy and exultation, and with her cousin's prayers, Mary made the journey back to Nazareth.

On her return she recounted what had happened. Ben, Abigail and Joseph were amazed to hear that Zechariah had also had a visitation from an angel. They all wondered whether it was the same angel who spoke to Mary and Joseph. If so, they concluded that he must be a very busy angel.

'He doesn't do much of anything else!' snorted Caleb.

During her absence Ben, Abigail and Joseph had been busy preparing the wedding. When the day finally arrived, it seemed the whole of Galilee and nature itself had made a special effort to look their best. Almond, fig and olive trees showed off their rich deep colours with the lush pasture providing a verdant background that only enhanced the vibrant colours of the flowering trees. Well-wishers were bathed in bright sunshine, the sun majestic in the cloudless azure sky. After the ceremony, crowds flocked to them, joyously applauding the newly-weds, while Joseph proudly held Mary's hand in public for the first time.

Ben, watching from afar, smiled to himself. He said a silent prayer of thanks to Yahweh for giving him such a daughter, and for giving her such a husband. He admired their determination and at the same time committed himself to them for the duration. Abigail was standing beside him. Since she had accepted Mary's part in the impending virgin birth, mother and daughter's relationship had blossomed. They had grown closer as a family and intimacy had returned to Ben and Abigail's marriage. It seemed as if they had fallen in love with each other all over again, and the second time was sweeter than the first. Like her husband, she made a silent pledge that she would be with her daughter every step of the way. Little was she or Ben to know, that neither of them would get to keep their promises.

That night, when the festivities finally came to an end, Joseph took Mary, his wife, home. He shut the door on the world outside. Gilchrist and his four warriors thought it prudent to absent themselves. Joseph turned to look at Mary. He took her by the hand, and led her to the matrimonial bed.

He sat on it and pulled her down to sit on his lap, his arm wrapped around her.

'You know that there'll be no love making tonight,' he said.

'Yes, my love. I'm sorry.'

'Don't ever apologise for this, Mary. We mustn't, however hard it'll be for you to keep your hands off me. Let's be honest, ask yourself, have you ever seen a more handsome and more desirable creature in your life?'

'I know. How am I going to manage it?' she asked, putting her hand on her chest and rolling her eyes heavenwards.

Joseph was serious again.

'You and I know and understand that it has to be a virgin birth.'

She looked lovingly into his sparkling eyes, and put her hand on the side of his face.

'Oh, Joseph, I love you so much.'

He pushed her to stand up, and stood before her.

'Now then, Mary. Let me hold you close.'

With that, he embraced her, and lifted her off the floor, her feet dangling half way up his shins. It took her breath away. She looked at him. They were both floating on air, she, literally, both relishing the moment of intimacy and privacy longed for, for so long.

'Are you going to carry me everywhere I go? I could get used to it, you know.'

'Enjoy the ride,' he advised her.

He put her back on her feet.

In the dark still of the night, she lay on their matrimonial bed. Then, he lay beside her, and looked into her dazzling eyes that seemed to sparkle more than ever tonight. He gently brushed some strands of hair that had strayed on to her face and revelled in her beauty. He could not believe that she was his wife. With his body he wanted to show her that he loved her, that he would care for her come what may and would stand beside her forever. He felt his mouth suddenly go dry, nervous at what he was about to do. He wanted to physically honour her, after all, this was their wedding night. So, he drew her to him, and with his eyes still gazing into hers, he kissed her lips. Then he held her hand. That's all.

Chapter 17

Gilchrist was the first to see them coming. His eyes were drawn to around twenty iron helmets, glistening in the hazy, late morning sun, bobbing, floating in the air. The small detachment of Roman soldiers made its way up the slopes from the Valley of Jezreel towards Nazareth. As they approached, the inhabitants heard the heavy step of the hobnailed sandals and the rhythmic jangling of the metal discs dangling like grossly oversized jewellery from the cingulum around the legionaries' waists. On entering the village's small market place, men, women and children gathered, wondering why these representatives of the Roman Empire had ventured to such an inconsequential place. Roman soldiers were hated by most Jews for they were an army of occupation, and in Galilee they were despised more than in any other part of the country. Jewish people had been conquered before, and would be conquered again, but however many times it happened, it didn't make the experience any easier. All Jews yearned for the day when the Messiah would finally arrive and drive their enemies away.

Gilchrist, on the other hand, had been waiting for this moment. He watched as the centurion leading the men, resplendent in his colourful ostrich plumed helmet, brought them to a halt. He had long respected Roman soldiers because of their resilience and persistence in the heat of battle. Gilchrist still wondered at what he witnessed in the Battle of Alessia some fifty years earlier when the Roman army under Julius Caesar, heavily outnumbered by Gauls, won the day. These were men of the Roman Sixth Legion – the Iron Clads – which had been formed by the present Caesar Augustus. The centurion waited a while for the villagers to gather.

'Well, let's get on with it,' Gilchrist said to himself.

As if responding directly to his murmured entreaty, the centurion reached for a scroll, and after unrolling it, began to read its contents to the gathered knot of people.

'Notice is hereby given that a census of all the people of the Roman Empire will be held in a three weeks' time. For this purpose, all males and their families are ordered to return to their home towns to present themselves to the census taker. Anyone disobeying will be severely punished. By order of Caesar Augustus.'

Then, he called for the village leaders to come to him and informed them that they were to feed him and his men before they made their way back to Tiberias, by the Galilean Sea.

It was a short address, telling in its ramifications. Instantly, the inhabitants began to speak amongst each other. Gilchrist was unconcerned. Rather, he looked over at Joseph, who, on hearing the tense but excited shouting outside his workshop that the Romans were approaching, had made his way briskly to the market place. He pondered the significance of the announcement for a while before returning home. He walked slowly contemplating the implications of what he had just heard meant for him, but for Mary in particular. She was just over eight months by now, and the thought of her having to travel such a long journey frankly worried him.

He arrived back home to find her sitting on some cushions. Despite the bleariness in her eyes from a slumber she had just woken from, she could see the concern in his furrowed brow.

'What's wrong?'

He sat beside her, putting his arm around her shoulders.

'I'm going to have to go to Bethlehem.'

'What?'

'Some Roman soldiers have arrived in the village. They announced that a census is to be held and every man is to go to his home town. And you've got to come with me.'

'Why?'

Ben and Abigail appeared in the doorway, as if from nowhere.

'You've heard the news?' asked Ben.

'Yes,' replied Joseph, getting up from the cushions.

Abigail rushed to take his place and put her arm around Mary.

'You're from the House of David, aren't you?' Ben asked Joseph.

'Yes.'

'You've got to go to Bethlehem.'

'Yes.'

'The other end of the country.'

'Yes.'

Abigail held her daughter tightly. She was getting impatient with her husband's pointless questions and her son-in-law's monosyllabic answers. She brought things back to the practicalities of the situation.

'We can't come with you: Ben is from Sepphoris,' she said, despairingly.

Sepphoris was only a short journey the other side of the mountain, to the north of Nazareth.

'But why do I have I got to go with you, Joseph?' asked Mary.

'Every man has to take his family with him. You're my wife.'

'If you hadn't married, you could have come to Sepphoris with us,' stated Abigail.

She looked at her husband who was by now lost in his thoughts.

'Well, say something, man!'

Stirred from his musings, Ben looked at Abigail and started reciting from the scriptures.

'Bethlehem, Ephrathah,' he said, looking at her fervently, 'though you are small among the clans of Judah, out of you will come for me one who will be ruler over Israel, whose origins are from of old, from ancient times.'

She was taken aback by how impassioned he was.

'Don't you see, Abbie?'

There he was again, calling her by her diminutive. Why did he only do this when he was talking scripture with her?

'Seven hundred years ago, the prophet Micah prophesied that the ruler of Israel – the Messiah – would come from Bethlehem, David's city, and Joseph here is a direct descendant of King David.'

Mary looked up at her husband.

'You didn't tell me.'

He shrugged his shoulders and offered a weak defence.

'You err, didn't ask.'

'No,' she smiled giving herself a light slap on the forehead. 'I should have thought to ask whether you had royal blood in you. Now, why didn't I think of that?'

He smiled back at her. Abigail was resigning herself to the situation.

'So, the pieces are falling into place.'

'They have to go to Bethlehem, Abbie.'

She turned to Joseph.

'How long do you think it'll take you?'

'I'd say ten days, but the condition Mary's in, it'll be more like a fortnight.'

'Which way will you go?' asked Ben.

'Best to go to Jezreel, and then down the Jordan Valley and cut across towards Jericho and head south for Bethlehem.'

Ben nodded his head in agreement. The other option was to go over the hilly terrain of Samaria. Going down the Jordan Valley would be much easier, albeit longer, and replete with difficulties and dangers of its own. Most people travelled that way when they were going south to Jerusalem and Bethlehem was not far beyond the capital.

'Well,' he responded, 'if you're going to be in Bethlehem in time, you'd better leave in a few days.

'I was thinking that myself.'

He turned to Mary.

'We have no choice: Rome tells us we must go to Bethlehem.'

'More than that, Yahweh wants you there,' added Ben.

All four were struck by the inevitable nature of these events and that they were mortal players in an immortal drama.

Abigail got up from the cushions.

'So, tell me: how did you know Joseph was from David's house?'

Ben shrugged his shoulders.

'I talk to people.'

'*I* talk to people.'

'Yes, but I listen, as well.' he replied pointedly with a provocative smile on his face.

'Didn't know you could do two things at the same time,' she retorted.

'You should try doing it some time,' was her husband's ready response.

Abigail narrowed her eyes at the perceived slight.

'On the way home, you can tell me whether you have any other gems of scripture you haven't told me that I should know about, regarding our grandson.'

Ben smiled again, this time to try and hide his unease. He hadn't the heart to tell her that when God had promised the coming of the Seed of a woman – Jesus, the Messiah, their grandson, as she had referred to Him – He also declared that Jesus's heel would be bruised: code for a savage and vicious attack perpetrated on Him by Satan's seed. But by doing that, Satan's head would be crushed by the Seed. Despite his despair at what was to happen to Jesus, therein lay Ben's hope; indeed, the hope of the whole world.

'Right, come along, Ben, we've got so many things to do before they leave.'

'Have we?'

'Yes,' she answered, pushing him out of the door.

Chapter 18

Antonin, flew down and landed by the gates of Bethlehem in front of around twelve demons. It was way past midnight. All was quiet since the city's inhabitants had long hunkered down after another day's hard endeavour merely to make both ends meet. Everyone, save for Nathanael, the captain of the guard and Shobal, his deputy, who were standing on the wall above the city gates. They were on night duty. For the demons the cloak of silence added to the menace that now pervaded the air with Antonin's arrival.

'Anything to report?' he asked curtly.

Sandon shook his monster head. As quick as lightning, and with the force of the same, Antonin struck him a brutal blow across his pitted cheek with his lacerated fist. He went sprawling to the ground, in the process knocking some of his own subordinates over. It took him a few seconds to gather himself before he could get to his feet.

'Well?' Antonin asked again.

'No, sir, nothing' he replied.

He thought he heard a few of the other demons under his command snigger at his discomfort. He'd get them later. For now, it was best to pay attention to Antonin.

'When did you take over from the previous guard?'

'Three years ago.'

'No single, pregnant women since I was here last time?' queried Antonin.

'No, sir.'

Antonin smiled at him. He took a step nearer. Suddenly, he took hold of his throat and squeezed it.

'Are you sure?'

He then bent Sandon's neck to the side and his head followed. Sandon could hardly breathe and certainly couldn't speak. He managed to nod his head.

'Good,' said Antonin, releasing his grip.

Sandon rubbed his throat, coughing as he did. Antonin stared at the city walls and gates that were now closed for the night. He seemed to be admiring the architecture. The demons stood adjacent to him, heads bowed, in respectful silence, like pall-bearers at a funeral. They were amazed to hear Sandon venturing to query Antonin's orders.

'Are you sure she'll be on her own, my lord?'

They lifted their heads. Had he lost his mind or had he simply had enough of living?

Antonin turned to look at him. He held his gaze for a few seconds. Normally, questioning him was like baiting a wild bear or poking a lion. However, Sandon's question made him ponder the matter. He was convinced that a virgin giving birth – as the prophet Isaiah had said – meant that this woman would be coming to Bethlehem on her own. No man would make her pregnant; no man would be involved. So, why would any man see fit to be with her? She had to be on her own. It was ludicrous to think otherwise. However, as the demon put in charge by Satan of keeping an eye on Bethlehem he had to consider all possibilities. One could not be too careful.

'Very well,' he said. 'Keep your eyes open for any couple where the woman is pregnant, but above all,' and he looked at them all threateningly, 'be on the lookout for a single, pregnant woman. That is your main priority. And remember, it could be tomorrow or fifty, a hundred years or more from now, and she could be coming from anywhere.'

With that, Antonin took off, satisfied that he had put the fear of, well... hell into the demons who were watching the comings and goings in Bethlehem.

He was headed eastwards for the Dead Sea, in the Jordan Rift Valley. For some time now, the sea had endeared itself to him. It's high levels of concentration of salt – greater than any ocean in the world – and the harsh hot climate meant that it was free of vegetation and any animal life. When any branches or tree trunks were washed up on its shores, they were all stripped naked of their bark by the saline waters. They always reminded him of white human bones lying haphazardly on top of each other. As he flew over the sea, towards his base, Antonin chuckled at the thought of Herod the Great's intention of building a health resort, of all things, on the shores of the sea. How ironic! A health resort on the shores of the Dead Sea! Soon, he arrived at his temporary base deep under the surface of the Lisan Peninsula on the south eastern side of the sea. The peninsula, or The Tongue as it was commonly known, was a horn of land protruding into the sea from its south eastern edge, which narrowed as it turned in on itself at its northern most point, like an upturned tongue: hence the name. The Tongue itself was made of strata of clay, chalk and gypsum, with sand and gravel embedded between them. Antonin had set up his headquarters here ever since Micah's prophecy, that the Messiah would make His appearance in David's city.

He savoured the thick, polluted air. Stretching his crooked body as best he could, he walked over to the mirror hung on the opposite wall to admire himself yet again. He stroked his hideous face, pockmarked and pitted with lesions and abrasions. He adored what he had become, especially his fiery red eyes and the snakes that writhed on his head. His heavenly beauty and elegance had been replaced by something much more attractive to him: a malignant, masochistic exchange of epic proportions. This existence was far superior, given authority and free rein by Satan to thwart the plans of the enemy. Such power and influence had never been accorded to him when he was in heaven. He thought of Gilchrist, who had once been his best friend. They had spent so much time together. Antonin smiled to himself as he remembered the look of consternation on his ex-friend's face when the rebellion began, and even more when he realised that Antonin, was a major player in that uprising.

For centuries, all he had been doing was leading a small band of warrior angels – that ridiculous Melon Head amongst them – on minor tasks for God, like guarding that horrible merchant, Abdallah, who had been on his way to Memphis. Granted, they had looked after King David throughout his life, but why guard such a worthless man as Abdallah? He had interrogated every one of the demons caught up in the skirmish with Gilchrist and his warriors. When he had asked one of them about the attack, it was nigh on impossible for Antonin to understand his answer since his face was still smarting from the pasting he had endured, strangely, at his own hand. In the end, the demon staggered to the wall of the cave, and with his talon drew a gleaming sword and Antonin knew immediately who it was. He then smashed the demon in the face with his fist for having the temerity to vandalise his wall. Antonin was left wondering, though. He could not understand: why had Gilchrist, such an accomplished fighting angel, been given such a menial task? It was like commissioning a master builder to build a simple straight wall.

Antonin sat down again, and let his mind stray to more important matters. He knew the scriptures better than any other demon. Like many Jewish scholars, he had wondered at the promise God had made soon after what His followers had quaintly called, 'The Fall' that the 'Seed of a woman' would come. He presumed that this 'Seed of a woman' would be the long-awaited Messiah, God's own Son. For centuries he had tried to deduce what those four words meant. There was no such thing as the 'seed of a woman'. But could it possibly be that a woman would be made pregnant without the agency of a man? It was a mystery that was beyond him. Like Ben, Mary's father, he was also familiar with Micah's prophecy regarding Bethlehem. So, he knew the where, the how was unbelievable, but he had no idea as regards the when. That was why the gates of Bethlehem were under surveillance by his demons, and they had been there for centuries, but nothing had happened.

Once Antonin had left Bethlehem to return to his lair by the Dead Sea, a welcome tranquil peace returned to the city, other than the intermittent bleating of the sheep in the surrounding hills. Lorcan, not taking his eyes off the demonic guard, spoke in a barely audible whisper.

'Gilchrist needs to know about this, Abida. Get up to Nazareth and tell him that Antonin's made an appearance.'

Lorcan was in command of a clandestine group of four angels lying silent and still, in the hollow in the ground some ten paces from where Sandon and the other demons stood – the one Gilchrist had looked out on from the top of the city gates, on his lone reconnaissance trip to Bethlehem nearly nine months earlier – their bright raiments shrouded in a sandy camouflage, obscuring them from sight. They had been sent there by Gilchrist, just before Jesus had entered Mary's womb, and had been monitoring the demons carefully ever since, from this, their Forward Observation Post. Although Lorcan hardly made a sound when he spoke to Abida, he heard him loud and clear. As a matter of fact, he would have heard him if he had been standing with the sheep grazing the lush pasture on the hills, opposite. Angels could communicate when they spoke in whispers in a certain low register, even over long distances, as if using a frequency known only to them.

Tonight, was the first time Antonin had been seen by them. They knew him by sight and reputation. He was a formidable agent of the enemy. His appearance was a significant development, worthy of Gilchrist's immediate attention, especially since it was now just over a fortnight before Jesus was to arrive in Bethlehem. No sooner was the word said than Abida, the fastest and nimblest angel in the Armies of Heaven, slowly lifted himself from the sand covering so as not to draw the demons' attention. While still watching them, he climbed backwards out of the hollow, but as he got to its rim, his foot tripped over a small rock and he fell down the slope sending billows of dusty sand into the air. He managed to stop his sharp descent and lay still as did the other three angels left in the hollow, hoping against hope that none of the demons on guard had noticed. For a second or two, they thought they had got away with it. Sandon and a few of the others with him looked over but were not inclined to do more than that. Then, Shobal, who had worked for years as a guard at the gates, and was renowned for his alertness, looked to where the dust cloud had appeared.

'Did you see that?' he asked Nathanael.

'What?'

'A dust cloud over there,' he answered, pointing his finger.

Nathanael turned to look. He saw the remains of a dust cloud dissipating into nothingness.

'I've told you before, Shobal, I've never come across any soldier with eyes as sharp as yours. It was probably some animal. You need to cool down.'

He said this more to reassure himself rather than to quieten Shobal's concerns. Night time duty made him nervous at the best of times.

'Strange, though,' persisted Shobal, still looking at where the cloud had first appeared. 'Never seen anything like that before. And there's no animal there.'

Shobal's concerns aroused Sandon's suspicions. He decided what had just happened warranted further investigation.

'Habilah and Marzan! Go over there and have a look.'

Lying face down in the hollow, completely motionless, Lorcan's concern multiplied exponentially. His whole being became very tense. He sensed the same from Jonathon and Peleg, the two angels lying beside him, hardly daring to breathe. Fear gripped them. It was not fear of the demons, rather fear that they would soon be discovered. The whole purpose of this mission was to keep an eye on things in Bethlehem, but to do that covertly. If they were detected now then the whole operation would be blown apart. More than that, the enemy would know that something was afoot, as regards the coming of Jesus. But other than lie still and hope, they could do no more and Lorcan could only imagine that Abida was doing the same. That's exactly what Abida was doing. He lay still in the sandy soil hoping the covering of dust he had gleaned from the previous eight and a half months in the hollow was enough to camouflage him.

By now, Habilah and Marzan were standing nearby, looking around. The few seconds they were there seemed like hours. The three angels lay completely still: they did not want to disturb the fine sand covering them. Habilah and Marzam stepped forward and were now standing directly above them. Lorcan was exerting himself so much he felt his head starting to pulsate and throb. He knew Jonathon and Peleg as well as Abida, wherever he was, must be feeling the same sensation. Then, he heard a loud, exasperated shout come from the top of the city battlements.

'You again! What do you think you're doing up here?'

He recognized the voice. It was Nathanael.

For some reason, Jedah and Nidab, the two vagrants who had arrived in Bethlehem the night of Gilchrist's reconnaissance tour had strayed on to the battlements. Nathanael was furious with them. When these two beggars had suddenly appeared in front of his eyes, first as shadowy figures he had very nearly jumped out of his skin, as had Shobal. After a few seconds he recognized them. He reacted aggressively, marching up to Jedah and violently grabbed him by the rags on his chest and pushed him hard against the stone battlements.

On hearing the commotion, Habilah and Marzam turned to look. Sandon and the other demons who had been standing at the gates, flew up to get a better view of the sport. Not wanting to miss out on some honest to goodness violence perpetrated by one human on another, Habilah and Marzam flew up to join the others. They arrived just in time to see Nathanael throw Jedah on to the floor of the battlement. Then, he grabbed hold of Nidab and threw him on to the stone floor beside his friend. Nathanael proceeded to kick them and stamp on their arms and legs. He seemed to enjoy inflicting maximum pain on the unfortunate beggars. The watching demons admired his efforts.

'Get back down there, back to the gutter, where you belong!' shouted Nathanael.

'Didn't we tell you to keep out of our way, when you arrived here?' thundered Shobal.

'We only came to look out,' cowered Jedah, holding his hand up, failing miserably to shield himself from the blows.

'None of your business,' snarled Nathanael. 'Get back down there!'

Jedah and Nidab half ran, half crawled to the top of the stairs. They raced down them but as they reached the final three steps, they fell over each other and landed in a crumpled heap on the ground.

Looking down at them from above, Nathanael and Shobal laughed loudly, while behind them, the demons hovering in the air joined in the merriment.

Back in the hollow, Lorcan, Jonathon and Peleg raised their heads from the sandy soil.

'That was a close one,' said Lorcan, smiling broadly, his teeth made all the more visible by the sand and dust that covered his face.

'Too right,' replied Jonathon.

'Could have been serious if they'd seen us,' was Peleg's opinion.

'I know,' agreed Lorcan. 'But they didn't.'

He had never been one to ruminate over what might or might not have happened. What was the point in mulling over such things? They hadn't happened; the milk had not been spilt, so that was that.

'Now then, where's Abida?'

He turned to look down the slope to where he'd last seen Abida slide down. He couldn't see hide nor hair of him. Had he gone already? Surely not. He wouldn't have risked it. He would have realised that Habilah and Marzam would have seen him.

'Abida!' he whispered.

No answer.

'If you're there, it's safe to go, now. The demons...'

Before he could finish, Lorcan caught sight of him as he shot up from the ground like a grasshopper. Unlike that insect, he didn't come back to earth as he sped further away in the distance. In no time, Abida, who could fly so fast, it was said he left lightning bolts in his wake, was out of sight, flying over Jerusalem headed through the night sky, for Nazareth.

Chapter 19

In a matter of minutes, Abida landed in the small Galilean village. Although he had flown faster than the wind it had hardly dislodged the grit and sand he had allowed to amass on his being during the previous eight and a half months' vigil. Dried sand covering his face highlighted his green eyes. He met Gilchrist and the others outside Joseph and Mary's house.

'Anything happened?' asked Gilchrist.

'Lorcan thought you should know: Antonin has been sighted.'

The other four angels looked intently at their commander. The hardened warrior showed no emotion on hearing the news that his one-time ally and close friend had been spotted.

'In Bethlehem?'

'Yes, at the city gates. He gave Sandon a bit of a going over.'

It came as no surprise to either Gilchrist or his small band that Antonin had been present at Bethlehem. Indeed, they had been expecting this.

'When was he there?'

'I came as soon as he left.'

'Does he know what's afoot?'

'He's expecting something to happen in Bethlehem, but they've been waiting there for centuries.'

'Are they looking for a pregnant woman?'

'Yes, but he wasn't very sure of himself.'

'Does he know where she's coming from?'

'No.'

'Are you sure?'

'Positive. But there's been another development.'

'What?' asked Gilchrist, an urgent look in his eyes.

'They're to keep an eye open for any woman who is pregnant, married or single.'

Abida could not hide the slight panic in his voice. The five angels looked at each other.

'This makes Sabteka's job all the more important,' responded Joram.

'A lot more depends on him now,' added Ebin.

'Do we need to let him know?' asked Caleb.

Gilchrist thought for a while.

'No, this doesn't change anything for him. Maybe puts a bit more pressure on what he has to do, but he doesn't need to know. Is Kandar still there?'

'Yes, still poking his nose around.'

'Okay, thanks, Abida. Remember me to Lorcan, and the others. You can go now. We'll see you, soon.'

Abida didn't move. Gilchrist looked at him.

'Err...I was wondering...if I could see her,' he said, his eyes dancing with excitement.

'You'll get to see her when she comes to Bethlehem.'

'I know, but...'

'What do the rest of you think?'

They all looked sternly at Abida.

'I don't think we should disturb her,' piped up Joram.

'Best not,' was Ebin's opinion, whilst Cadman shook his head doubtfully.

Abida was disappointed. He had hoped to see the woman who was carrying his Lord in her womb.

'Didn't we hear her tell Joseph earlier on that she'd had enough of us angels following her everywhere she went,' offered Caleb, 'and if she saw another one she wouldn't be held responsible for her actions?'

Abida looked at him disbelievingly. Joram turned on him exasperatedly.

'What a dumb thing to say,' he said. 'Now he knows we're winding him up.'

'How?' Caleb asked innocently.

'He knows she doesn't know we're even here! She can't see us!'

Caleb laughed to himself.

'Didn't think of that.'

Although renowned for his infinite patience, Ebin's forbearance was constantly tested by Caleb. Despite being best friends, their relationship could also be construed as two siblings, with Ebin playing the part of the older brother. He felt it was his place to guide and admonish Caleb, as the occasion arose: something he would never have dreamt doing to any other angel.

'Are you real or what? If you've not got anything credible to say, keep your mouth shut. How many times have I told you?'

'Well, I just wanted to join in the banter,' Caleb explained sheepishly.

Ebin shook his head in despair.

'So, I can see her,' said Abida eagerly.

'I always like a bit of banter,' Caleb mumbled quietly.

The others ignored him.

''Course you can,' smiled Gilchrist. 'Just, don't be long because I need you back in Bethlehem.'

'A few seconds, that's all,' Abida assured him.

True to his word, Abida didn't stay long. He came back through the wall, his face aglow with wonderment.

'I can't believe He's in her womb,' he whispered.

The others were agreed. Even though they had been beside Mary for so long, they were still amazed by it all. Abida broke the silence.

'When are they leaving?'

'Tomorrow,' answered Gilchrist.

'Could be tight – timewise.'

'Not with our help.'

Abida nodded.

'Right, best be gone.'

'We'll see you, Lorcan and the others down in Bethlehem.'

'We'll be waiting for you.'

With that Abida shot off into the air. Within seconds he was out of sight, skilfully manipulating the buffeting night winds to his advantage to speed him on his way back to Bethlehem.

Chapter 20

The summer harvest had been especially fruitful throughout Israel. Wheat and barley had been gathered in abundance during the spring and early summer months and bunches of grapes had drooped heavily from vines, ensuring that the land of milk and honey would flow with wine as well. The almond trees, their strikingly vibrant white on Mary's wedding day, vouching a plentiful crop, had made good on their promise.

With just over a fortnight before the census date, Joseph and Mary, were at home, getting ready to bid farewell. Ben and Abigail were in attendance, as were the five guardian angels. Abigail, as all mothers do during emotional departures of their children, was nattering aimlessly.

'Right, have you packed the bread I made, and the olive oil?

'Yes, Eema,' Mary answered patiently.

'And have you got enough water?'

Joseph lifted the wineskins, full of water.

'Eema, we've been through all of this a thousand times.'

Her mother looked at her grimly.

'Don't exaggerate child, else in time, no one will believe a word you say,' she said, admonishing her daughter.

Ben and Joseph smiled at each other. Abigail looked into Mary's eyes.

'Come here,' she said, opening her arms to embrace her daughter tightly.

She wanted to be with her, to help her give birth; she should be with her, and Abigail felt the pain of not being able to fulfil her motherly duties all the more keenly. Just as quickly, she disengaged herself.

For the first time in nearly nine months of being with this small family the angels felt that they were intruding. They all sensed the worry and concern that pervaded Abigail's heart at that very moment. Gilchrist wished that he could let her know that they would guard them every step of the way, that they had been chosen by the Lord of the Angel Armies to protect her daughter and son-in-law.

'Right, well, there's no more to say,' Abigail said.

The words brought an end to the postponement of farewells. Up until now, Abigail had been walking along a narrow path of emotion and agitation. Uttering those fateful words, she felt herself come to the end of that pathway.

'Let them go, Abbie. They have a long journey ahead of them,' said her husband gently.

She embraced her daughter again, but more intimately. It was an embrace that said so much even though words were not spoken. She told her how much she loved her; she told her how sorry she was for the squabbles and arguments they had had over the years. They all seemed so unimportant now, like autumn leaves floating downstream, never to return. She also told her how she wished she could be going with her on this journey that would change her life forever. Mary heard every word, loud and clear.

They separated, and Abigail, not able to look her daughter in the eye, stepped towards Joseph and embraced him. He was so surprised he stood stock still, his arms hanging limply at his side. She leant up and whispered in his ear.

'Look after her... and Him.'

When she released him, he nearly saluted such was the authority she had managed to convey in her still, quiet voice. He nodded his head.

Ben stepped forward and gave his daughter a warm but heavy-hearted embrace. Then he shook hands with Joseph, before charging them, his voice choked by the emotion of the moment.

'Take care of Him. We're all depending on you two,' he said,

Joseph and Mary looked at each other. Those last few words from Ben made them realise the magnitude of what lay ahead. It dawned on them that the whole of humanity, past, present and future was relying on them. It struck them like they'd been hit in the forehead by the smooth stone thrown at Goliath by Joseph's most famous of ancestors. All Joseph could think to say in response was, 'We'd best be on our way,' which sounded completely inadequate.

Ben made way for them to leave.

As they began to walk down the slopes from the village towards the Valley of Jezreel and the Jordan Valley beyond, Joseph's arm around his wife's shoulders, Ben and Abigail couldn't help thinking how forlorn, helpless and defenceless they looked. They were so young, venturing on a long journey that would eventually take them to Joseph's mighty ancestral home down south. They did not see, they could not see, the two formidable warrior angels who were walking either side of Mary and her husband and the shorter, bow legged one behind – warrior guards of the royal womb – who would be with them every step of the way. Even if Abigail had been aware of their presence she would not have been satisfied and would still have argued that an expectant mother needed her own mother to look after her. After all, what did angels, and in particular warrior angels, know about the vagaries and dangers inherent in childbirth? Frustration engulfed her, so she comforted herself by picking on her husband.

'Why were you born in Sepphoris, of all places? Couldn't your mother at least have arranged for you to be born somewhere nearer Bethlehem?'

Ben gasped at her unreasonable questions, but said nothing.

Chapter 21

The route chosen by Joseph down to Bethlehem along the Jordan Valley was easier to travel than the hilly terrain of Samaria. But he had another reason for following this route down south. He hoped they could tag along with some merchants on the way, and maybe cadge a ride for Mary on one of their camels or cart even. However, he would be disappointed.

There had been some merchants on the road, but they were few and far between. To his deep dismay and frustration, even though Joseph begged, pleading Mary's pregnancy, not one agreed to help. They were more concerned that they arrive at their respective destinations before the onset of winter. Consequently, progress was slower than he had expected, and all the while Mary was feeling the strain more and more. The changing weather was another thing that worried Joseph. Since they had left Nazareth, the nights had got longer and colder. The days remained warm, hot even – as the autumnal sun could be – and the woollen cloaks they wore were burdensome. They were grateful for them at night though. They stayed, for free, in little khans, small unmanned fortress-like buildings dotted along the way, built as resting places for weary travellers.

Joseph was also anxious about their safety. The wooded valley of the River Jordan was a well-known haven for bandits and ruffians. Travelling as they were, on their own, they were easy prey. But Gilchrist and his angels kept these robbers at bay. One evening, as darkness was descending, they still had not arrived at a khan a local woman had assured them was not that far away. Mary was tired and Joseph had stopped to let her rest. Unbeknown, and unseen by them, a gang of four itinerant thieves was lying in wait in the thick forest of the Jordan, ready to pounce. Gilchrist walked up to them.

'Okay. Everybody ready?' asked their leader.

The others nodded their heads smiling malevolently, anticipating the twisted entertainment they were about to enjoy at Joseph and Mary's expense.

'Let's go,' ordered the leader.

Just then, Gilchrist struck. Lifting his hand, he rendered them all blind.

They were gripped with panic, baffled by what had just happened. One minute, the man and woman had been in their line of sight, the next their world had been turned dark and unseeing. Some held the palms of their hands out flat, trying to feel their way in the darkness. Then, they started talking loudly and some shouted at each other in their alarm.

Gilchrist raised his hand again. He didn't want Joseph and Mary disturbed. This time they were struck dumb.

Panic morphed into sheer fright and horror. They were losing their senses, one by one, or so it seemed to them. They stood stock still, too fearful to move. Gilchrist left them there to re-join the others. By the morning they would have regained full sight and voice but Joseph and Mary would be long gone by then.

Then, for three days a pride of lions seemed to be following them, their leader roaring loudly throughout the night. It struck fear into the hearts of Joseph and Mary, and kept them awake for hours. When the lion started his thunderous roaring from the depths of the surrounding forest the third night, Caleb had had enough. Without a word of warning, he left the small troop of angels, and marched off into the woods to look for the irritating beast.

'Don't be too hard on it,' Gilchrist shouted after him.

He thought he heard a feint, 'Yeah'. Gilchrist wasn't convinced.

'Joram, go with him,' he ordered. 'Make sure he doesn't do too much damage.'

It was Ebin's turn to be on aerial duty that night. Located, as he was, some hundred and fifty feet above ground, he could scan the land for miles and keep an eye on the skies in case any demons were in the vicinity. From his commanding position he could see Caleb make his way through the vegetation towards the lion.

'Oh, oh,' he said to himself, foreseeing that trouble lay ahead for the unfortunate creature.

It wasn't long before Caleb came across the lion. He strode right up to the offending creature and waited for it to start opening its jaws, ready to roar again. Just as Joram arrived, the beast whipped its tail majestically in the air and swung its head in a proud arc in preparation for another roar. As it was about to open its mouth, Caleb swiftly lifted his index finger, like a teacher admonishing an unruly pupil, and the lion's lips were sealed. The creature was dumbstruck. It shook its head, as if doing so would free its lips. Nothing doing. Exacerbated, it stomped its feet on the ground, its eyes shifting from side to side, looking in vain for whatever or whoever had done this. Alarm took hold and it began to salivate. Once it stopped its stomping, Caleb bent down in front of it and gently took hold of its mane, either side of its head. The creature began to stomp again, trying to free itself, but to no avail. Caleb waited patiently for the lion to still itself. Then, looking deep into its eyes, he spoke softly.

'Now listen puss, I know you think you're king of the jungle, and I'm ready to play along with that... up to a point. But I sorted some of your fore-fathers out back in Babylon when they were supposed to eat Daniel alive. I'm not prepared to let you scream and bawl about how great you are and letting everyone know that this is your territory when there are two friends of mine over there trying to get to sleep. So, you and your harem can push off – now!'

Whether the lion heard and understood him not even Caleb knew. He certainly got his message across though, for the animal suitably chastened, turned and shakily trotted off, without so much as a backward glance at its pride. Lying in the thick ferns and thinking they had settled for the night, the lionesses looked at each other with bemused faces. Seeing their leader dis-appearing in the distance, they got up and followed him through the dense overgrowth.

Caleb turned to make his way back and saw Joram.

'Joram! You okay?' he asked nonchalantly.

'Yes, fine. You?'

'Never better,' he answered, walking past him. 'Joseph and Mary should get some sleep now, don't you think?'

'No reason why not,' he responded, falling in behind him.

When they arrived back with the others, Joseph and Mary were fast asleep, as Caleb had predicted.

'Everything okay?' Gilchrist asked Joram quietly, looking at Caleb as he lay down on his back on the bare earth, gazing at Ebin in the sky above. Cad-man was sitting against a tree trunk, rhythmically sharpening the heads of his arrows on his whet stone.

'No problems. Just, I never knew Caleb had such a way with words. And I certainly didn't know he was the one who'd been with Daniel in the lions' den.'

'Yes, well, he was on sabbatical from our unit. Remember?'

'We've all been on temporary leave – away on other missions. And he was away in Babylon?'

'Yes. Michael sent him to deal with the lions.'

'I knew someone had been sent, but I didn't know it was him. He never talks about it.'

'I know there's a lot of bravado with Caleb, but he pretty much keeps his exploits to himself. That's what I like about him.'

'Does Ebin know?'

'Probably, but he won't have told anyone else.'

'Why did Caleb get that gig?'

'Don't you remember how he was with those lions when they tried to kill David's sheep?'

'Yeah, I know, but...'

'He likes animals: he's good with them.'

Joram looked at his captain disbelievingly.

'Could have fooled me.'

'You know I can hear you,' said Caleb.

'Talking *about* you, not *to* you,' replied Gilchrist.

'That's a' right then,' responded Caleb.

He closed his eyes, the back of his head lying in the palms of his hands, making himself comfortable, the best he could on the hard earth. A few seconds elapsed.

'Hey, Caleb! Are you going to sleep?' whispered Ebin in a low register, from way above.

'Last time I fell asleep was about two hundred years ago.'

'I know,' said Ebin longingly.

'And that was only for ten minutes – a power nap!'

'The best ten minutes I ever had,' Ebin muttered to himself.

Caleb opened one of his eyes.

'I heard that, as well.'

Chapter 22

Jesus's arrival on earth was fast approaching, and the excitement in heaven was palpable, especially amongst the angels in the choir. None more so than Dylan. He could hardly wait and as for a child, time seemed to go slower as that first Christmas drew nearer. Despite his increasing exhilaration Dylan continued his secret missions to differing people all over the globe. And still, his friends, Sabta, Gether and Dumah wondered where on earth he would get to. Many a time they discussed the matter amongst themselves. They knew there was no point asking him, as they had done before, for he always refused to say. Eventually they decided they would have to follow him to find out. It would be so easy since he flew so slowly. However, he had the uncanny knack of being able to seemingly disappear into thin air. On other occasions, he would slip away at the most unexpected times, quite often during choir practice and it would be impossible to follow him. Besides, everybody, especially Axa, was relieved when that happened.

As it was, more and more rehearsals were held, Axa wanting to ensure that no stone was left unturned in his search for perfection. However, whenever Dylan was present, his singing was still making waves. With only days to go before the royal performance Axa's temper was frayed virtually to breaking point. During one of the latter choir practices, he could take no more.

'Dylan!' he shouted, his indignation turbo charging his voice.

Instantly he regretted it. He had shown how fragile he was in front of the whole Angel Choir. As any choirmaster worth his weight, Axa knew that maintaining composure in front of his choristers was essential. The slightest hint of anxiety or tension on his part would be picked up by them and would affect their singing. Dylan smiled nervously back at him. There and then, Axa decided he had to do something drastic: he had to see Archangel Michael and Gabriel. Once practice had finished, he went to speak to them.

He found them staring into space, admiring the stars and constellations in all their brightness. They had done this a thousand times and more before, and they were still mesmerised.

'Archangel Michael! Gabriel!'

They both turned sharply. They had been so absorbed with the beauty of what they were watching, they hadn't heard Axa approaching.

'Ah, Axa,' greeted Michael, 'how's the choir coming along?'

'Well, that's why I've come to see you.'

'There's nothing wrong is there?' asked Gabriel.

'There's a problem... a big problem.'

They both looked at each other. What could be the matter? There were only days to go before the big event. Everything had been running so smoothly.

'Well?' Michael asked, concern etched on his face.

'It's Dylan,' Axa explained.

Michael and Gabriel sighed with relief.

'Dylan? The angel who can't sing?' asked Gabriel.

'Yes.'

'Oh, thank goodness,' said Michael. 'We thought there was some major problem.'

A sudden surge of indignation frothed from Axa's mouth.

'I can assure you both, this is a major problem. He is completely and utterly out of tune. Since he sings so loud...'

'...and joyously, no doubt,' interjected Michael.

'Well, yes, I'll give him that,' conceded Axa grudgingly. 'As I was saying, he sings so loudly, he affects everybody else. His singing spreads through the choir like wildfire, and soon, no one knows what they're singing and choral carnage ensues. Frankly, I don't know where I am either. I can't tell the difference between my top tenors and baritones, and last rehearsal I even heard the basses sing counter-tenor, and until then I hadn't thought the thing possible.'

Axa's voice had got louder and louder and more high-pitched as he related this to the two angels.

Neither Michael nor Gabriel seemed to be listening much, though. They were more interested in watching the stars in their glory.

Axa persisted. This was a serious situation, and his reputation was on the line. He didn't want to be made a laughing stock in the heavenly realms, just because of one angel who couldn't sing.

'Michael,' he said in a slightly irritated voice that made both angels turn around to look at him again. 'I can't let Dylan sing in the choir.'

'But he so enjoys a celebration, and especially one where he gets to worship God,' replied Gabriel.

'Couldn't we tell him to come along but not sing?'

Michael thought for a few seconds before he replied.

'And by saying, "Couldn't we..." what you really mean is, "Couldn't I or Gabriel tell him to keep quiet?"'

Axa's face quickly turned a fiery red.

'Well...' he started.

'Neither of us would be prepared to do that,' said Michael emphatically. 'Besides, there's no way we're going to tell him that he can't sing in the most important event the Angel Choir has ever performed. It would simply break his heart.'

Gabriel coughed a little.

'Err...Not that we angels have hearts, of course. A mere slip of the tongue...a manner of speech...a coin of phrase.'

'But I really can't have him there,' persisted Axa. 'He spoils everything for the rest. We will be announcing Jesus's arrival. Nothing must go wrong!'

Michael heard the slight panic in his voice. Putting a hand on the choir master's shoulder, he said, reassuringly,

'Don't worry Axa, it'll be all right on the night.'

Axa couldn't believe what Michael had just said. 'It'll be all right on the night! All right on the night?!' Here was Michael telling him not to worry about the angel who had taken singing out of tune to a whole new galaxy, and that everything would be 'all right on the night'!

Before Axa could think of a reply, Michael, with an apologetic smile on his face, said,

'If you could leave us now, Axa? We're very busy, what with the final arrangements for our Lord's coming. Things are getting quite delicate.

'But...'

'I'm sure you'll understand.'

'Of course,' he smiled weakly.

Axa slowly turned and began to leave, quietly seething inside. '"We're very busy! Very busy!" My foot, my legs, my everything!' If they were that busy, why had they been admiring the stars when he walked in? He left the hall muttering an irritated, 'Management!' under his breath.

Chapter 23

It was Christmas Eve; the very first Christmas Eve. Mary was getting weaker and Joseph knew it. He feared that they would not reach Bethlehem – the designated birth place of the Saviour – in time. Over a fortnight had passed since they had left Nazareth and Mary was getting increasingly exhausted. The last two days progress had been slow, every step a climb. Joseph was also feeling the strain. He would often carry her for long periods, and although he was used to lifting heavy objects in his line of work as a builder and carpenter, he was faltering.

In the early afternoon sun Mary was worn out. Joseph helped her to lie down on the dusty soil. Thick forest and lush vegetation had given way to the semi-arid landscape at the southern edge of the Jordan Valley. He sat beside her and offered some water from a wineskin, which she gratefully accepted. He lay back and felt the searing heat on his weather worn face.

'I'm tired, Joseph.'

'I know my love.'

'How much further have we got to go?'

'Not long now.'

The truth of the matter was they were a mere half a day's journey from Bethlehem, but they had already expended so much energy, they felt they were wading in a river of honey – against the flow. He was beginning to doubt whether they would even be able to get to David's city and the thought of failing to fulfil the Messianic prophecy was playing on his mind: it would be all his fault. Over the last few days the number of travellers on the road had dwindled to a trickle and by now they were alone: a sure sign that others had reached their various destinations. In all of this, Joseph's love for Mary had grown though. He was amazed at her strength and will-power. She had not uttered one word of complaint until now, but that was because her time was getting closer and Joseph could hardly hold that against her. Would she have to give birth to Jesus by the wayside here, he wondered?

Mary's five guardian angels were concerned for her as well. It was clear for all to see that her strength was draining from her. Standing in a circle, towering over the married couple, Gilchrist, Cadman, Joram, Ebin and Caleb discussed the situation.

'She's getting more and more tired,' stated Joram.

'I can't see she'll be able to make it,' was Ebin's opinion.

'And Joseph can't carry on much longer, either,' pointed out Caleb.

'Everyone agreed?' asked Gilchrist, looking at each one.

He caught Cadman's eye.

'No choice,' was all he had to say.

Gilchrist turned to Joram.

'Joram?'

He nodded his head.

'Okay,' said Gilchrist. 'We haven't much time. They've got to be in Bethlehem before nightfall and we need to rendezvous there with Sabteka.'

Chapter 24

With the sun beating on her face and tiredness getting the better of her, Mary slid into a troubled sleep. Joseph let her be for a few minutes. He was exhausted himself. He had carried her most of the way the last day during which, they had turned in a south westerly direction. Having left the Jordan River behind, they were now traversing the fringe of the inhospitable Judean desert, a vast expanse of flaking limestone and jagged, distorted ridges that seemed to rush hither and thither in any and every direction. No wonder the ancient scriptures called it The Devastation.

He tightened the woollen cord that held his linen head-dress in place. Although he was grateful it shaded his face he still felt the sun's heat on his head. He got to his feet, collected their things and strung them across his back for the umpteenth time. Rallying himself, he gathered Mary in his arms, and headed towards Bethlehem. Progress was slow though, and he stumbled rather than walked. His faltering steps took him no more than a few yards before his knees gave way, shattered by the exertion. He bent forward and carefully laid Mary on the soft sand. There was no oil left in his inner flame; it was flickering its last. His head dropped in desperation. The hopelessness of their situation hit him hard. For the first time since they had left Nazareth he began to believe they were not going to make it to Bethlehem: he had failed his God. He had never felt so alone.

'Stop that,' he berated himself. 'You have a wife and child – the Messiah, Jesus, Saviour of the world in your care – and you need to get them to Bethlehem.'

Try as he might though, kneeling on the ground, with Mary sleeping fitfully in front of him, he felt that circumstances were getting the better of him and he could see no way out. They should have started from Nazareth much earlier; he shouldn't have expected her to make the journey in such a short time; shouldn't have expected so much of her and so much of himself.

'Are you praying or what?'

Joseph turned his head sharply. At his shoulder was the head of a large mule. Was he going mad? Had the animal just spoken to him? He'd heard about how spending too much time in the desert, short of water could play tricks with one's mind. Then, he noticed that the mule was tied to a moderately sized cart. On its seat sat an old man. Joseph saw his bald head shining in the sun and what little teeth he had were a disgusting shade of yellowish brown. Wizened skin hung from his throat and thin forearms, while his scrawny hands held on to the reins. Joseph wondered how on earth had he not heard them come up behind? He strained his eyes to look behind the cart and he saw the tracks of the wheels and the mule's hooves stretching far into the distance in the dry soil. He must have been too tired to have heard them. He staggered to his feet.

'No. I was resting if you must know.'

The old man looked around.

'Resting?! What a dull thing to do. Why would you want to rest in a place like this?'

He didn't bother answering him. The old man persisted.

'Are you going anywhere?'

Joseph's indignation energised him.

'Of course, we're going somewhere. Do you think we travelled all the way from Nazareth just to come here?'

Joseph was surprised at his own sarcasm which was completely out of character for him. The old man was not deterred.

'Nazareth,' he mused, 'never heard of the place.'

Mary stirred. She looked around.

'Joseph, where are we? Help me get up.'

He helped her to her feet. The old man pointed a crooked finger at her.

'What's wrong with her?'

'Nothing,' answered Joseph.

'Doesn't look too good to me.'

'If you must know, she's pregnant. She hasn't got long to go.'

The old man was quiet for a few seconds.

'You didn't answer me.'

'What?'

'My question.'

'What question?'

Joseph had never met such an irritating man. His thin high-pitched voice was particularly annoying. Even the angels were wide eyed at the old man's exasperating manner.

'Where are you going?'

'Bethlehem. Have you heard of *that* place?'

'Joseph,' Mary admonished, putting her hand on his. She had never seen her husband so impatient.

'Yeah, sort of.'

He looked around again and ran his hand along his neck.

'That's why I asked you.'

'Asked me what?!'

'Joseph had had enough. It was high time for this grouchy little man to be on his way.

'Where were you going?'

Joseph felt the old man's questioning was taking him round and round in circles.

'Why?'

'Coz that's where I'm going.'

'Where? To Bethlehem?'

'Yeah. Hop on if you like. I'll take you there.'

The flame inside Joseph flickered once again. He looked at the old man in a completely different light.

'Are you sure?'

'No. So, you'd better get on quick, before I change my mind,' he replied, giggling loudly to himself. He climbed gingerly down from the seat. Limping slightly, he led Joseph and Mary to the open-ended back of the cart. Their hearts danced with joy as they saw a thick heap of straw on its floor.

'There you are. You can have a proper rest, or even pray there if you want... all the way to Bethlehem.'

He laughed his irritating laugh again.

He helped Joseph lift Mary on to the cart. Joseph averted his face. Mary felt a tightness in her throat and stomach, as if she was about to vomit. The old man's foul-smelling mouth was as nothing they had ever encountered. Joseph quickly levered himself up on the cart whilst Mary lay her weary body on the straw. It felt like the softest cushion imaginable.

'We can't thank you enough,' said Mary.

'Are you sure you're going all the way to Bethlehem?' asked Joseph. His voice had changed its tone to one of acute gratitude and appreciation.

'All the way,' he reassured them, 'got to deliver this straw to Izzy the blacksmith: should be there before nightfall, now. That is, if you stop asking questions.'

Joseph and Mary smiled at him gratefully.

He limped back to his seat smiling to himself. Once aboard, he gently shook the reins and his mule started walking again.

Gilchrist and the guarding angels, appreciative of the old man's timely assistance, relaxed as they walked behind. Now they would get to Bethlehem on time.

Chapter 25

With barely hours to go before Jesus's birth, an increasing excitement suffused the whole Angel Choir. The prospect of welcoming Jesus to the world thrilled them so much they could hardly wait. Everyone in the choir wanted to give Him the best greeting anyone could imagine. They would sing as they had never sung before.

Axa was very pleased with them.

The final practice had just finished that first Christmas Eve. The angels in the choir had left to prepare for the journey down to the hills outside Bethlehem. Axa was speaking to Tiras, his assistant.

'Well, what do you think?'

'They sound out of this world, Axa.'

'Tiras, they *are* out of this world,' he answered drily. Axa was known to be a little difficult when discussing his choir, especially when a performance was about to happen. 'We're in heaven, aren't we?'

Tiras decided on a different tack.

'They sound positively angelic,' he ventured.

Axa looked sideways at him. He wasn't sure whether his assistant was patronising him or not. After deciding he wasn't, he said,

'Yes, they do sound rather good, don't they?'

He said this in the kind of self-congratulatory voice, believing the excellent sound of the choir was all his doing.

'When they hit that top C and hold it for what seems like an eternity,' said Tiras, 'I'm taken away somewhere on a bed of clouds. I don't know where, I don't care. I just let myself be smothered by their voices.'

Axa was quite touched, and felt a sudden surge of pride.

'Why, Tiras, I didn't know you could be so emotional.'

The assistant choir master's face turned a shade of red.

'Of course,' he said, 'when Dylan attends practice, which isn't very often, it's a completely different matter.'

It was as if someone had taken a sharp pin and popped Axa's bubble.

'Don't remind me.'

'At least he hasn't been to many practices this week,' said Tiras, trying to comfort Axa.

'No, he hasn't.'

'He didn't even come to this final rehearsal.'

By now Axa was hardly listening, his mind wandering to the announcement he was to make that night.

'I wonder where he gets to,' wondered Tiras.

'I know,' agreed Axa absently.

'You know?' asked Tiras.

'What?'

'You said that you know where he goes.'

'No, I didn't.'

Tiras was in awe of the choir master, but this time he was adamant he was right, and Axa was wrong.

'When I asked, "I wonder where he gets to?" you said, "I know".'

'I wasn't saying that I know where he goes. I was trying to say that I agree with you, not that I know where he goes.'

Tiras could be very trying sometimes.

'But "I know", doesn't mean "I agree", as well.'

Axa finally snapped.

'Tiras!' he hissed. 'I was agreeing with you. I don't know where Dylan goes. Frankly, I don't care. Does anyone care? Whatever he does, it can't be as important as what we are about to do tonight. Now, let's leave it at that.'

Tiras decided that discretion was the better part of valour... for the moment. Then he continued.

'He's always on an errand. He's gone somewhere now – hasn't been seen for a while – and if he doesn't return soon we'll have left and he'll have missed the celebratory announcement.'

Axa's mood suddenly lifted at the thought that maybe Dylan wouldn't be able to make it back in time. Maybe that's what Michael had in mind when he had said, 'It'll be all right on the night'. Axa felt himself warm to the archangel. Maybe he did know better, after all.

'Right,' said Axa, 'let's make sure that the choir is ready. We haven't much time before we leave.'

Chapter 26

'Right, you two, wake up! We've arrived.'

Joseph and Mary woke with a start. Having forgotten their earlier encounter with the old man, they couldn't understand why they were lying on a mound of straw in the back of a cart. They looked around through bleary eyes. Above them they saw his wrinkled, leathery face complete with his near toothless grin. Then it dawned on them.

'Are we here?' asked Joseph.

'What kind of question is that? Of course, we're... here. You're always here! She's always here! I'm always here! Everybody's here, we're never over there, coz we're always somewhere, here, aren't we?'

'He's lost none of his ability to infuriate,' Joseph thought to himself. He really was the most annoying man he had ever met.

'Have we arrived in Bethlehem? That's what I meant.'

'Yes, we have.'

He climbed down from his seat and limped to the back of the cart.

'I can't see Bethlehem,' said Mary, looking around.

'It's just the other side of this steep slope to the right,' he said, pointing behind her.

Joseph jumped down and Mary pushed herself along on her bottom until she sat at the end of the cart, her legs dangling over the edge. Joseph stepped in front of her, put a hand under each armpit and gently lifted her on to the ground. Both were comforted by the fact that they were not alone since other people were walking past, evidently on their way to Bethlehem.

'I thought it best to drop you off here, coz the guards at the gates will ask too many questions.'

Mary pulled her head back to avert standing too near to his reeking mouth.

'We must thank you again,' she said. 'We'll be forever in your debt.'

'I know,' he said, and gave a short burst of squeaky giggling.

He climbed back on the seat of the cart. Suddenly, his demeanour changed, seemingly more reticent. It seemed as if a veil had come between him and the couple.

'Right then, I'll be off.'

Joseph and Mary walked to the front of the cart.

'We may see you there,' said Mary hopefully, rubbing the sleep from her eyes.

'Maybe, maybe not.'

'We don't know your name,' said Joseph.

'Seth,' he answered.

'Joseph, Mary,' he said, pointing at each in turn.

'Fine. Better be off. They'll be closing the city gates before long. The day's coming to an end, and you'd better get a move on as well,' Seth advised, encouraging his mule to move.

Mary looked at Joseph.

'Did you get the feeling he was in a hurry to leave?'

'Yes,' he answered, watching the old man and his cart round the slope. 'He didn't even wish you well with the birth.'

'We've got to be grateful. If he hadn't turned up, I don't know what we'd have done.'

'I know. Right, come then, Mary. The sooner we arrive, the sooner we can find somewhere to stay.'

Feeling invigorated after his sleep, he hoisted their things on his back, and with his arm around Mary's shoulders, he led her to Bethlehem. As they rounded the slope the city was revealed to them, situated as it was on a hill. Joseph stopped and took it all in. This was the first time he had seen his ancestral home since the last census, when he'd come here with his parents. He was slightly surprised by how small it looked. Then again, he had seen it through the eyes of a child.

'What's on your mind?' Mary asked.

'Just thinking.'

'About what?'

'Oh, you know, family, forefathers, ancestors.'

By now, Mary had come to accept that her husband thought a lot and lived much of his life inside his head.

'Come on,' she smiled, 'we'd better get going.'

Together, they started the final stretch of their tortuous journey. Ahead of them, some people were hurrying through the city gates. Along with these folk, Joseph and Mary were the last remnants of a multitude that had made their way to Bethlehem from all over the country, some having travelled from beyond Israel's borders.

Gilchrist and the angels, aware that demons were standing at the gates, hid behind the steep slope Joseph and Mary had just rounded. They watched carefully as the couple made their way up the hill. Either side of the road they saw a huge number of tents, sheltering those who had already arrived for the census, spilling down the slopes. The scene would have been mirrored all over the land, indeed all over the Roman Empire.

In the distance, Gilchrist saw Seth, approaching the city gates. He was still a little stunned, as were the other angels, at how he had spoken to Joseph and Mary. The guards stopped him at the gate.

'What business gave you got here, old man?' asked Nathanael, the captain of the guard.

'Some straw for Izzy, the blacksmith,' Seth answered, jerking his head over his shoulder.

A guard went to the back of his cart to check its contents. He was waved through, no more questions asked.

'Right, we can't stand here gawping: we've got things to do. Time for you two to leave, I think,' said Gilchrist, looking at Ebin and Caleb. 'We'll see you later.'

They both nodded and left the hiding place.

'Have you seen Sabteka?' Gilchrist asked Cadman.

The angel had been carefully scanning the area ever since they had arrived at the outskirts of Bethlehem. He shook his head.

'He must be here,' he said.

'If he's not...' started Gilchrist.

'Well, we'll soon find out,' reasoned Cadman.

They watched intently as Joseph and Mary made their way up the hill. They were around a hundred yards from the city gates and were in full view of the demons. Tension gripped Gilchrist. He felt a tight knot in his stomach. Lorcan and the other three angels in the Forward Observation Post were on heightened alert. The success or failure of all the planning and preparation on their part as warriors in the Angel Armies of the Lord, boiled down to these crucial seconds. Were Mary to be rumbled now there was no knowing what would happen. The warrior angels and those in the Observation Post were ready to spring into action at the slightest hint of danger to her.

At that precise moment, Sandon became very excited; two or three demons that were standing beside him were suddenly more animated, like famished dogs at mealtimes. One of them kicked some of the others that were lounging on the ground at the base of the limestone buttress nearest the city gates. They quickly got to their feet. Every demon present stared excitedly at the few last weary travellers making their way up the hill. The demons must have seen Mary, and realised who she was, else why had they reacted as they had? All warrior angels present breathed quicker. They tightened their grip on the hilts of their swords, readying themselves for action.

They needn't have worried.

Sandon and his demons had seen someone, but not Mary. A young woman was walking slowly towards the gates. She was heavily pregnant, and was travelling alone. It was plain to see that the birth was imminent. One hand cradled her stomach, trying to lighten the load for her exhausted body as the other hand rubbed the base of her tired back. She was struggling to complete the last part of her journey. Her clothes were dirty and rumpled and her hair was tousled and unkempt. Blood trickled from her feet from treading on jagged stones, or sharp thorns. Breathing heavily, she veered from the main path that led to the gates and walked right up to where Sandon was standing. He moved aside to make way for her as she leant her hand on a buttress to rest a while. The short, sharp incline had proved too much for her. She had to rest.

Standing a mere arm's length away, Sandon eyed her carefully and became very excited. This was what they had been waiting for. As she looked at her stomach lovingly, he heard her whisper quietly to herself,

'Not long to go now. God the Father will look after us.'

At last! This was their reward for the decades of vigilant waiting and watching. Sandon gave a prolonged sigh such was his relief. He couldn't believe how close she was standing to him. He looked at her intently. So, this was the woman chosen by God to deliver the Messiah to the world. As he studied her, he noticed the deep pain of her long, lonely pregnancy etched across her face. She had a deep cut on her lip and the skin around her left eye had a pale, yellow tinge: obviously the healing remains of a bullying fist that had struck her eye some days previously. Her body was in hardly better shape, ragged and worn out from the energy she had expended to get there. A depraved smile spread across his face. He was gratified that she – whoever she was – had finally arrived during his watch. And he was delighted at her physical suffering. It was obvious her time was fast approaching. Antonin would be pleased.

Having regained her strength, the lonely woman pushed herself from the buttress and walked past the soldiers at the gates. Instantly, she made her way to the well situated just inside and sat down to drink copiously from its sweet waters, before walking wearily, with faltering steps to look for somewhere to stay.

Immediately, Sandon dispatched one of his demons to inform Antonin of the latest development, whilst Habilah and Marzam were detailed to follow the woman as she walked the streets of Bethlehem. He was elated: he had seen the woman who was carrying the Messiah. During the last few days, a few expectant mothers – each one with a husband beside her – had passed through the gates. Sandon had ordered his demons to follow them, as per Antonin's orders, but evidently not one of the women was carrying the Messiah. This was different though. Obviously, this was the one they had been waiting for; it had to be! Sandon leant back against the buttress and along with the remaining demons that were with him, he relaxed. There was no need to be on their guard any longer.

Consequently, when Joseph and Mary approached the gates seconds later, they slipped through unnoticed by the demons. They made for the well. Mary gratefully sat down in the exact spot vacated by the young pregnant woman. Neither did the demons show any interest in a timid elderly couple, the husband's arm holding his wife tightly, as they walked slowly through the gates shortly after. Once inside, they too made their way to the well and sat down beside Mary. The old couple looked around fearfully, intimidated by the thick throng of people pushing around them.

Not far from the well, Jedah and Nidab, the two vagrants who had been kicked by Nathanael at the gates of the city nine months earlier and mercilessly assaulted by the same just over a fortnight earlier, happened to be leaning against the side of a house. By now, they had been joined by five other homeless beggars – birds of a feather flocking together. Since arriving in Bethlehem, they had spent their time wandering its streets begging for whatever they could get their hands on. More often than not, they had to endure a frequent kick or a verbal insult from the good people of Bethlehem and had to content themselves with morsels of food thrown from tables, treated no better than dogs. They would eat them ravenously as if there was no tomorrow. These last few days, things had looked up since the city's population had grown like wild rabbits in springtime so there were more people to prey on. Even so, Jedah was still as surly as ever.

For a good five minutes prior to this, he and his fellow malcontents had been standing near the gates watching the new arrivals, wondering who looked the most susceptible to their especial charms. Now, as Jedah stood by the house he happened to make eye contact with the old man and his wife.

He looked at them threateningly, sneering, as if to say, 'Who are you looking at?' The old couple hastily averted their eyes. They didn't want any trouble, especially from these unpleasant low-lives.

As she turned her head, the old woman looked at Joseph and Mary. She watched him as he carefully gave his expectant wife some water to drink. After filling his wine skin with water, he helped her to her feet. He put his arm tenderly round her shoulders and they trudged southwards along the streets of the city. Presently, the old couple, themselves fortified by the liquid refreshment afforded by the well, also turned left to wander the streets of the city, thankful that Bethlehem's down-and-outs had lost interest in them.

Outside the city Gilchrist relaxed. He looked across at the four angels in the hollow. Abida blew through his lips and Lorcan whispered, 'No problem', smiling at him.

'You think so, Lorcan?' whispered Gilchrist back.

'No worries whatsoever: I knew all along. You need to lighten up, Gilchrist.'

'Lighten up?! Right, we'll meet up with you four later.'

'That sounds like a threat to me, boss,' he grinned.

'Get going... and don't get caught,' replied Gilchrist.

Making sure they were not seen by the demon guards, the four angels stealthily left the Forward Observation Post that had been their home for the last nine months, and headed to the north side of the city.

'And we need to meet up with the others,' said Gilchrist.

Chapter 27

Seth guided his mule through the crowded streets of Bethlehem. It wasn't long before he arrived outside Izzy's forge. Although the streets were teeming with people, no one paid any attention as he climbed down from his seat. He tickled the skin below the animal's eye with his crooked fingers and whispered an affectionate, 'Goodbye' in its ear. The mule snorted and jerked its head in response, as if imploring him to stay. Then Seth limped along the street, leaving the mule and cart with its load of hay behind.

After a short while, when Izzy came to shut the doors of his forge he scratched his head when he saw the mule and the cart, their owner nowhere to be seen. They were still there hours later. So, just before he went to bed, he brought them into his yard intending to keep them safely until the owner returned. He had already begun to calculate the significant advantages of owning the mule if no one were to claim the beast, though. Maybe not as attractive, a mule was much stronger, more intelligent and its stamina far exceeded that of any horse. And by the look of him this was a magnificent specimen. No one did return for the mule and cart and its contents, so Izzy took grateful possession of them.

The sun had already started its steep descent, casting long shadows on the narrow streets of Bethlehem. Despite his limp and obvious age, Seth walked with an assured step: he knew exactly where he was going. On and on he went, through congested streets, past noisy households and crowded inns. Eventually he arrived at the entrance to a narrow alley, hardly visible in the gathering gloom. He was at the furthest point away from the city gates. The alley, about twenty yards in length, was completely deserted, a world away from the buzz and excitement in the rest of the densely populated city. Hidden behind the towering city walls, the sun could not penetrate the dim half-light between day and night, so this particular spot was rendered perpetually dark, dank and musty. He walked into it and looked at the small house built as an appendage, a lean-to, onto the boundary wall at the other end of the small lane. Then he sat on a tiny ledge at the base of the city walls, and waited.

A few minutes later, Gilchrist and Cadman flew quietly over the city wall, and landed gracefully on the sandy ground between the house and the alleyway. They walked towards Seth. The old man slowly got to his feet. All three carefully looked around. Satisfied no humans or demons were present,

Seth transformed himself. He was no longer the grouchy old man, but Joram, chosen and committed guardian angel of Mary and Jesus, his Lord.

'You had a nerve, talking to Joseph like that,' said Cadman.

'Tell you one thing, you were no angel,' added Gilchrist.

Joram smiled broadly.

'Well, I thought I'd give the old man a bit of an edge.'

'"Bit of an edge"?!' exclaimed Gilchrist. 'It was more like a razor-edged sword!'

'They had no idea, did they?'

'No inkling at all,' Cadman assured him. 'Even I wasn't too sure whether it was you at the start. Then I knew it was you because your breath stank.'

'It was rank,' confirmed Gilchrist.

'Funny! What are you, rhyming poets?'

'Yes,' replied Cadman. 'We write epic poems in our spare time about heroic angel warriors. We've had no cause to write one about you... yet.'

'Glad all my hard work is appreciated.'

'No worries.'

'You met up with Candrell, then?' asked Gilchrist.

'Yes. He followed us all the way down the Jordan Valley with the mule and cart, but kept out of sight, just as you told him.'

'The best insurance policy you've ever thought of, Gilchrist,' said Cadman.

His captain grinned at him.

'So, now...?' asked Joram.

'Now? We wait, for Sabteka,' replied Gilchrist, as they all sat down on the small ledge.

Chapter 28

In the slowly descending darkness of the night, the young pregnant woman who had caused such a stir amongst the demons at the city gates, wandered the streets of Bethlehem. Laboriously, she trod the uneven roadways. As she made her way through the teeming crowds, once or twice a forceful shoulder of a careless passer-by would collide violently with her frail body It would render her breathless with pain, while she held on tight to her stomach. After leaning against a wall for a few seconds to collect herself, she continued her wandering with no particular destination in mind.

After half an hour of walking along endless narrow streets, on evermore painful feet, she came to a halt. Satisfied that she had wandered enough, she looked around, and caught a glimpse of the two demons that had been following her ever since she set foot in the city. They were brazenly standing at the corner of a street, less than a stone's throw away. Satisfied with this as well, she slowly made her way to a narrow alley, at the furthest point from the city gates.

Gilchrist and the two warrior angels were aware she was approaching. As she rounded the corner and entered the dank corridor, they stood up, as if paying her respect. Then they walked backwards up the alley towards the lean-to. The woman followed and walked past them once they had all exited the alley.

'Two of them – not far behind,' she whispered, looking straight ahead.

They escorted her towards the open door of the house that Seth, aka Joram had looked at a little earlier. By now, Habilah and Marzam, the two demons tailing her had arrived at the other end of the alley. What they saw stunned them. She was at the door of a house accompanied by three warrior angels. When one of them turned to look round, they were breathless: it was none other than Gilchrist, the mighty warrior of the angelic host! The other two turned to face them and were immediately recognised: Cadman and Joram. They could only be here for one thing. This pregnant woman, here to give birth to the so-called Messiah was being protected by them. They watched as the woman walked through the open door, followed closely by Gilchrist, leaving Cadman and Joram standing guard outside. The two demons hid from their view and looked at each other in elation.

'We've got to get news back to Sandon,' Marzam whispered.

'More to the point, Antonin needs to know,' said Habilah

'You go. I'll stay and keep watch.'

Habilah took off in the air and flew back to Sandon who was still standing at the city gates.

Chapter 29

Once inside the house, the young pregnant woman looked at Gilchrist and smiled broadly. The house was far from empty since, waiting for them were Lorcan, Abida, Jonathon and Peleg. They all greeted each other warmly. The door opened and they turned abruptly, hands on the hilts of their swords. They soon relaxed as in walked Cadman and Joram. Cadman closed the door behind them.

Joram took the young woman's hand and shook it gleefully. He was especially glad to see her.

'Sabteka: nice to see you again! A masterful performance, even if I say so myself.'

Many a time in the past he and Sabteka had worked together, both renowned as the most accomplished of all disguisers of the angels of heaven.

They certainly took your bait,' Gilchrist said.

'Did they?' Sabteka asked.

No one paused for a second to consider how incongruous it was for a young, piteous, pregnant woman to be speaking in such a rich baritone voice.

'Sandon couldn't take his eyes off you.'

'No?'

'He couldn't control himself, he was so excited. His eyes were all over you,' answered Gilchrist.

'Mind, I couldn't believe it when you went and leant against the wall, right beside him,' said Lorcan.

'Just making sure he could hear and see me,' smiled Sabteka.

'Habilah's left to report to Sandon,' said Cadman.

'And Marzam's still at the end of the alley,' added Joram.

'You could have picked a bigger house, G,' pleaded Lorcan, eyeing their immediate surroundings.

'I think it's quite cosy,' responded Gilchrist.

'Cosy? When did you become all domesticated?'

Sabteka transformed himself back into a warrior angel.

'Well, thanks, Sabteka. We couldn't have done this without you, said Gilchrist.'

He shook his hand.

'A pleasure, G. Wouldn't have missed it for the world.'

'Until when are you with us?'

'Until tomorrow.'

'Where are you off to then?'

'Somewhere in Samaria. Deep undercover – can't tell you where. Sorry.'

'That's okay,' Gilchrist smiled. He understood, as did the others, that the work they did often called for the utmost discretion. There were no more questions.

'Better get going, boss,' said Cadman. 'We don't want to be here when Antonin arrives.'

Gilchrist agreed. He turned to Lorcan and his angels.

'Now, remember, if things get too hot and you need help, just call.'

'No problem. You go and take care of her,' responded Lorcan.

'Right, you two,' said Gilchrist, addressing Cadman and Joram. 'They'll be at the cave soon.'

All three walked through the wall facing away from the watching demon, and then strode quickly towards the south side of the city.

Chapter 30

While this was all happening, the other side of the city, Joseph and Mary walked the streets in the twilight. Their next problem was finding somewhere to stay. It was going to be difficult since so many people had arrived that day. The impending night time compounded their situation as well. Mary was getting worried, too. She had felt a few tremours in her womb, which made her think they needed to get somewhere sooner, rather than later. She didn't tell her husband because it would have been like adding an extra weight to an already overburdened packhorse.

'You okay?' he asked.

'Well... you know, my feet are aching, my thighs are sore, my back is hurting and I'm carrying the Messiah, the Saviour of the World in my womb. Besides that, I'm fine,' she replied, smiling gamely at Joseph.

He squeezed his arm around her shoulders a little tighter.

'We're nearly there,' he comforted her.

Once in the city, Joseph had asked around for places to stay. He had been directed to two or three inns in the south side. Slowly, they made their way through the teeming streets. They were both amazed at how alive Bethlehem was. It seemed it had got its second wind after the efforts of the day. Noise and light spilled out through half-closed doors of houses that were tightly packed side by side. The seductive smells of early evening cooking, suffused with herbs and spices wafted out through loosely shuttered windows of houses making Joseph and Mary's already painful hunger all the more acute.

Neither of the first two inns they called at had any room at all. The second innkeeper, mindful of Mary's condition had suggested they try an establishment right at the southern edge of the city wall, run by a man called Benaiah. He hadn't long started his business and the innkeeper thought that maybe he would have room for them.

Wearily, they headed on. As they trod the streets, they noticed that that part of the city was poorer. The houses looked tired and uncared for. Long broken shutters dangled freely from their hinges and wooden doors were rotting at the top and bottom. Their inhabitants were unruly, noisier than other parts of the city and the darkness of the night sky seemed palpable, the streets more menacing. They walked a little quicker, keeping their heads down, avoiding eye contact with the inhabitants. Eventually, they arrived at the inn. They had been told it was easily recognizable, even at night, since it was situated right next to a huge rock, with an unexpectedly wide clearing in front of it.

Joseph knocked on the door and waited. Mary was beginning to feel more than tremours in her body.

Meanwhile the old couple that had followed Joseph and Mary into the city and had sat beside them at the well were having words.

'Get your hands off me!' the woman whispered irritably.

'Why?' asked her husband innocently.

'This is the last time I play the wife to your husband.'

Ebin and Caleb, in the guise of the old couple had followed Joseph and Mary as they climbed up the hill towards Bethlehem's gates. From a safe distance, they had watched them call at the first two inns, carefully keeping to the shadows of the city's narrow streets.

'What's wrong?'

'What's wrong!?' Ebin was plainly aggravated. 'You were holding me so tight around my waist, when we walked in through the gates you were squeezing the life out of me, and you're still doing it.'

'I was just trying to show Sandon I was lovingly taking care of you.'

'"Lovingly taking care of me"?! Ebin whispered a little louder. 'How could anyone expect you, to "lovingly take care" of anyone when your hands are more used to holding lions by their manes?'

'If you're acting the old wife,' remonstrated Caleb, 'it would look really strange for me as a caring husband not to help you. Look at Joseph, how he cares for Mary.' He nodded towards the couple who were walking ahead of them.

'But he isn't trying to strangle her waist, is he?'

'You strangle someone's throat, not waist,' corrected Caleb.

'Just keep your hands to yourself. Anyway, there aren't any demons here. They're all concentrating on Sabteka at the moment, and Sandon is still at the gate and...'

'Look!' exclaimed Caleb.

They both watched as Joseph knocked the door to Benaiah's inn.

'We'd better get going!' said Ebin, having forgotten his irritation at Caleb's cack-handed attempts at tenderness.

They turned to their right and walked along a street that ran directly parallel with, but out of sight of the front of the inn. Taking advantage of this, and the fact that the street was deserted, they turned themselves back into warrior angels. Both felt more comfortable in their supernatural states. Playing the human was very constricting, like being mummified by thick, heavy bandages. They turned left and hurried along a narrow alleyway, much like the one where Sabteka had met Gilchrist, Cadman and Joram on the other side of town. The alleyway opened out to the clearing adjacent to the inn, and they took in the huge limestone rock that rose majestically in front of them. At its base, they saw an entrance to a cave, wide and high enough for a donkey, a horse or even a moderately sized camel, at a push. They contemplated in mutual silence what was about to happen here in a few hours' time. Their eyes strayed upwards, and saw the cloudless inky blue sky dotted with sparkling stars, seeming to glow more brightly in anticipation, and in deference to their Creator who had put them in their place so many centuries earlier. It seemed they'd all decided to come out that evening in His honour. Both marvelled at the inventiveness and artistic creativity of their Lord, but they were as nothing compared to His unparalleled and unprecedented, imminent Incarnation.

Soon, Benaiah, the innkeeper, opened the door. He was a tall, rangy man, in his early forties, with a full crop of hair and a bushy beard, although the hair on his temples had already begun to turn grey. His kindly face was comforting, though he looked at Joseph and Mary with dark, slightly earnest eyes.

'No,' he said, and made to shut the door.

Joseph put his hand against it. Benaiah looked at him.

'Please,' said Joseph, turning towards Mary, who was standing behind him. 'My wife is heavily pregnant. Her time is getting very near.'

'My inn is full. We've no room,' he answered holding the door firmly, sensing the force of Joseph's hand, whether it was from his physical power, or his emotional strength owing to his wife's desperate condition. Somehow, the door had become the focus of their contention rather than whether he had room for them.

'We have nowhere else to go,' Joseph half-reasoned, half-pleaded with him.

The innkeeper looked at the young woman who hadn't uttered a word. She had no need to. Her eyes seemed to look deep into his as they searched for his heart. Once found, he was powerless, as she delicately unwrapped it and discovered him to be both charitable and bountiful, prone throughout his life to acts of immense kindness and at times, insane generosity.

'She can't be much older than my own Deborah,' he thought.

He relented.

Joseph felt the door give way, and Benaiah opened it wide to let them in. Ebin and Caleb, standing in the clearing, smiled in admiration of the innkeeper as they saw the couple step into the main courtyard of the inn, just inside the door.

Benaiah led them to the well situated in the centre of the courtyard. They sat on its rim, heads downward, completely exhausted. She did not look very good. She was in obvious discomfort. He ran his fingers through his hair. What on earth had he done? For goodness' sake, he ran a respectable establishment for travellers, not a maternity unit for expectant mothers!

'Look, you can rest for a while, but you'll have to leave.'

He tried his utmost to sound firm.

'Have you no room at all?' asked Joseph.

'I have twelve cells,' he answered, holding his arm out as if showing them to a prospective buyer, 'but all are taken.'

Joseph became more forward in his desperation.

'No room in your house?'

Benaiah hid the offence he felt and responded in a hoarse whisper.

'Had I room in my own home, I would have offered you shelter there, my friend. My family have arrived, ready for the census. Even my guest room is full.'

'I'm sorry,' replied Joseph, bowing his head in shame, for having suggested such a thing.

Suddenly, Mary grabbed her husband's arm tightly.

'Joseph! He's coming,' she exclaimed.

Instantly, he sensed the panic in her voice.

What was happening to her body mirrored what had happened to every woman who was about to give birth ever since Eve gave birth to Cain: her waters had just broken. The Messiah's birth was that much nearer, a matter of hours away. For a moment, Joseph was motionless, unable to move. His blood turned cold.

'Joseph!' pleaded Mary, her voice echoing the alarm bells ringing in her heart. 'I need somewhere, now!'

He looked at Benaiah in desperation. Realising the urgency of the situation, the innkeeper thought of somewhere for her, but he was loathe to make the suggestion. He could think of nowhere else though. He ventured his solution, fearing their reaction.

'Well, I do have a cave outside.'

Sensing they hadn't dismissed him completely out of hand, he was encouraged.

'It's dry.'

His mood lightened as he thought of other advantages.

'You'd have complete privacy: no one else would dream of going there.'

He could have put that better he thought, as he saw Joseph look at him quizzically. He tried to make amends.

'And it's warm, because there are... erm... animals in there.'

In his mind he was wishing he was an ostrich, and could bury his head in the sand. He quickly thought of a more practical reason to make it more appealing.

'And I won't charge you anything.'

Joseph looked at Mary. Without hesitation, she nodded. Frankly, she would have agreed to pay a thousand shekels of silver for the cave the way she was feeling.

'Right, take us there,' said Joseph as he slowly helped Mary to her feet. 'Could we trouble you for some food as well. We haven't eaten properly for days.'

'My wife will get you something. Now, come with me,' he said and led them towards the door of the inn.

Ebin and Caleb had been waiting patiently at the end of the alleyway on the edge of the clear piece of ground. Their eyes were fixed on the door to Benaiah's inn.

'What's up?' asked a deep voice from behind them.

They both jumped before swiftly turning round.

'G!' said Ebin reprovingly. 'Stop doing that!'

Gilchrist, Cadman and Joram were bent double, laughing at their comrades' edginess. Using the same alleyway that Ebin and Caleb had walked a little earlier, they had silently come up behind them.

'You look like you've seen an angel,' said Joram.

'Funny,' retorted Caleb. 'On my back and my stomach aches as well, coz I'm laughing so much.'

'Well, tell us, what's happening?' pressed Gilchrist.

'They're inside Benaiah's inn,' answered Ebin. They all looked expectantly at the door. 'They've been there for some time.'

'Did things go off okay with Sabteka?' asked Caleb.

'Perfect. Marzan's focusing on the lean-to we walked into, waiting for Antonin to arrive,' answered Gilchrist.

'Did you see Sandon when he saw Sabteka?' asked Joram. 'He suddenly began pacing about like an angel possessed.'

'Yeah, well, when you think about it, that's what he is, isn't he?' reasoned Caleb.

They looked at him in silence for a while.

'I've got to say, Melon Head,' said Joram, 'you may not know how to start a conversation, but you certainly know how to end one.'

Caleb beamed with pride and delight.

'Here they come,' said Ebin. He'd been keeping a vigilant eye on the door.

Sure enough, Benaiah, lantern in hand, appeared, leading Joseph and Mary out through the door of the inn. She was moving much slower than when they last saw her, and was leaning heavily on her husband.

'Not long to go, I'd say,' observed Gilchrist.

The others murmured their agreement.

They all watched as Mary covered the last few painful steps of her long journey from Nazareth. She and Joseph followed Benaiah into the cave. By the flickering light of the lantern, they could just about distinguish the shadows of other travellers' animals as they moved to the back of the cave. All five angels were deep in thought, not quite believing that the Dayspring from on High had willingly abased Himself to be born in a cold, dirty cave in front of an audience of animals.

Gilchrist turned to the others.

'Okay, one package delivered. I'm going back to heaven to pick up the other one.'

'Don't you want to be here for His birth?' asked Joram.

'God wants me there. Besides, thanks to Sabteka, I don't think you'll be troubled by Antonin or Sandon, or any other demons, now that they think Jesus is going to be born in that house the other side of the city. By the time they realise what's happened, it'll be too late for them to do anything. You four take your guard outside the cave. And remember don't hesitate to call for help. This isn't the time to be heroes.'

With that, Gilchrist took off. He was careful to fly behind the sizeable rock that housed Joseph and Mary, so as not to be seen by any demons that were about, and then flew as fast as he could back to heaven, to meet with God in the Eternal Throne Room.

Chapter 31

Antonin was on his way. As soon as he received the message from the demon sent by Sandon, that a young pregnant woman had been seen by his guards, he left his hideaway on the edge of the Dead Sea. He was accompanied by a small band of fifteen devils. Hand-picked by him for their exceptional fighting abilities, none more so than Ashtenaz, Riphthal, Tograman and Hazarm. Sadistic cruelty was their reason for living. Any way they could sate their unending craving to inflict pain on anyone, human or spirit, was pursued with a vengeance. All fifteen had been on standby for such an eventuality as this, ever since Antonin had set up his headquarters overlooking the Dead Sea. They had to get to Bethlehem, as soon as possible. The more Antonin thought about it, the more astounded he was that a mortal woman should be carrying Jesus in her womb, and that God should have imperilled his Son's life in such a way. It was imperative they get to her before He was born. She was key. They had to kill her, and so terminate Jesus even before His life on earth had begun. Antonin smiled to himself at the thought.

They flew through the early evening air in perfect triangular formation. Antonin had placed himself in the most advantageous position: in the middle, behind the three demons that formed the arrowhead. They thus cleared a path for him, taking the full force of the wind that was blowing against them.

From what the messenger had told him, this was a woman of ill-repute. How typical of God to choose someone like her to bring His Son into the world. If there was one thing Antonin knew about God, it was that He always enjoyed confounding and doing the unexpected. Soon they saw the lights of Bethlehem. In the light of the bright moon that was in its ascendancy, Antonin could see the mass of tents spilling down Bethlehem's hillside. And even though the gates had been closed there was plenty of noise coming from behind as the city was bursting at the seams from the travellers who had arrived the last few days.

Sandon and his fellow demons saw them as they approached and shuddered at the sight of those who accompanied Antonin. They recognised them and knew them from reputation as demons of the worst kind who had committed the most hideous and heinous acts in the name of Satan, and that, without compunction or forethought. Just as Gilchrist and his small band of warriors were highly revered and admired by the heavenly host, these demons were feared and loathed in equal measure by the hordes of hell. And they gloried in their exalted status. Sandon was afraid, and so were the other demons with him. They stood to one side to make space for them to land.

'I take it you got my message, Lord Antonin,' he said bowing.

'No, I've just come to pay you a social call,' he replied sarcastically, his rasping voice grating the cold evening air.

Sandon smiled half-heartedly. Ashtenaz, one of the demons in Antonin's entourage came and stood behind him.

'Well, have you anything more to report?' asked Antonin.

Sandon looked past Antonin, into the distance. He still remembered the pummelling he had given him the last time they had spoken.

'Two demons followed the woman and in a back alley, she was met by three warrior angels, sir.'

Antonin took more notice.

'And?'

'They recognised one of them as...' he paused, '... Gilchrist.'

He stole a glance at his commander. He noticed a slight shudder in Antonin's being as he heard the name of his one-time friend.

'Did they recognise the others?'

'Yes – Cadman and Joram.'

Antonin was silent, pondering what Sandon had just told him. Then he asked,

'How did they get in to the city? Did you not see them?'

Sandon had been looking forward to informing Antonin what his demons had discovered. He had even let himself envisage that he would be rewarded for their vigilance in finding the pregnant woman. Suddenly, he had been backed into a corner, from which there was no escape. He had no answer.

'I...erm...uh...'

He let out a short breath of despair. Ashtenaz, the demon standing behind hit him a vicious blow in the base of his back that sent him reeling to the ground. As he did he made sure that his talons had dug into Sandon's back. Sandon was overcome with panic as he gasped for air, feeling himself sinking in a sea of breathlessness. Presently, he began to breathe normally and slowly got to his feet.

Antonin calmly turned to the other demons who had shared the vigil with Sandon at Bethlehem's gates.

'Who followed the girl to the house?'

Habilah tentatively stepped forward.

'Me, sir.'

'Pretty obvious it was you, else why would you have stepped forward.'

'He never gives up,' the other demons thought to themselves.

'Show me... oh, and the rest of you? Make yourselves scarce. You don't want to be here now.'

Habilah took off, with Antonin and his personal entourage close behind. They flew over the wall of the city and made their way through the air to meet up with Marzan, who was still keeping an eye on the small house from the other side of the alley.

Unbeknown to any of them, inside, five warrior angels were lying in wait.

Chapter 32

Meanwhile, Dylan had just been comforting a lonely old lady in northern Europe. Not that he knew where he had been. He depended on his internal radar to respond to the pull of people's sadness. Compassion was his compass. He was hurrying back to heaven so that he could go with the Angel Choir to the celebration to mark Jesus's arrival on earth and was relieved he had not been called upon to minister to some other unfortunates. He realised that this was his special calling and was ready to respond any time, but singing a welcome to Jesus as He arrived in earth was something else. He had been looking forward for such a long time, and there were only a few hours to go.

Just as the vast rehearsal room was coming into view, he sensed a faint tug. He carried on, ignoring the all too familiar sensation. He simply had to get back to heaven to go to Bethlehem. On he sped, but the pull became stronger. He stopped and stared ahead. It was someone new, he hadn't been to before. He could make out some members of the Angel Choir congregating in the hall. Meshek and his warrior angels were there, ready to escort them to Bethlehem.

Dylan hung in space for a few seconds, breathing heavily, his legs swinging back and forth. The pull weakened. Maybe the pain felt by that person – whoever it was – had been eased by a hug or a warm embrace or just a smile from someone on earth. Dylan was relieved. He began to fly heavenwards once again. Then, he stopped. It returned and was much stronger. He hung in space again, his legs swinging as before. He realised that he had to turn back. If he went with the choir now it wouldn't be right. No way would he be able to enjoy himself, knowing that someone, somewhere on earth, was hurting. He had been the one called for and he had to respond.

He reasoned that if he hurried and flew faster than he'd ever flown before, he could get back just in time to catch the choir as it was leaving for Bethlehem, or at least he would be able to follow them from afar. Hundreds of thousands of angels travelling together through space would surely leave some kind of trail.

Dylan looked towards heaven. The angels were still gathering.

Slowly, he turned his face towards earth and began the long journey to the one in need. He flew faster than the wind. Immediately, he felt the pull grow stronger. He saw no other angels. Every one was back in heaven preparing to leave for earth.

Eventually, Dylan arrived in a little village, situated on the edge of a prairie of big, blue stem grass. It was a sunny morning, and he found her: a little girl no more than seven years old. He could see the other children of the village, playing in the stream that ran nearby. She was kneeling on the floor where she slept inside her parents' tepee enviously watching the others squealing and shrieking as they threw water on one another in the warm autumn sun. All the children of the village were there except for her. This was how things had always been since she could remember. She didn't know why they didn't want her to play with them, but inside, her little heart was screaming for one of them to ask her to come and play. That never happened. Dylan could hear her scream though and felt her pain. He had come across so many children whose best friends were they themselves, and no one else.

So, he did the only thing he could do and that was to sing to her. The pain of her loneliness made his voice all the sweeter and it lifted her heart and somehow, deep inside, she knew she was not alone. In an instant Dylan forgot about the choir of mass angels that would soon be leaving heaven and the party that was about to happen in the skies above Bethlehem. His mind was totally focused on the little girl. He was there to serve her in the only way he could, and that was to sing her a lullaby, quieten her fears and dissipate her loneliness.

Although no one on earth could see him, he glowed a warm light that grew so strong it would have blinded any human eyes that saw it, such was its intensity and brightness. Dylan felt a joyous pleasure wash over the little girl. He smiled softly to himself.

Thankfully, it was time to return to heaven.

He had never flown so fast. High mountains, wide rivers and thick forests flashed underneath him. Before long he was climbing high above the clouds. Stars and planets came into view, but Dylan hardly saw them. He flew swiftly. His mind was thinking of one thing only: get back to heaven as soon as he could to catch the choir. He was hoping against hope that they had not left yet. Occasionally he would look around, trying to catch a glimpse of the choir's trail, just in case they had already left. But to his great dismay, he saw no one.

At last, he could see the rehearsal room where the choir had been gathering. This spurred him on and in what seemed like no time to Dylan, he landed in the rehearsal room. He could see no other angels. He listened intently, but other than his own deep breaths, everything was silent. He felt a slight dread inside him.

It was obvious to him that those angels he had seen congregating earlier on in the rehearsal room had left. Then, he had an idea.

'Of course, Archangel Michael's Great Hall!'

Maybe some of them were in Michael's Great Hall. Why hadn't he thought of that before? He began to hope again. He ran as fast as his short legs could take him, his heavy footsteps resounding through heaven's empty corridors.

However, even before he arrived, he knew there was no one there since there was no hubbub of noise or the excited chatter of a huge choir of angels congregating. It was completely deserted.

He felt himself plunge into a black hole of despair. There were no angels in heaven. He was on his own. The loneliness Dylan felt was magnified by his helplessness, since he did not even know the way to Bethlehem. He was engulfed by the sudden, awful realisation that he was going to miss the great celebration to welcome Jesus to earth. His sadness knew no bounds.

Tears flowed freely now, as he wandered aimlessly around the wide corridors and vast, empty halls. In a few hours all the angels would return full of joy, full of stories of the greatest party that was ever held on earth and he had missed it. He would have to rely on their descriptions of what had happened. He had wanted to be there himself, to see the wonder of the arrival of Jesus on earth and to sing His praises, regardless of whether he was in tune or not.

Then Dylan began to feel very cross. They had left without him. He would never have done that to any of them. Why had Sabta, Gether and Dumah not waited for him? It was obvious that they, and everyone else had not wanted him there.

He continued wandering aimlessly along heaven's huge corridors. He felt he was carrying a great burden on his back. Eventually, he stopped and leant back against a wall. He didn't know where he was, and he didn't care. Silently, he let himself slide down to sit on the floor. He pulled his knees up tightly resting his forehead on them. Powerful waves of loneliness and despondency crashed against him and he felt unable to withstand. He sobbed uncontrollably, his round shoulders heaving to the rhythm of his sorrow and the beat of his aching heart. He lifted his head. He wished that someone would come and sing to him, but there was no one there. Heaven was deserted and its emptiness weighed heavily on his small shoulders. He had never felt so dejected.

Chapter 33

Cadman, Ebin, Joram and Caleb, standing guard outside the cave, eyes constantly monitoring the air around them, were becoming more concerned. For some time, the peace of the night had been shattered intermittently by the sounds issuing forth, from inside the cave. At times there were shrieks of an unearthly nature, which made them turn to look at the cave and then look nervously at each other. This was followed by loud pants of relief as the pain of a prolonged contraction subsided once again. After one particular scream that seemed never ending, Caleb turned to the others.

'Things seem to be going well.'

'You're joking,' was Ebin's opinion.

'She's making a lot of noise.'

'Were you expecting a silent night?' asked Joram.

'No, but...' mumbled Caleb.

A few more seconds of heavy breathing went by.

'Do you think we should go in?' Caleb persisted.

'And do what?' asked Joram.

'Do you want to go in there?' asked Cadman. 'We all know what's happening. Hearing it is bad enough: seeing it would be ten times worse.'

'I know, but...'

'We're safer here,' added Ebin. 'Besides, what can we do to help?'

Involuntarily, they all jumped in unison, as another sharp piercing scream punctured the air. Once again, they turned to look at the cave and then at each other. Nervously, they returned to their vigil. They didn't know exactly how long they had been there, but they knew that it was way past midnight. All four secretly wished that the birth would happen sooner rather than later. They envied Gilchrist who had gone back to heaven and was missing this most daunting and unnerving part of their mission on earth.

Dylan didn't know, demoralised and disheartened as he was, that he had sat right outside God's Eternal Throne Room. Maybe his tears had blinded him to exactly where he was in heaven, engrossed as he was in his own grief.

Certainly, he did not hear the footsteps approaching from the Throne Room. They were the steps of a majestic warrior angel, wearing a crumpled, dirty tunic, a captain's cloak draped over his shoulders. A powerful voice burst in on Dylan's silent sobbing.

'Dylan! Get up.'

He didn't answer.

'Dylan! You've got work to do.'

Through his sobs, he declared,

'Don't... want to... work.'

He felt as if he was drowning in the depths of despair, gulping for air, finding it nigh on impossible to speak properly. He ran two fingers along his wisp of hair.

'We need you to sing.'

'I can't... sing.'

'Yes, you can,' persisted the voice.

'Don't... want... to... sing,' Dylan responded, hanging his head stubbornly, sobbing breathlessly between each word.

Then he felt two strong hands take hold of his heaving shoulders, lifting him up on his feet.

'Come,' said the voice.

Then with some authority, it said,

'The Lord of the Angel Armies wants to see you.'

Slowly, Dylan looked up. He saw the sword shining brightly through its sheath. He raised his eyes some more and saw the mighty arms that had fought so many battles throughout the centuries.

'Gilchrist,' he whispered.

He stopped crying.

'Come,' he said, holding his hand out, walking towards the entrance to the Eternal Throne Room.

'What are you doing here? Why aren't you at the party?'

The warrior angel turned back to look at Dylan

'I've been waiting for you.'

'What?'

'Dylan, we haven't much time and our Lord wants to see you.'

'Wants to see me? But why?'

Gilchrist didn't answer. He just stood at the doorway to the Eternal Throne Room, holding his hand out again, inviting Dylan to follow him.

Dylan quickly wiped his tears away. A dreadful fear welled up inside him. He had been summoned to see the Lord of the Angel Armies Himself. God was probably going to give him a severe dressing down for missing Jesus's arrival on earth. It was the biggest blunder any angel could have made.

How could he have been so stupid? Who else would have put a little girl before Jesus?

He gingerly walked behind Gilchrist, his eyes cast down, not daring to look up. What was God going to say to him, or worse, do to him?

Antonin was standing at the far end of the alleyway from the little house that Marzan and Habilah had seen the young pregnant woman enter, accompanied by Cadman, Joram and Gilchrist. Behind him, the demons who had travelled with him waited impatiently.

'Are we going to see some action?' whispered Ashentaz, the demon who had nearly fatally injured Sandon. Antonin felt that his tone of voice was a little threatening. Keeping his eyes on the house, he answered him.

'I have to make sure that she's the one.'

'There can't be any other. She fits the bill: a pregnant woman, on her own, and what's more, Gilchrist and the others were sighted with her.'

'I know, but...'

'We could strike a deathly blow tonight. We could get Philip that malignant Pharisee who lives here to do our bidding: work on his twisted mind like I did with King Manasseh, even getting him to send his own son into the fire. You, yourself said he would be very compliant, willing to toe our line.'

'It's not as easy as that...'

'Can't see the problem myself,' Ashtenaz retorted. 'All we'd have to do is let him know that there's a pregnant woman in town, with no husband. His hypocritical indignation would do the rest. We could just sit back and let him do our work for us.'

Antonin thought to himself that this demon was trying to take control, when it was he who had been put in charge by none other than Satan himself. He looked down the alley. It was a sorrowful even dolorous birthplace for God's Son. This was so typical of how God worked. Yet, some things were gnawing at him. He had been watching the little house for some time now and could detect shadows moving from under the door by the weak light within, but things seemed too quiet to him. Surely the woman should have been making much more noise, especially since Sandon had told him that the birth was imminent. And why had she only been accompanied by three angels, albeit three warriors who were amongst the deadliest and most proficient in the whole Angel Armies? Shouldn't there have been much more?

He questioned Marzam again.

'Are you sure no one's left the house?'

'Sir.'

'And you haven't left your position here at all?

'No, sir.'

He was adamant.

Antonin pondered for a while longer and then he came to a decision.

'I'm in charge here and we move when I say so.'

'And so?' Ashtenaz asked expectantly.

'We wait.'

Ashtenaz and the others let out a long, impatient groan.

The four warrior angels were getting more anxious. The screams of pain emanating from the cave behind them were more regular with the time between much shorter. Mary could only relax for a few short minutes before her young body endured further suffering greater than the last. They heard another growl and an almighty grinding scream more prolonged than the others and then, an abrupt silence once again.

'I can't take much more,' said Caleb. 'I'm a soldier in the Angel Armies of the Lord. I'd rather fight twenty demons, with one hand tied behind my back, than this, any day.'

The others said nothing, so Caleb continued. He always felt more at ease in difficult situations if he could give vent to his thoughts and feelings.

'I mean, it all seems so unreal. It's the early hours of the morning, there's not a soul in sight, the night is still and yet, here we are, not a stone's throw away from the birth of the Messiah, and no one's taking a blind bit of notice. The whole world is getting on with its business and the only people who know about it are Joseph and Mary!'

'Not quite,' piped up Cadman.

'What do you mean?'

'Well... there's Ben and Abigail – Mary's parents – for starters. They know.'

'Okay, another two. That's it.'

'Before long, the Angel Choir will be up on those hills opposite, telling the shepherds of His birth,' added Joram.

'And they will tell,' assured Ebin. 'News will spread.'

They heard a short slap come from inside the cave and then a baby cry. They looked at each other. Their furrowed faces lit up as the weight of the world slid from their shoulders. It was as if they had literally disrobed a heavy piece of armour. They were elated, smiling at each other, thankful that their helpless ordeal was over, slapping each other on the back as if they had just become fathers themselves.

Inside the cave Joseph, even more relieved than the angels outside, worked quickly in the light of a lantern. Still holding baby Jesus in the crook of one arm, he picked up the small pot of hot water that Benaiah had thoughtfully provided earlier, although it had cooled considerably by now. He placed it beside Mary. Gently, he passed the small, naked and bloodied baby Messiah to her. There was no midwife present so Mary had to perform those offices usually undertaken by her.

She knew exactly what needed to be done. Hadn't she been present when Elizabeth had given birth to John and she had very carefully watched the midwife at her work? So, she tenderly washed the blood away, as He kicked His legs and flailed His arms. Then she motioned Joseph to pass her the bag she had carried with her all the way from Nazareth.

From inside, she brought out a smaller bag, and on opening it, Joseph could see there was some salt there. Carefully, Mary rubbed it all over Jesus's little body in order to cleanse it. Then, she stretched into the bigger bag and brought out a sizeable bundle of cloths and strips of linen her mother had given her. Joseph watched in silence and awe as she tenderly wrapped Jesus's body and arms and legs with the cloths, until He was completely bound, as was the custom of her society. Throughout the whole operation, Jesus made some baby noises, His head jerking from side to side as His mouth searched for some nourishment. Once she had finished her midwife responsibilities, Mary placed Jesus in the crook of her arm, and brought His head up to her breast. Joseph looked at Him in wonderment.

'I can't believe it, Mary: God made flesh; a baby! In front of our very eyes.'

'And I can't believe that I'm about to feed Him, the One who created the world.'

Joseph gazed at her. Mary's cheeks, still red from her physical exertions somehow made her more attractive than ever to him. He leant forward and kissed her sweat, sodden brow. She looked up at him lovingly, grateful that he was by her side and had been there throughout.

'Well, you'd better get on with it,' he smiled at her. 'He looks really hungry to me.'

Just then, Cadman appeared at the mouth of the cave and stared in wonderment. He was looking at the incarnate deity; God made flesh. Slowly, he fell to his knees, and worshipped the babe.

Mary steered Jesus's head closer to her breast and felt His lips on her nipple. She winced from the pain. She pulled Him away, surprised at how strongly His gums had squeezed her nipple. She clenched her teeth, then gingerly pressed her breast to His searching lips and for the first time of many, He sucked His mother's milk. He, the life force of the world, the fountain of life, drew sustenance from her. She lay her weary head on the straw: it was over. For nine months she had carried the Messiah in her womb and after hours of prolonged agony, when the pain had been incessant, like the waves of an incoming tide, she had given birth to the Saviour of the world. Even now, she did not know where the strength to endure the unimaginable physical hurt had come from. She had been wholly unprepared for it. But she had survived and like a ship that had eventually reached safe harbour after passing through the teeth of the storm, she could rest. She looked at Jesus and delighted in His beautiful face. She suddenly felt great elation as she realised once again, the honour that had been bestowed upon her and she would indeed be blessed. Yes, it was over, but it was not all over. For with the honour came a terrifying responsibility for His physical well-being during His childhood and adolescence.

After He had had His fill of her milk, Mary took out some of the milkweed leaves she had got Joseph to pick when they had travelled down the Jordan Valley. Cadman raised his head, but he soon lowered it again for he could not watch owing to the deep shame he felt when he saw what she did with them.

Chapter 34

As soon as Dylan stepped into the Throne Room, all his fears vanished in the blink of an eye. He couldn't believe it. The cold fear that had been coursing through him a second before was replaced by a warm peace. Not only that, strange things were happening to him. He couldn't help himself from having good thoughts. It seemed he had been overpowered as he relaxed in the goodness that flooded through. He was completely alive, sensitive to the slightest touch, feeling the power of the everlasting, boundless joy of God. He gazed at the floor. It was a sea of glass coloured blue and turquoise with gently rolling waves playfully lapping his feet. He looked up and around in wonderment. Above him were galaxies and constellations, star systems and universes all stretching out in far-flung expanses, but yet, so close. Dylan felt he could stretch out and touch them. It was as if distance was of no consequence here.

Then, a silly smile spread all along his wide mouth. He was going to see God! He was awash with excitement at the thrilling prospect of meeting the Lord of the Angel Armies, face to face.

Dylan looked ahead expectantly, but try as he might, he could not see God at all. He was walking so close behind Gilchrist, the warrior's back hid Him from sight. However, his being was framed by the light that emanated from the six cherubim that encircled the Eternal Throne, fluttering their wings, creating a blinding blaze of worship of their Lord. Dylan could also see the emerald rainbow that formed a perfect bow above the throne.

Gilchrist stopped, stood for a second, before falling on bended knee and then bowed his head.

Dylan was so lost in his elation he did not notice that Gilchrist had suddenly knelt down. He walked straight into the warrior's left shoulder and promptly fell head over heels onto the floor before God. Gilchrist quickly looked up and saw Dylan floundering on the floor. He stole a glance at God. There was a faint smile on His face and His shoulders rippled slightly.

With his feet pointing towards the throne, Dylan, with some difficulty – since his belly prevented a smooth, elegant action – rolled himself onto his front. He planted his feet on the floor, used his hands to push himself up and straightened his legs. Unfortunately, as he did so, his bottom faced God.

Gilchrist was both ashamed and embarrassed. This was how this angel had presented himself to the Lord of the Angel Armies? He hastily looked up at God, half expecting Him to throw lightning at Dylan.

He, however, was still smiling, enjoying the entertainment that Dylan was providing. As for the object of His mirth, he brought his head up and looked in front of him. Where had God got to? He swiftly looked to the right and left. No sign of Him. He swivelled a hundred and eighty degrees. There He was!

'How did You get there?' he asked, pointing at God.

Gilchrist shook his head. Was this angel stupid, as well as clumsy?

God was still smiling. However, when He saw the little trickles of dried tears on Dylan's face, He stretched down, held his head gently, in the palms of His hands, and softly wiped the tears with his thumbs. God then held his hand out in front of Dylan.

'Would you like to come up?'

Dylan could only nod his head in response.

'Then, climb on,' He said, as the happiest, broadest smile stretched across His face.

Dylan looked up and clambered on board, losing his balance for an instant. Without thinking, he put his hand out and held on to God's thumb to steady himself. He looked at God apologetically, but He continued to smile at him. Once he was safely in the palm of His hand, God lifted him up slowly. Instinctively, Dylan looked down and although God had only lifted him past His knees, the floor, was already a long way away. He began to feel a little dizzy: something he had never experienced before and it made him a little frightened.

'Look at Me, little one,' whispered God.

Dylan did just that and he was carried up to meet Him face to face. His dizziness disappeared and he felt completely relaxed. He looked down again and was amazed to see that Gilchrist was a mere speck, far below. How could it be that he had been carried so high in such a short space of time? Then he was standing directly in front of God's face. Starry eyed, he looked in awe at its loveliness and radiance. Dylan had never been this close to His face before. He was struck dumb. He felt joy and kindness and peace flow through him, all emanating from his Lord, but above all he saw an overwhelming love in His beauteous countenance. The stars and constellations still sparkled in their wondrous beauty, but Dylan was oblivious to them all, lost in the comeliness that was his Lord's.

'So, what have you been up to?'

Dylan stirred from his wonderment. The questioning and scolding were about to start in earnest. Why did you go and sing to that little girl? Why weren't you here on time? Didn't you realise that nothing was more important than welcoming My Son to earth? Dylan blurted out his answer, nearly falling over his words.

'I was on my way back to heaven, ready to join everybody else to go to the party, but I felt a strong pull from someone new. I hovered in space for a long time, in two minds. Then I decided to go and help the little girl. I tried to get back in time, but they had all left and now I'm the only one here... well, besides You...'

Suddenly remembering Gilchrist, he looked down adding,

'... and Gilchrist of course.'

God did not respond. Things went quiet.

Dylan thought to add,

'I was so disappointed to have missed the party – honest,' he said, thinking this would placate God.

'Yes,' said God, looking deep into Dylan's eyes.

An awful thought struck Dylan.

'Has Gilchrist missed the party because of me?'

'No. He had to wait for you. He has more important work to do than to go to the celebration, and you, are to go with him.'

'Me?'

'Yes, you.'

'With Gilchrist?'

'Yes.'

'But he's a warrior angel. How can I help him?'

'You're not to help *him*.'

'Then who? What can I do?'

Dylan was beginning to panic. He didn't want to fight, he couldn't fight. He had never been a warrior angel like Gilchrist and Cadman and the other warriors he had heard so much about.

'Go with him now. You have important work to do, as well' God said tenderly, as He leant down and gently put him on his feet beside Gilchrist.

'My dear, faithful Gilchrist,' started God.

It seemed to Dylan that He was making an announcement and was very excited about it.

'He has been born.'

Gilchrist's face beamed with delight.

'You and your warrior angels have already done much and you have much to do yet.'

Gilchrist stood tall.

'They are your warriors my Lord, and I, and they cannot do enough for You or your Son.'

God was visibly touched.

'Go now, there's not much time.'

'My Lord,' said Gilchrist, as he bowed and turned to leave.

Dylan following his lead bowing deeply and trotted after him.

As they reached the door of the Eternal Throne Room, God's voice cascaded towards them.

'Dylan!'

Both angels stopped and turned.

'What you did for that little girl, you did for Me, and to Me. I, the Ancient of Days, acknowledge and recognize you, and I thank you.'

Dylan was open-mouthed. For a few short seconds, he was rooted to the spot. The Lord of the Angel Armies had just thanked him; had thanked him for going to the little girl. He looked up at Gilchrist in wide-eyed wonderment.

'Did you hear that?'

'Come on, we haven't much time.'

He put his hand on Dylan's shoulder and led him out of the Throne Room.

'Where are we going?' he asked.

'Bethlehem.'

'But that's where Jesus is to arrive on earth.'

Dylan's hopes were quickly raised.

'So, we *are* going to the party?'

'No, we're not.'

He didn't understand.

'Why are we going there, then?'

Gilchrist took Dylan by the arm and hastily led him along the empty corridors of heaven.

'No time to explain, I'll show you when we get there.'

Chapter 35

'We can't stand around here all night, Antonin.'

Much as he despised Ashtenaz, who hadn't stopped berating him since they had arrived at the alleyway, Antonin had long realised the truth of what he had to say. Other than the slight movement he could detect from under the door, there was no sign of life inside the small house. For some minutes, he had reasoned that there was nothing to stop him opening the door to see inside. After all, she wouldn't be able to see him. Even so, he waited a few more minutes. He hated his own indecision, and he knew the demons accompanying him were getting very impatient. Finally, he decided on a plan of action.

'Okay, here's what we'll do,' he announced. 'I'll go to the house and slowly open the door as if the wind has caught it. She won't be able to see me and I'll get a good look inside. Then, we'll stir our friend, the Pharisee and get him to do his worst: a single woman who's pregnant in his city, David's city. What does their law say? Such a woman must be stoned to death.'

The listening demons smiled sadistically. This was too good to be true. They were going to see a lonely, scared woman killed in such an appealingly brutal way, thus terminating the baby Jesus.

Antonin walked purposefully up to the house as the other demons watched excitedly. Holding his breath, he slowly opened the door.

Sensing what he was doing, the five warrior angels inside quickly drew their swords. The weapons pulsated a sharp light that momentarily blinded Antonin.

'Antonin!' greeted Lorcan, joyfully. 'Come to join our little gathering?'

Regaining his sight from the dazzling light, he looked inside for the woman. There was no sign of her: she wasn't there. Rather, he was faced with these five warrior angels, whom he knew, and remembered well enough. Above all, he recognised Sabteka, master disguiser, and in that instant, he realised what had happened: he had been duped. Gilchrist, Cadman and Joram were nowhere to be seen. They must have slipped out unseen through the wall the other side of the house from where they had been watching. He slammed the door shut, and let out a thunderous roar. How could he have been so stupid? Of course, they had led him and the other demons to her. They had made her so blindingly obvious to them they had not seen the real woman who was carrying Jesus. Sandon and those other idiots had been fooled, and he, Antonin, had gone along with them. For the second time in as many minutes he was blinded, this time with fury, spitting obscenities and blasphemies. So incensed was he, he could not think properly and this merely added to his frenzy. He let out another shriek of apoplectic rage. More than anything, his anger was driven by the fact that he, who had made a name for himself as deceiver-in-chief, next to Satan, had been made such a chump so easily. How had he been so stupid, so gullible?

The demons, at the other end of the alleyway, watched in bewilderment as Antonin quickly walked back to them, still spluttering profanities.

'What happened?' asked Ashtenaz.

'She wasn't there, was she!' he blurted, trying to control his anger.

'What?'

'She never was there!'

They were confused. Antonin continued, his fiery red eyes glaring threateningly at Marzam and Habilah as he announced,

'She was never there, never had been, because she...' and here he stopped, gathering all his strength as if to dredge the next words out from the back his throat. '... all along, was Sabteka!'

Marzam and Habilah quietly pressed themselves as far as they could into the shadows of the city wall.

It dawned on all of them what had happened. They all knew Sabteka from centuries past as a supreme disguiser, who could take the form of any human or object, like no other angel. So skilful was he at blending in that they could have literally been standing next to him and not realised that he was an unskilled labourer, a playful child, or in this case, a young pregnant woman.

'Is he on his own?' persisted Ashtenaz.

'No. Lorcan, Abida and two other warrior angels are with him.'

'What about Gilchrist? Was he there?'

'No, neither were Cadman or Joram,' he shouted, his rage gaining a second wind.

'I don't understand,' said Ashtenaz. 'They were seen going in and they haven't left.'

'Am I surrounded by complete imbeciles? Didn't anyone realise that they can walk through walls? Phasing is nothing to them. They made sure they walked in through the door so that anyone watching them would forget that they can phase!'

As he said these last few words he glared threateningly at Mirzam and Habilah.

The demons were silent for a while. Ashtenaz was still up for a fight though.

'There are five of them, right. Well, there are plenty of us here. We could take them on.'

'What would we gain by doing that?'

Antonin was beginning to think more clearly now that his initial fury was subsiding.

'I'm ready for it,' replied Ashtenaz.

A few of the others murmured their approval.

'We came here to find the woman carrying Jesus and that's what we can still do. She must be somewhere in Bethlehem. Why go to all the bother of getting Sabteka to fool us. More than that, Gilchrist, Cadman and Joram have been sighted and Ebin and that idiot Melon Head can't be far away. No, we find Gilchrist and the others, and we find the woman, wherever she is.'

He thought for a while

'Ashtenaz, get over to Lord Kandar. Tell him to go to that Pharisee's house and be ready to wake him. The rest of you, split into three groups and spread out. We may still have time, before she gives birth to the Messiah. Once you find Gilchrist and his warriors, let me know.'

As the demons dispersed, Antonin, still furious that he had been made to look a fool by Gilchrist and his angels wanted to hurt someone. He walked up to Marzam and Habilah, the snakes on his head spitting venom at them. He swung a forearm against their faces with such ferocity they smashed their heads against the wall. Their whole beings then bounced back, before collapsing and lying motionless on the ground. Antonin felt much better.

Chapter 36

Seconds later, Ashtenaz landed on the walkway on the city wall above the gates. Less than a yard away, Shobal, the deputy commander of Bethlehem's guard was leaning over the battlement surveying the multitude of tents sprawled across the land before him. Around thirty paces away, another guard stood on duty.

'Lord Kandar,' Ashtenaz said.

Shobal hardly reacted, other than shifting his weight from one leg to the other.

'A message from Lord Antonin. The Pharisee needs stirring. She is in the city.'

Speaking not much louder than a whisper, Kandar, senior commander amongst Satan's hordes, in the human guise of Shobal, answered him.

'I know that. I saw her with my own eyes earlier on. I was expecting someone to come and tell me to fetch the Pharisee some time ago.'

'There was a problem. It wasn't her. It was Sabteka.'

Kandar turned his head towards him slightly. Ashtenaz could see his eyes turning a raging red. Kandar controlled himself before answering calmly.

'You mean, you were duped.'

Ashtenaz didn't reply, although, he thought Kandar couldn't say anything because he had obviously been tricked as well. Instead, he stepped back, not wanting to bear the brunt of Lord Kandar's wrath.

'So, she's somewhere in the city?'

'Yes.'

'How are you going to find her?

'Gilchrist is here, to protect her.'

Kandar let his head drop.

'As well as the other four?'

'Cadman and Joram have been seen, and we presume Ebin and Melon Head must be around too.'

'But we don't know where the woman is,' stated Kandar, plainly irritated.

He had spent years at these gates, as Shobal, under the incompetent leadership of Nathanael. He had also had to endure Sandon's dire vigilance. He still couldn't believe that he'd had to prompt him to investigate that dust cloud that had suddenly appeared a few weeks earlier. Ashtenaz, sensing his frustration tried to steer Kandar's annoyance away from him.

'Antonin believes that once we find Gilchrist and his angels, we find the woman.'

Kandar pushed back from the wall and straightened himself. Ashtenaz took another step back. Without looking at Ashtenaz he called over to the guard.

'Nature calls – been screaming for a while, in fact. I'm going to call on Philip the Pharisee then, so I'll be gone a while. It's quiet here anyway.'

'Not like him, to leave his post,' the guard muttered to himself. Even so, he waved his hand in acknowledgement.

As Kandar walked towards the steps he suddenly stopped. A thought came to him. That old couple that had arrived late on that evening: there was something about them that had made him look twice. The husband seemed to be holding his wife a bit too tight. Maybe it was nothing – still. He remembered the direction they'd gone.

'Tell Antonin to send someone to the south side.'

'Why?'

Kandar gave him a vicious stare.

'My lord,' said Ashtenaz, terror in his eyes.

'Find them, and be quick about it. I'll be at Philip's house. You know where it is?'

'Yes, my lord.'

Kandar, aka Shobal, deputy of the city guard, then ran swiftly down the steps.

Chapter 37

Gilchrist sped through space dragging Dylan along by his shoulder. The little angel felt Gilchrist's iron grip and imagined how countless demons must have felt when they fought the angel warrior. He was glad Gilchrist was on his side. He had never flown this fast before. If he thought he had sped quickly back from the little girl earlier on, it was as nothing compared to the speed they were travelling at now. Indeed, they were flying so quickly he had to close his eyes. As they flew through earth's atmosphere, Dylan jerked his being involuntarily as if he was suffering from something akin to grass burns. If his eyes had been open, he would have seen the Angel Choir approaching the hills above Bethlehem, since he and Gilchrist had caught up with them. As it was, he felt like he had a ship's sail, full of wind, inside his mouth! He'd been told centuries earlier that the best way to breathe when flying was in through the nose and out of the mouth. Dylan had never bothered to master this since he always made a point of flying at an unhurried pace which suited him. This, though, was a completely new experience. And all the while he was wondering why was he going to Bethlehem, but not to Jesus's welcoming celebration?

Approaching the outskirts of Bethlehem Gilchrist slowed down considerably. Dylan was thankful. They had been travelling so fast, he was convinced he had no face left. He prodded it with his finger, to make sure it was still there. It was, but he couldn't feel it very much. Travelling at a speed Dylan was more accustomed to, he could take in his surroundings.

He turned round and looked up to the hills in the distance, opposite the city. He jumped for joy. He could see a never-ending stream of angels descending from the sky. As Dylan watched them touchdown – a multitudinous throng of divine messengers in gleaming raiments – they seemed to him like a boiling white effervescence at the bottom of a huge waterfall.

'Gilchrist!' he shouted, pointing at them. 'The choir! They're arriving; up in the hills. Look!'

'Dylan! We have other things to do,' was Gilchrist's curt reply.

As they flew on Dylan looked longingly at the choir. Then, below, he saw the banks of tents streaming down from the walls of Bethlehem. Most of the people were asleep inside their temporary homes, keeping warm from the cold night air. There were a few hardy souls still out, talking and nattering.

Gilchrist slowed down and looked down at one large circle of tents. Dylan saw around thirty men and women gathered around a small camp fire, drinking hot soup, discussing some matter or other. Their clothes were drab and their head-dresses threadbare, with frayed edges from years of use. Suddenly, the group burst out in raucous laughter.

Then Gilchrist sped off again and headed past the city gates to his right. They flew all the way round to the south side. Eventually he stopped and landed in front of an old inn, inside the city walls. Dylan landed beside him. He was unimpressed with the dilapidated building.

He turned to look up to the hills. Angels were still arriving in their thousands.

'Gilchrist!'

He looked at Dylan.

'I want to go up there,' he said, pointing at the host of angels.

'I've told you, we're not going there.'

Dylan had had enough.

'Gilchrist, I want to sing and worship my Lord,' he said, raising his voice, emphasising every word.

'But...'

Just then, the silence was shattered by the sound of a baby crying. Gilchrist turned his head and gazed somewhere the other side of the inn.

'We need to go.'

'What baby is that?'

Gilchrist began to make his way towards the side of the inn.

Dylan could not hold his frustration any longer.

'You've brought me here to see a baby?' he screamed. 'You're not listening to me! I haven't come to Bethlehem to see a baby. I don't want to see a baby. I want to be in the choir,' he demanded, pointing his finger towards the hills.

Gilchrist stopped, and walked back to him. Dylan hadn't finished.

'Jesus is about to arrive, in all His glory, with all the Angel Armies escorting Him. The choir of angels is there, waiting to greet Him and here we are, outside this stupid inn and you're taking me to see some baby!'

His voice rose to a crescendo when he uttered those final three words. With his eyes downcast and hot tears streaming down his cheeks, in a quiet voice virtually pleading, he said,

'All I want to do is sing in the choir. Jesus is up there, and that's where I want to be.'

Gilchrist wisely weathered the storm. When it eventually subsided, he bent down, placed a hand on both of Dylan's shoulders and looked intently into his eyes. Gently, he said,

'He's not up in the hills. And there are no Angel Armies up there either.'

Dylan looked at him in shock.

'But... why is the choir up there?'

'They've been sent there to announce His arrival.'

'So, what are we doing here?'

'I and a few other angels have been given an enormous honour by the Lord of the Angel Armies, but yours, yours is so much more. I have no words to describe it.'

'What honour is that?'

Gilchrist paused before answering.

'You too, have been chosen by the Mighty One.'

'Me!?'

'Yes. Just, come with me.'

With that the warrior angel straightened himself to his full height and strode quickly towards the back of the inn. This time, he didn't look back. He needn't have done, for Dylan was trotting behind him, like a dog faithfully following its master.

Once they rounded the corner of the inn, Dylan could see the huge rock that rose above the inn. By now the baby had stopped crying. What took his attention though was the sight of four warrior angels standing guard, in front of a cave, at the foot of the rock. A weak light spilled from it. It was difficult for Dylan to see who they were. Then as he and Gilchrist got nearer, Dylan took a sharp intake of breath. These were none other than Cadman, Joram, Ebin and Caleb, four of the greatest angel warriors, save for Gilchrist, and Michael. He couldn't wait to tell Sabta, Gether and Dumah. Intrigue trumped indignation. What were they doing here?

Gilchrist approached them.

'Anything?'

Cadman, standing nearest to him turned.

'Nothing. He has arrived though – a couple of hours ago.'

'Yes, we heard.'

Cadman looked at Dylan, but spoke to Gilchrist.

'So, this is he.'

'Yes,' replied Gilchrist.

'Pleased to meet you, Dylan,' he said, offering his hand.

Cadman knew his name! He was known! Slowly, Dylan shook this great warrior's hand. He felt its sheer power as it clasped his hand. In fact, he lost all feeling in it, as it all but disappeared in its mighty grip. Indeed, Dylan was slightly surprised when his hand reappeared, whole, once he let go of it.

'Have you seen Him?' asked Gilchrist.

It took Cadman a few seconds to answer. Something was bothering him.

'Yes. I just can't believe it.'

'What can't you believe?'

He took a moment to compose his thoughts.

'We're talking about the King of Kings here, Gilchrist, the Prince of Peace. You know, once, when I was still in Dedan's unit, before we came together, we flew to what we thought was the outer edge of the universe. We never arrived. We couldn't get there! We could see other planets and galaxies in the distance but however fast we flew we were no nearer them. The universe was perpetually expanding, never standing still. We had never been so far from heaven, but all the while, we always felt God's presence with us. Galaxies and constellations went on and on, further than our eyes could see and all of them, every one...'

He pointed a finger at the cave. Gilchrist was surprised. This wasn't the Cadman he knew.

'...every one of them was made through Him. The world and the heavens were all created at His say so, and she... she...'

His voice shuddered to a stop. He couldn't go on. He looked at his three brothers in arms. They only looked away. They knew what was on his mind. Gilchrist could feel his friend's discomfort.

'Tell me, Cadman.'

The warrior angel lowered his head and looked down to the ground. Gilchrist had never seen Cadman so emotional and animated. He could barely hear the words as his friend struggled to speak with tears of shame welling in his eyes.

'She... she had to guide His lips to her breast so that He could suck her milk. She had to wipe His mouth when the milk spilled down His chin, and...'

Cadman lifted his head and looked Gilchrist in the eye, his cheeks damp.

'... and that's not all.'

In a voice only slightly audible, he continued.

'You know Mary got Joseph to pick all those milkweed leaves a few days ago, and none of us knew why? I know, now. She... she used...' he let out a long sigh and then forced the words, 'she used them to make a nappy for Him.'

Cadman had said enough.

Gilchrist looked skywards. He took a deep breath.

Although he had known for some time that his Lord would come to earth as a baby, it was only now, on hearing what Cadman had just said, that the realisation of what Jesus had allowed to happen to Him, hit Gilchrist with a force that weakened his whole being. He had to steel himself. For a few seconds he was lost in his own thoughts, contemplating the enormity of it all.

Dylan could not make head or tail of things.

'What's happened, Gilchrist?'

The warrior angel looked at him.

'Let's go see Jesus,' he replied.

With that, he turned towards the cave.

By now, Dylan was completely confused.

'Why are you taking me to that cave Gilchrist? Jesus isn't in there,' he pleaded. There was panic in his voice.

He looked at Cadman. No words were exchanged, but Cadman waved him to follow Gilchrist.

Once again, Dylan trotted after him. He was fearful of what he was about to see in the cave, afraid his illusions were about to be shattered.

Meanwhile, another angel's misconceptions were about to be righted.

Chapter 38

As Dylan and Gilchrist had already witnessed, Axa and the choir were arriving safely in the hills above Bethlehem. Axa had been gratified to see that they had been accompanied all the way by Gabriel and the Archangel Michael. Axa was delighted at the arrangement, for it showed the great significance that had been attached to what his Angel Choir was about to do as well as the importance of his announcement.

By the light of the clear white moon, he could see Bethlehem, its lights flickering gently on the opposite hillside. A multitude of tents clustered around the city. Other than the occasional bleating of the sheep nearby, Axa was struck by how still and quiet everything was. An ethereal majesty pervaded the scene. The darkness of the night sky with its endless stars and planets arrayed in iridescent glory was like a splendid royal cloak that had been flung around Bethlehem. This would indeed be a worthy stage for the arrival of Jesus.

He smiled to himself at the thought of these poor shepherds, blissfully unaware of what was about to happen. They were going to have the shock of their lives. He could hardly wait. This was the culmination of so much preparation on his part. The choir was ready to sing at its most beautiful and harmonious, especially since Dylan had not managed to make it in time – thankfully. He felt a tingling excitement inside.

Three things were bothering him though, as he looked down on Bethlehem. That was one of them: why Bethlehem of all places?

'What a pathetic little excuse of a city,' he murmured disdainfully to himself.

He looked around and saw the shepherds and their sheep. That was another problem that was eating away at him. He simply could not understand why he was announcing Jesus's arrival to some shepherds. Why were they to be the first people to get in on the act? Everybody knew shepherds were the most untrustworthy people around. No one believed a word they said because they were known as deceitful liars. What was the point in making this proclamation to them? It would be like throwing pearls in front of swine.

As more and more angels arrived, the third matter came to mind. In fact, this issue had been preying on him for quite some time.

Where exactly had Jesus been lately? He hadn't been seen by anyone in heaven, according to Axa's approximations, for about nine months in earth time. Over the centuries He had been known to heaven to go to earth as He'd done when He met up with Abraham at the trees of Mamre, or when He appeared in the fiery furnace with Shadrach, Meshach and Abednego, in Babylon, but those occasions had been very few and far between and only for a short space of time. He had asked around but everyone was as mystified as he.

Lost in his own thoughts, he was unaware that Michael had landed beside him. He and Gabriel had been mopping up the stragglers, ensuring no one got lost on the way.

'Okay, everyone here, said Michael, 'including Dylan,' he added, straight faced.

Axa turned a paler shade of white.

'What?!'

'Only joking,' smiled Michael triumphantly. 'Got you going, there, though, didn't I.'

Axa let out a long sigh and relaxed his shoulders that had suddenly become very taut.

'He didn't make it in time,' continued Michael, gazing fixedly at Bethlehem. 'Can't help thinking about him, wondering where he is right now.'

Axa tried to sound sympathetic.

'I know, but it's all for the best. The choir will sound... well, heavenly...'

'Without him,' volunteered the archangel.

'Well, yes...' stuttered Axa. 'After all, this is such an important event, it was crucial that the choir be at its best.'

'Yes, quite.'

Axa quickly averted his eyes, as Gabriel approached.

'Axa, good to see you.'

'Gabriel,' he acknowledged.

'Right, I'd say we're about ready,' ventured Michael.

Axa was confused.

'Ready!? *We're* ready, but where's Jesus? I mean, we can't start without Him. He must be arriving soon.'

'Oh, He's already here,' said Gabriel.

Axa was stunned by the Gabriel's response.

'What?!' he asked, open-mouthed.

'He's already arrived.'

Axa felt a quick panic rise from the depths of his feet.

'B...b... but where is He?'

'Down there,' said Michael, pointing towards Bethlehem.

'In Bethlehem?'

'Yes.'

'But... what's He doing down there?'

'You'll soon find out.'

Axa did not quite understand.

'But I thought Jesus was arriving here, at the head of the Angel Armies.'

'What made you think that?' asked Michael.

'Well... this is... invasion earth, isn't it?

Michael smiled wryly.

'Yes, this is an invasion...'

'So, where are the warrior angels?'

'They're here,' Michael answered reassuringly, although Axa wasn't comforted by his response, especially when he added, 'well, they're down there, actually,' nodding his head, this time, towards Bethlehem.

Axa looked intently at the city.

'Oh, you won't be able to see them Axa.'

Axa closed his eyes for a few seconds, trying to make sense of what Michael had just told him. He opened them again. Looking behind the archangel, he could see the angels lining up, banks and banks of them, resplendent in their bright finery. He had this uncomfortable feeling inside that the expectations he had been harbouring for so long, expectations that were to be fulfilled that very night, were about to be shattered before his very eyes.

Michael reiterated what he had started saying earlier.

'You're right. This is an invasion, but like no other invasion.'

'Hang on now Michael. I think I must have missed something here.'

He took a few seconds to gather his thoughts.

'You're telling me that Jesus is down there,' he said, pointing towards Bethlehem.

'Yes,' nodded Michael.

'Well, what's He doing down there?'

'This very minute?'

'Don't mess around, Michael. Just tell me.'

In a matter of fact sort of way, which added to Axa's astonishment, he replied,

'Lying in a manger, I suspect.'

'Lying in a ...!' Axa was incredulous. He'd been shaken to the core.

'Yes.'

'B... but He can't be lying in a manger,' he objected, with half a smile on his face. 'That's absurd!'

'Why?'

'He's too big!'

'No, He's not.'

'How come?'

'Because... He's a baby.'

'He's a what?!'

Chapter 39

Just as Gilchrist, with baited breath, stepped into the cave, Dylan caught up with him. He was reminded of walking into God's Throne Room, since he could hardly see anything, for the warrior angel's frame hid everything from his sight. However, Dylan could smell a distinctive agricultural aroma, the fresh air of the countryside. To his left, he could see two donkeys and a cow, its nose dribbling and its eyes somehow managing to shine in the dim light of the lantern.

Suddenly, just as he'd done back in the Eternal Throne Room, Gilchrist fell on one knee and bowed his head low.

Dylan could now see over his shoulder.

Instantly, he also fell to the floor.

On bended knee, with head bowed, a thousand thoughts raced through his mind. He had just seen a baby. Maybe a baby, but he recognised Him as none other than Jesus, his Lord! Slowly, he raised his head and took a sideways glance at Him; somehow it didn't feel right to stare.

Dylan was dazed and confused.

What was Jesus doing here, a baby? Why wasn't He up in the hills where the angelic choir was waiting to welcome Him? And what was Gilchrist doing there, as well as those crack warriors standing guard outside?

Gilchrist stood up. Dylan followed his lead. For a few minutes they stood in silence. Dylan was the first to speak.

'Why is Jesus here, Gilchrist? And why is He here, a baby? Has there been a change of plan? Axa won't like that,' he whispered.

Not taking his eyes off the baby, Gilchrist answered.

'No, there's been no change of plan, Dylan. Jesus, the Wonderful One, has come down to His earth and is invading it with His love. An infant has brought infinity to the world and this very instant, the immortal is kissing the mortal before our very eyes.'

Dylan turned to look at Jesus. The initial sense of shock was receding, and he was beginning to get accustomed to the sight of his Lord confined by earthly flesh. He smiled as he saw Him yawn, open His eyes slightly and looked straight at him. Then He closed them just as quickly and snuggled back to sleep on the straw. He was tired, as if He had just arrived after a long and arduous journey. Dylan's eyes wandered from Jesus to the man and woman who were reclining on the straw before the manger. Who were they?

He was older than the woman, but as Dylan watched him, he perceived an innocence and mischievousness in his eyes.

The woman looked totally exhausted. Her hair straggled around her head, with pieces of straw hanging limply from it. Some strands of hair still stuck to her face. Dylan put his hand to his mouth; he was shocked to see her hand gently stroking Jesus's head, as He lay asleep in the manger.

'Who is she, Gilchrist?'

'She is Mary, our Lord's mother on earth. She was made pregnant in a way that is beyond our comprehension. Jesus took up residence in her womb and for nine months she carried Him. She accepted the responsibility as well as the difficulties that lay before her.'

'Difficulties?'

Gilchrist watched Mary as he answered the little angel.

'Think about it, Dylan. A single mother. She was also betrothed to Joseph here, at the time. He thought she'd been unfaithful to him – been with another man. He could have had her stoned to death.'

Dylan's podgy little eyes were wide open with horror at the thought. He felt a little afraid, fearful of what this man could have had done to Mary. He sidled a little closer to Gilchrist.

'He could have, but Joseph is a great and good man. He loved her. He couldn't entertain the idea of having her stoned, so he just broke the engagement off, but only for a short while.'

'Why, what happened?'

'I flew back to heaven to tell Michael and...'

'Wa...wa... wait. You flew back to heaven?'

'Yes. I and the other four had been sent to protect her. So, when Joseph broke off the engagement, I reported back to Michael. Gabriel went to see him that very night and sorted him out. He told him that Mary hadn't been unfaithful and that she really was carrying the Son of God. They married soon after.'

'But Gilchrist. Why am I here?'

Gilchrist turned to look at Dylan.

'Isn't it obvious? To...'

With that, baby Jesus began to cry.

Chapter 40

Axa was traumatised.

He was sitting on a small rock, at Michael's feet, his head in his hands. Beside him lay a shepherd, sound asleep, his head resting on the stone. Axa's dreams for the night were in tatters.

'A baby!' he muttered to himself. 'Jesus has come to earth as a baby!'

'Why are you so surprised?' asked Michael. 'You're familiar with the prophecy in scripture that speaks of His coming?'

'Yes.'

'It also says a child would be born.'

'Yes, but...'

'But what, Axa?'

'I didn't think He would come as a baby!'

'He had to – there was no other way – if He is to identify Himself with the people of the world.'

'But what's He doing in a manger?'

'Well, that's where you end up when you get born in a cave-cum-stable,' Michael answered.

A look of sheer dread spread across Axa's face. He stood up.

'You mean to tell me that Jesus – our Lord – has been born in a stable.'

Then, his horror multiplied when a new thought struck him. He closed his eyes, before saying,

'Please don't tell me there are animals in there with Him.'

Axa peered anxiously through half-opened eyes. Michael didn't say anything; he didn't have to: a slight nod of the head was enough.

'Cows?' asked Axa, half fearing the answer, yet knowing what Michael's response would be.

'Probably.'

'Donkeys?'

'One or two.'

'Mice?'

'I would have thought so, but I couldn't tell you exactly how many.'

'How could He allow such a thing to happen to Him, Michael?' asked Axa.

He looked around in disbelief. Tiras was busily arranging the excited angels. How many precious hours had they spent preparing for this moment?

More than that, how many times had he practised his announcement making sure every word was enunciated perfectly, knowing that all eyes would be upon him? It had all been to no avail. Even poor Dylan, who had blighted Axa's endeavours for so long with his tuneless singing could have come along.

'There's no need for me to announce His arrival, then. No need for the choir to sing' he said flatly.

'On the contrary,' replied the archangel enthusiastically.

'There's no need Michael, if He's already here.'

'Yes, but *they* don't know,' he said, pointing to the shepherds. 'In fact, no one knows. They need to be told; the whole world needs to know, and that's why you're here, Axa.'

Axa wiped his brow as he listened.

'You will tell these shepherds that the Saviour of the world has been born in Bethlehem and that they will find Him in a stable, wrapped in swaddling clothes. Then, Axa... then, they will go; they will go down to Bethlehem to see Him. And they will see Him, face to face; the first of many who will have the honour and pleasure of doing that. They'll fall on their knees, as you and I have done countless times in heaven whenever we see Him. But that will not be the end of it, for they will go home to their families, to their friends and neighbours and tell them what they've seen, and so, the news will spread, like cold, refreshing water coursing through furrows and ditches in a field long left parched.'

On hearing this, Axa lifted his head. Maybe all his preparations had not been in vain. Maybe Jesus had not come to earth in the way he had expected, but from what Michael had just said, not one person in the whole world knew that He had arrived. How were they to know, unless the good news was announced by someone, namely, him? And it was his great honour to make that announcement. He realised that all was not lost, after all. He would be seen!

He quickly got to his feet and with a renewed purpose in his voice he turned to Michael and said.

'You said that everyone had arrived and the choir was in order.'

'Yes,' replied the archangel.

'Give me a minute to explain things.'

With that, Axa strode over to the choir and stood before them. In a loud voice, he called for quiet. This took a while since they were all so excited. Eventually silence descended. Axa stood before the hosts of heaven and for a few seconds he was awestruck as he admired the angels standing in front of him, their raiments white as snow, their faces gleaming expectantly for the great moment when Jesus was to arrive and they were to burst into song to welcome Him to earth. Axa could feel their exhilaration, which made him choose his words very carefully.

'Members of the Lord's Angelic Choir: we have arrived!'

At this, every angel promptly applauded, whilst some hollered and others whistled. Axa held his hands up, asking for quiet again.

Before we begin, may I say that we have misunderstood what is about to happen here tonight.'

An audible murmur could be heard as the angels turned to one another in puzzlement.

'Please,' Axa said, raising his voice as well as his hand. 'Let me explain.'

One of the angels shouted.

'We thought we were here to welcome Jesus as He arrived on earth.'

At this, Axa paused a while. Then he took a deep breath and said,

'That is not why we are here.'

The choir was silent, until one shouted out,

'Then why *are* we here?'

'Have we all flown here for nothing?' another shouted.

Yet another gave voice to the concern of many.

'We thought Jesus was coming here. Isn't He coming?'

At this, Michael stepped forward. All angel eyes turned to look at him.

'Fellow angels: Jesus has already arrived on earth.'

The angels were thunderstruck. Little discussions broke out, like a thousand seeds sprouting in the ground.

Michael waited patiently for the chatter to stop.

'Where is He?' someone shouted.

Michael braced himself for what he was about to tell them. Pointing towards Bethlehem, he said,

'He's down there, in Bethlehem, in a stable, lying in a manger. He has come as a baby.'

Consternation swept through the angels. They were awash with incredulity.

Chapter 41

Gilchrist and Dylan watched, as Joseph, on hearing Jesus cry stirred himself. Mary, exhausted, had drifted off into a deep sleep, and had not heard her baby's whimpers. Joseph got to his feet and gingerly lifted Jesus and held Him close. This was his first child, even though he wasn't the father and everything was new to him. What was he to do? Was Jesus crying because He wanted some milk? He didn't want to wake Mary since she was so tired. The animals in the cave looked at him with their big sparkly eyes and wafted their tails indicating impatiently for him to quieten his baby. He started to walk around the cave, rocking his body in an awkward rhythm that did nothing to comfort Jesus. He thought of singing to Him a lullaby that he remembered his mother had sung, but thought better of it: he was trying to get Jesus back to sleep, not upset Him. So, he contented himself with shushing and dancing clumsy, inelegant steps around the cave. Still, the baby cried. Like many a father before and after him, Joseph felt that he was the only person who was awake in the whole wide world.

Joseph heard a chuckle behind him. He turned and saw that Mary had woken and was smiling broadly.

'How long have you been practising that awful dance?'

He smiled, relief etched across his face.

'Longer than you think.'

She stretched her arms out.

'Here, give Him to me. I'll give Him some more milk.'

Joseph did as he was told. He was amazed once again at the deftness with which Mary held Him in her arms, as if she had been trained to do so. Gently, she guided Jesus's lips to her breast. The whimpering stopped, but only for a few seconds, for Jesus shied away, shook His head to and fro and started crying again, but louder.

'Oh. He doesn't want any,' Mary said.

'What's the matter then?' asked Joseph, a touch of panic in his tired voice. 'He shouldn't be crying – He's the Son of God.'

Not for the first time Mary wondered at her husband's humility. Ever since she had told him that she was pregnant from the Holy Spirit, not once had he claimed this wondrous baby as his own. He had always referred to Him as 'God's Son', never 'my son'. Even though he had not been part of her miraculous pregnancy, excluded from the intimate and heavenly contract

God had made with her, he had faithfully played his part as an expectant father. Not once had he presumed on his legitimate marital rights as a husband even, and had looked after her on the arduous journey from Nazareth. Here he was now, a willing attendant at her Son's birth. She sought to reassure him.

'He's a baby, Joseph. He can't speak. Something must be troubling Him, but He can't tell us. We'll just have to go with it.'

Then, the baby in her arms began to cry even louder.

Gilchrist's discomfort escalated just as Jesus's crying increased. Frustration poured over him. His natural instinct was to serve his Lord, to try and alleviate the distress He was obviously experiencing. He was helpless though. In desperation, he turned to look at Dylan with imploring eyes.

In that instant, it dawned on Dylan why he had been brought here. Yes, Gilchrist and the other warrior angels standing guard outside had their part to play and the Angel Choir was about to play its part up on the hills, but there was no way they could do what he was about to do. He felt Jesus's sad longing for heaven.

Dylan connected with baby Jesus; fed on His loss and he did the only thing he could do: he sang from deep within, a song of comfort to His Lord. He did what no other angel or human had ever done: he sang a lullaby to Jesus. Only he, of all the angels in heaven, could do this.

He sang a song more marvellous and beautiful, than he had ever sung before. Gilchrist looked around, for he swore that he was hearing a choir, but the only one singing was Dylan. A soaring, uplifting melody resonated throughout the whole cave. He harmonized with the tune and left notes dancing in the air. New refrains and harmonies were introduced until a great symphony of voices saturated the cavern. Instantly, Gilchrist was taken back to the first time he had heard Dylan sing and as then, he felt a deep connection with heaven. He was overcome with the emotions that Dylan's song had released in him. He fell to his knees and tears of joy and contentment flowed freely down his cheeks. Outside, Cadman, Joram, Ebin and Caleb turned from their vigil awestruck by what they were hearing.

Although she couldn't hear it, the sound surrounded Mary and she felt her whole body enveloped in a warm and delightful caress. She was a little startled. It reminded her of the times Joseph would suddenly give her one of his hugs and she would feel safe, secure and hidden, deep in his clothes. She would ask him why had he done that? 'No reason... just,' he'd reply sheepishly, 'I wanted to.' She looked around. Had Joseph come from behind and put his huge arms around her? No, there he was, still standing in front of her. Then, she looked down and saw that her baby had fallen into a peaceful sleep.

Joseph relaxed again and knelt before Him. Mary ran a finger along His forehead and then down to His nose while Joseph gently stroked His cheek.

'Know what, Mary?' he asked in wonder, as he let his fingers ripple across Jesus's head. She looked up into her husband's eyes.

'Remember, the story of Hagar, Abram's servant girl, who was amazed that she was still alive after seeing God? Then there was Moses, who hid his face because he was afraid to look at God when the bush was on fire. And Manoa, Samson's father who was convinced he was going to die when he'd seen God.'

Looking at Jesus's face again, Joseph continued.

'Here we are, stroking God's face, as if it was the most natural thing in the world to do.'

'And we have been entrusted with His care! You and I, Joseph.'

'I know. If I think too much about it, I'll be honest with you, Mary, it scares me.'

Mary smiled and nodded her head.

Dylan, seeing that Jesus was asleep, stopped singing, but the notes and harmonies he had left hanging in the air still reverberated around the cave for a few minutes until they slowly died down. The little angel had expended so much of his energy upon his Lord, he was exhausted. Gilchrist got up from his knees, put his arm round his shoulders and led him out of the cave. Joram, Ebin, Cadman and Caleb had gathered in a huddle in the middle of the clearing outside, like sheep waiting to be fed by their master. They looked at Dylan in amazement. They had heard the heavenly melodies emanating from the cave. They knew that it had been Dylan. All four were in awe of him.

Gilchrist led Dylan over to them. All were silent for a while before Joram spoke on behalf of them all.

'Dylan... when we were told that you, the angel who was out of tune, were coming to join us here tonight, we couldn't understand why. What could you have to offer? We were the warrior angels who had been sent to guard our Lord. We didn't need any help from you. We were so, so wrong.'

He put his hand on Dylan's shoulder.

'We heard you shouting at Gilchrist earlier on that you wanted to be up in the hills with the Angel Choir singing and worshipping Jesus. Remember this: you had far more important work to do, to comfort Jesus – the

Dayspring from on high – and only you could do this, for you live your life close to God.'

Dylan gazed at Joram for a few seconds, transfixed.

'I can't be that close to God if I shouted at Gilchrist.'

Joram shrugged his shoulders.

'We sometimes feel like shouting at him, but he is our captain.'

The other four angels chuckled quietly. Gilchrist stood in front of Dylan and uttered a few short words, telling in their impact.

'Dylan, you are one of us.'

The little angel nearly collapsed. For so many centuries, he had been an agency of one, a division of the angelic order that was made up solely of Dylan: the head, deputy, lieutenant and rank and file all in one; the only lone practitioner in heaven. And here were these legendary warrior angels paying tribute to him. Gilchrist said he was one of them! For the first time ever, he felt that he belonged.

In that instant, Dylan understood that every mission and errand that he had undertaken to each one of his 'clients', had had a purpose. They had all been a preparation for tonight, and their fulfilment was his lullaby of love to baby Jesus. Most of all he realised he had been given a mission by God. And what a mission! It meant that God knew what he did and had wanted him in Bethlehem to sing a song of comfort and encouragement to His Son.

He lifted his head and looked at Gilchrist.

'I'm sorry.'

'For what'' asked Gilchrist.

'For shouting at him? You needn't worry about that, we've already told you,' said Ebin.

Dylan smiled.

'No, no. Not for shouting, but for telling you that I had not come to Bethlehem to see "some baby". Some baby, eh?'

Bathed in the silvery moonlight, the six angels stood together in a dedicated huddle. Peace descended on them like a thick, silken, soft blanket. However, within a matter of seconds, the tranquil atmosphere was maliciously rent by a despicable rasping voice.

'Gilchrist! How nice to see you after all these years.'

Chapter 42

If such a thing were possible, the angels were mortified at what Michael had just said. Jesus! Their Lord! A baby! Again, Michael waited calmly for the jabbering to stop.

'If you'll let me, I'll explain everything. He arrived safely a few hours ago. In fact, He has been on earth these last nine months. Our Jesus abased Himself of his rightful dignity, became an embryo like every man and woman that has ever lived...'

Axa stepped forward.

'Save for Adam and Eve, Michael. Sorry to correct you, archangel.'

Michael stole a glance at Gabriel. The messenger thought he detected a slight look of irritation in the his eyes. Humbly, he answered,

'Quite right, Axa. I stand corrected.' Turning back to the vast choir, he continued. 'Nine months ago our Lord left heaven, to become nothing more than a small embryo.'

Audible gasps were heard amongst certain members of the choir. He continued.

'Since then, a young woman by the name of Mary has been carrying Him in her womb. She has cared for Him as He grew inside her. A few hours ago she gave birth to our Lord.'

Some of the angels, who had been blessed, or not, as the case may be, to have witnessed a woman giving birth, were open mouthed. This was unheard of.

'She has a husband, Joseph; a good man, Gabriel will vouch for that,' he said, turning his head towards the messenger angel. 'He has spoken to him: he is kind and caring. They will look after Him as He grows. Now, I know most, if not all of you thought that our Lord was coming to smite His enemies once and for all, and then establish the kingdom of heaven here on earth.'

They all nodded and murmured their agreement.

'Let me be clear: it is still His intention to invade earth...'

There was a loud sigh of relief from the congregated crowds.

'...but not in the way you or I expected.'

Michael did not want to dwell on that. They were on earth now, constricted by the demands of time and it would not stop, or slow down even, for any man or angel. There were still things to do that night: Axa had to make his announcement, the choir had to sing the arrival of Jesus and he,

Michael had to confront Gilchrist with his final orders and that wasn't going to be easy. Finally, he said,

'My dear angels your time has come to shine.'

Chapter 43

Gilchrist knew whose voice it was. Thus, he wasn't surprised when he turned and saw Antonin standing before him. What did surprise him though was how he looked. It all but took his breath away. Before the rebellion, no angel displayed a greater beauty, other than Lucifer. And here he was, a grotesque abomination, a hideous, crooked distortion of what he once was. Vipers writhed on his head and his eyes were a fiery red. And all the while his whole being emitted a foul, acrid odour.

Gilchrist quickly stirred himself. He counted a dozen or more demons standing behind Antonin. He looked back at his comrades.

'Looks like we're going to have some fun of our own down here. With me?'

'All the way,' replied Joram.

'I'll stand in front of you, if you want,' stated Caleb.

Gilchrist smiled, before decreeing,

"And no messing around. We do it quickly and as silently as possible: we don't want to wake Him, on this most holy of nights, the night the Saviour of the world was born.'

The warriors nodded their heads.

Then, he turned to face Antonin and his small horde a second time.

Joram looked at Dylan.

'Get in the cave, little one. You'll be safe there.'

Dylan was petrified. The demons looked menacing. Moreover, he had counted them and they easily outnumbered Gilchrist's warriors.

'Do you want me to help?' he asked in a faint voice, wishing with all his worth that Joram would not take him up on his offer. He smiled at Dylan's fortitude.

Gilchrist faced Antonin, a mere ten paces from him.

'No, we'll be fine.'

'But Joram, there are fifteen of them.'

The warrior put his hand on Dylan's shoulder.

'Yes, but we have something they haven't.'

'What?' asked Dylan, innocently expecting Joram to make a short speech about having right on their side, or that they were fighting for the Lord of Lords. He winked at him, as he answered,

'We have Melon Head on our side.'

'Who?'

'Caleb! I mean, look at him. He's frothing at the mouth with wrath. Would you want to fight that?'

From his demeanour, Caleb was plainly irritated that these monsters should have presumed to have gate-crashed a select gathering, such as this one. Dylan watched him as he touched the hilt of his sword, reassuring himself that it was still there. Then he adjusted his tunic. He was intrigued when he saw him loosen the hair at the back of his head and tighten the bun. It was all done, as if he was making himself look presentable for battle, although his general appearance was one of uncaring scruffiness.

'Go now, and stay in the cave,' Joram said, in a calm and reassuring voice.

Dylan did as he was told and scuttled along. He hid behind the wall at the entrance to the cave, although he poked his head round to watch as events unfolded.

Joram turned to join the other three warriors as they fanned themselves out either side of Gilchrist, their captain. Caleb still fidgeted with his hair, whilst Ebin stood beside him, resolute. Meanwhile, Cadman stood the other side of Gilchrist, and watched Joram as he came and stood at his shoulder. Cadman calmly moved the folds of his tunic behind his sheathed sword. Then he slowly turned his head and stared at Antonin's four lieutenants, his ice cold blue eyes exuding a violent threat that unsettled every one of them.

Angels and demons faced each other for what seemed an eternity. The tension laden air crackled and was so real that Dylan felt he could reach out and touch it although he didn't dare, for fear of burning his fingers.

Antonin was the one who finally broke the silence.

'So here you are, Gilchrist, still fighting forlorn little battles and skirmishes for your Lord.'

'I wouldn't call them "forlorn", not when you seem to have brought Ashtenaz, Riphthal, Tograman and Hazarm and their underlings.'

The ten demons at the back bristled with anger.

'So, tell me, why did you do it, Antonin?

Antonin feigned ignorance.

'What *are* you talking about?'

'You know.'

'Oh, the rebellion, you mean. I fancied a change,' he shrugged smugly. 'That's all.'

'You shone, Antonin. Of all of us, you were the only one we could begin to compare with Lucifer for beauty.'

'You sound like you envied me,' Antonin said provocatively.

Nothing could be further from the truth. Rather, it was a lament for what had been and what had been lost. He knew, as did Antonin, that some things were irreparable, irreversible. He and every other demon that had chosen their diabolical path had gone beyond. They knew it and gloried in it, even.

'I did look good, didn't I?' he smiled, contentedly. 'I dazzled, even. But it wasn't enough, was it?'

Gilchrist and the other four warrior angels looked at him in bewilderment, as did Dylan who was listening intently from just inside the cave. Gilchrist raised his voice blurting out the question on all their lips.

'Wasn't enough?'

'I wanted more!'

'There was no "more"!'

'Yes, there was.'

'What? Exulting in your status as one of Satan's high command, your authority based on violence, as is your relationship with your master.'

'And your relationship with your Master is based on your love and devotion,' Antonin sneered back.

They held each other's gaze.

'Are we going to stand here and talk all night?' asked Antonin.

'I thought you were waiting for more demons to arrive.'

'No.'

'Is that all you've brought?'

Gilchrist's confident manner made Antonin feel nervous. He quickly looked behind the five angels arrayed in front of him. Other than that little squirt of an angel he'd seen scurrying into the cave there were no others. He regained his confidence: there were much more of them.

'So, tell me, Gilchrist, I'm intrigued: how did you get her in here, without our guards seeing her?'

'Who? Mary?'

'Is that her name?'

'It was obvious you knew Jesus was to be born in Bethlehem and that He was to be born of a virgin.'

'A simple reading of the scriptures,' said Antonin. 'I'll give you that much.'

'In your mind, there was no way a man, much less a husband, would acknowledge her and stand by her as his wife, knowing that he was not the father. All along you were looking for a woman who was on her own. That was your mistake. She has a husband.'

Antonin bridled at the thought that he had blundered. The one thing he had discarded as too absurd, too bizarre even to contemplate had been his undoing.

'How did you get him to do it?' he snapped. 'What simpleton did you get to play this fool?'

At this, Gilchrist stood more erect somehow, standing up for Joseph.

'His name is Joseph. He's not a simpleton and definitely not a fool.'

'Did her father pay him?'

'No need.'

'Oh, yes?

'There's one thing you and your minions will never understand, Antonin.'

'What on earth could that be?' sighed Antonin, affecting boredom.

'Love, Antonin, love. It makes a man and woman do the unexpected, the unpredictable. You don't know what love is; that's how we played you and you couldn't have played your part any better.'

Antonin seethed with anger. He hated being made fool of, but he despised being made to look a fool in front of the other demons. Antonin scoffed, exhaling a deep acrid breath.

'Joseph knew what marrying Mary meant. He knew – still knows – that people will think he made Mary pregnant before they were married, or they'll pity him for being naïve enough to marry her knowing that he wasn't the baby's father. Either way, he can't win. Still he loved her – still does.'

'He's a fool, then,' Antonin accused.

'Maybe, but a fool for God.'

'And a loser. You, yourself said he couldn't win.'

'Losers don't stick around.'

Cadman, Joram, Ebin and Caleb murmured their approval.

Conversation came to a halt for a while, but the warrior and renegade angels still eyed each other tensely. Dylan, watching from the safety of the cave, was all too aware of the antagonism bouncing back and forth.

'And what about you lot?

Gilchrist looked at him questioningly.

'A ragtag bag of inconsequential warrior angels. I mean, who would want to have Melon Head in their gang?' he sneered.

Ashtenaz laughed derisively as he pointed at Caleb. Ebin noticed his friend was burning with resentment.

'Look at him,' said Ashtenaz in a patronising voice. 'He's spoiling for a fight.'

'Don't you get the feeling that you've been used all these years?' continued Antonin.

Again, Gilchrist's eyes questioned him.

'All those years you spent looking after David before he was made king, and then, there was hardly a moment's peace throughout his troubled reign. Then, when he died and Solomon, his son took over, you never got to enjoy the glories and splendour of his reign because you were sent away to look after some nobodies on the other side of the world.'

Gilchrist stared at him.

'And correct me if I'm wrong, but not one of you was in the hills surrounding Elisha, the prophet's house, when thousands of warrior angels were there, blazing in flaming glory on chariots of fire. Not invited. No, what do you get to do? Look after some obnoxious, little merchant like Abdallah, on his way to Memphis, a half-deserted village in the middle of the desert: the glamour of it all. Don't you think someone's been trying to tell you something?'

'I would rather stand at the door of my God's house than live in the house of the wicked.'

'Oh, please don't recite the scriptures to me,' answered Antonin, plainly irritated. He quickly regained his composure though.

'Tell me, do you still have those quaint little ceremonies in heaven where warrior angels who have accomplished great deeds get a silent ovation from the whole Angel Army. I can't imagine they've ever done anything like that in honour of you five.'

This much was true. Many warrior angels had been acknowledged over the centuries by their peers on completion of an especially onerous mission. Fellow warriors would draw their swords, hold them high above their heads, and stand in silence before the honoured ones. Gilchrist's unit had never been accorded such a privilege. Indeed, very rarely would they take part in such occasions since they were away so often. It was something that never really bothered them, although they had occasionally discussed the matter amongst themselves when it was brought up, more often than not, by Caleb.

The four warrior angels stole a glance at Gilchrist. He had visibly relaxed his shoulders, his arms hung easily by his side.

'Tell me, where's it all got you? You Gilchrist, are a mere foot soldier in the army of the Lord,' Antonin said scornfully. 'Leader of a bunch of failed irrelevancies, who never get the limelight, but are always called upon by your Commander when some fighting needs to be done, whereas I, I am in Satan's high command, commander of thousands, feared by all of them.'

He waited a short while, then, he said,

'What do you say Gilchrist? Come over to our side; the others will follow you.'

'Really!?' Gilchrist replied, trying to load that one word with as much incredulity as he could muster.

Gilchrist was astonished. Was he really trying to entice him to join Satan's armies and turn his back on the Lord of the Angel Armies? Slowly, he turned his upper body to look at Cadman and Joram who were standing to his left, ensuring his sword, hanging on his left hip was out of Antonin's sight. He bent his left arm back, his hand on the hilt. He smiled benignly at both of them. All four sharpened their senses. They were on heightened alert although they were completely relaxed. No word of command would be given.

Chapter 44

'Why don't you join us, G? You can stand next to me,' persisted Antonin.

Unseen by Antonin, Gilchrist swiftly whipped his sword out of its sheath with his left hand and flicked it at his throat. It flew flat and smooth, aimed unerringly at the errant angel's gullet. Even though this happened in less than a split-second, Antonin was aware of what was happening. He saw the tip of the sword literally splitting the air. That initial cut was made bigger by the razor-sharp edges of the sword as it proceeded to tear the air, creating an airless, timeless void between him and Gilchrist. Antonin froze. He was struck breathless. He could only close his eyes, expecting the worst. Just as the tip of the sword was beginning to puncture his outer pores it stopped. Antonin opened one eye... slowly. Gilchrist was holding the sword by its hilt once again, staring dispassionately at him. How had he managed to do that? How had he moved so fast? Then, he remembered being aware of two sudden flashes of translucent brightness either side of him before he closed his eyes expecting the worst as Gilchrist's sword homed in on his throat. He sneaked a look at Ashtenaz, Riphthal, Tograman and Hazarm through the corner of his eyes. All four warrior angels had replicated Gilchrist's action, and just like him, the four demons were standing helpless, with Cadman, Joram, Ebin and Caleb holding their swords to their throats. They were as stunned as he was by the speed of their movement. Antonin swallowed hard; the other four gulped.

Dylan stared, open-mouthed. How had they done that? It seemed to him they had moved faster than time. Now, as they stood still in front of the demons, it was as if they were waiting for the rest of the world to catch up with them.

'Just breathe easy and nod if you can hear me,' Gilchrist told Antonin, trying to sound reassuring.

Antonin did as he was told, but very gingerly. He could feel the diamond like sharpness of Gilchrist's sword tip on his throat. He feared that any movement, however small, on his part would have serious, maybe fatal consequences.

'You remember Axa, don't you?' Gilchrist asked in a light voice.

Antonin nodded his head again, just as carefully as before.

'He and the Angel Choir will soon start to sing God's praises up in the hills behind you. Let's listen to them, shall we? I'm sure you'll all enjoy.'

Chapter 45

When Archangel Michael had exhorted the angels to shine, they had hollered and whooped and whistled loudly. Michael and Gabriel stepped aside and Axa strode forward. With all the authority vested in him as choirmaster of the Angel Choir, he lifted his hands to command them all be quiet. They immediately fell silent. Michael was impressed. They stood noiselessly, even though the buzz of excitement amongst them was fit to burst.

With an extravagant flourish, Axa turned and looked at the four shepherds who were lying on the ground, one of whom was already sound asleep of course, whilst the other three were about to settle for the night. Then, he showed himself, gleaming from top to toe in the night sky.

The poor shepherds were thunderstruck, likewise the sheep. Some were grazing, despite the late hour, but most were sleeping on the ground. Once they caught sight of Axa, they scattered to all corners of the hillside, as far away as they could possibly get. As for the shepherds, they sat bolt upright, jolted out of their half slumbers. They tried to scream but failed pathetically: fear had gripped them by the throat. They raised their hands to shield their eyes as their temporary blindness added to the panic swelling inside. Axa realised that his light was shining too brightly, so he toned himself down. Sensing the light had diminished enough for them to be able to see Axa they started scrambling backwards trying to get away. Self-preservation was the order of the night. Seeing their dread, Axa tried to reassure them.

'Do not be afraid.'

Michael turned to Gabriel.

'Well, I'm glad he said that: nice touch.'

Gabriel gave a wry smile.

However, telling someone not to be afraid, when that person is plainly scared witless is much like telling a merchant who's just found out that his business is bankrupt, his house is in flames and his wife has run off with his best customer, to be joyful. Nevertheless, Axa continued.

He cleared his throat. Although he was only addressing the four shepherds it seemed to Michael and Gabriel that he was telling the whole world. In a way, he was.

'I'm here to announce a great and joyous event that is meant for everybody worldwide: a Saviour has just been born in David's town, who is Messiah and Master.'

The shepherds were confused. Seeing this, Axa sought to explain to them.

'This is what you're to look for: a baby wrapped in cloths lying in a manger.'

Michael nodded his head and pursed his lips. He was pleased.

Then, Axa turned around, raised his arms and bid the choir to appear.

The shepherds had stood on their feet, getting used to their heavenly visitor. When a whole host of angels appeared before them, it sent they fell backwards on the ground again. There were hundreds of thousands, banks and banks of them. Wherever they looked there were angels shimmering and filling the sky. Then they started singing God's praises:

'Glory to God in the heavenly heights,

Peace to all men and women on earth who please him.'

Over and over they sang these words in worship of their God, the Supreme Being. Even Michael and Gabriel were taken aback. Never had they heard such a heavenly sound. Although there were thousands of celestial tongues and countless delicious harmonies – Michael swore later in the retelling that he could literally taste them on his lips and tongue – they sang with one voice. Axa had indeed done his God and Jesus proud. As for the choir, they became even more glorious. Their lights shone brighter than they had ever done. This was a night like no other and they were making sure that the shepherds knew it.

On hearing the voices, the shepherds' fears were eased. They watched and listened open-mouthed. Angels danced and jumped, somersaulted, flew flamboyant formations and performed impossible acrobatics. Groups of ten, fifty and a hundred angels made angelic fireworks of themselves, exploding into avalanches of vibrant colours, that no human eye had seen before; sometimes a thousand or more got together and exploded into a huge flower of luminous glowing petals, falling through the sky in perfect unison. From the darkness, brightly coloured explosions flashed from nothing, like cluster bombs of bright fireflies, lighting the night like mid-day on the startled shepherds' faces. So many entrancing things were going on all at the same time, it was akin to sitting at a banqueting table, full of delicious food, not knowing where to start. They began to relax and enjoy the splendid spectacle that was unfolding in front of them and exclaimed their appreciation and admiration, with,

'Wwwww!' and 'Aaaaaaaa!'

The celebration continued with no end in sight. At the heart of it was the heavenly singing of the Angel Choir, and its subject was God's gift to the world. Axa conducted, while the Twelve led the way. Every note, every harmony and euphony pitch-perfect, as if lovingly sculpted by a renowned sculptor and now sent forth, not only in the hills above Bethlehem but to the whole world.

Antonin and the other demons hated every second of it. Seething anger built up inside them as they heard the angels singing God's praises. Inwardly, Ashtenaz, Riphthal, Tograman and Hazarm fulminated and swore vile threats at Antonin. It was his fault they were having to stomach this heavenly sound. It was like having their tongues stuck to blocks of ice, unable to tear free.

For their part, the five warrior angels revelled in the glory being heaped on their Lord by the Angel Choir. Dylan watched in awe from his hiding place. He knew the hymn of praise by heart and they were coming to the climax.

Gilchrist caught Antonin's gaze, the tip of his sword still pressed against his throat.

'Your window of opportunity has shut. You could have hurt Him when He was in Mary's womb, but you failed.'

Antonin was incandescent with rage. He had come so close to mortally wounding God's Son thereby destroying once and for all whatever plan God had in mind to save the people of the world. But he still had a card up his sleeve and could have some fun watching Gilchrist and his motley crew suffer. Besides the five back in the lean-to, there were no other warrior angels around and they were too far away to hear any cries for help. He maintained a cool demeanour as he addressed his one-time friend again.

'You know, Gilchrist, in all your smugness, from your ruses and artifices, you got one thing wrong.'

'Oh, yeah?'

'Yes.'

'And what was that?'

'You didn't think these were the only ones I brought with me, did you?' he replied, motioning towards the demons standing behind him.

At that, he lifted his head skywards and gave out a loud howl in the air. Within seconds, a horde of armed demons straddled the nearby city walls and strode towards them, cackling and squawking exultantly. Gilchrist and the others could only watch in stunned silence. The enemy's force had suddenly swelled to at least fifty or more. Gilchrist was evidently shaken. From the look on his face, and the other angels' faces it was obvious they had been caught unawares. Dylan, hiding at the entrance to the cave, noticed the look of shock and shrank back into the shadows. Antonin felt the pressure from the tip of the sword on his throat slacken as Gilchrist dropped it to his side. Antonin took a step back, a self-satisfied smile on his face. The warrior looked to his right at Ebin and Caleb. Like their leader, they had let the demons nearest them go and were now looking at him with some concern in their eyes. Gilchrist turned his head to look at Joram. He too had dropped his sword, shocked at what now confronted them.

Up in the hills the celebrations continued. Just as fear had gripped the shepherds a few moments earlier, now, they experienced an exquisite calm. Like Michael, they could taste heaven. They wanted to stay there forever, to bask and feast on this extravagant heavenly manifestation. Then, the choir stopped and vanished.

All was quiet. The sky returned to a dark, velvety blue and although the stars twinkled and sparkled as best they could, it all seemed very empty to the shepherds as they looked up now. The angels had vanished, but not into thin air, for they were still there, just invisible once again to the shepherds. Had they the most powerful magnifying glass in their possession they would not have been able to see them. They looked around, but saw nothing, even though one of them had wandered and was standing right beside Michael.

The angels, for their part, although they were on mute, were not silent. They knew they had played their part majestically. The Saviour's arrival on earth had been well and truly announced. There was a lot of back slapping, shaking of hands and hugging. Those who had performed the acrobatics congratulated each other and used their hands to re-enact each burst and dive of their heavenly bodies.

Axa stood in front of them, relief and pride etched on his face. His choir had sung wondrously. He couldn't have asked for more.

Chapter 46

Back in Bethlehem, the demons pressed in on the angels, taunting them. Inside the cave, Dylan cowered and panicked. There were so many of them. Gilchrist looked around in disbelief, as did the others, save for Cadman. Gilchrist's faithful lieutenant still held the tip of his sword to Tograman's gullet.

Gilchrist caught his friend's eye and flickered his eyes skywards: a barely perceptible movement. If Cadman had seen it he made no effort to acknowledge it.

'Game over, Gilchrist,' sneered Antonin. 'You're heavily outnumbered.'

The other leading demons, other than Tograman, looked on disdainfully.

Gilchrist didn't respond.

'One more chance, G. Come over to our side.'

Again, there was no reaction. Instead, the warrior captain stared serenely into the far distance, as if reminded of, and contemplating similar past encounters. A few more seconds elapsed. Antonin had had enough.

'Take 'em,' he ordered, in an indifferent voice. As he did, he took off, and flew backwards to stand at the back of his hordes. Ashtenaz, Riphthal, Tograman and Hazarm did likewise allowing the newly arrived demons to lead the charge. However, before they had time to react to Antonin's command, Gilchrist whispered,

'Now.'

He and the other four warrior angels sprang into action.

Cadman shot up into the air hovering some twenty feet above. He reached both hands back to the quivers slung across his shoulders and launched a burst of arrows at the demons below. Projected with pace, power and accuracy the arrow heads became hot, glistening a white heat from the friction as they sped through the air. The other four closed ranks, forming a tight semi-circle on the ground some ten paces in front of the cave. Even so, with vastly superior numbers, the enemy pressed in on them.

As Gilchrist's speed and agility had enabled him to get the better of the demons at the foot of the Scorpion's Pass, so his and his comrades' swift movements meant they had the upper hand now. The attacking demons' thrusts and lunges with swords in hand were laboured and ponderous. Whilst plunges were easily parried and swinging fists effortlessly eluded, the four went on the offensive. Close quarter fighting was the order of the day, so the warriors eschewed their swords, preferring to use their daggers. Cuts and slashes were delivered whilst precise hits were inflicted on their assailants' eyes, throats, noses and chests. Before the demons could let rip their unearthly screams at the pain they suffered, angel fists were hammered into their heads rendering them unconscious on the ground. Caleb was in his element. Next to worshipping God he fervently believed that this was what he had been created for. And all the while, Cadman continued his barrage of arrows at those demons waiting behind to join the fray.

Unhindered by a bow, he unleashed a constant shower of missiles. Shafts of white heat tore the air as the arrows sped towards the demons who were helpless in the face of the never ending onslaught. On point of contact they were hit with a force that propelled them onto their backs, the arrows pinning them to the ground through their shoulders. Unable to get up, they writhed on their backs letting out terrified howls of stinging, burning pain. Sometimes, Cadman would grab hold of three arrows between the four fingers of one hand, hurling them simultaneously, smiting three demons in one volley. Some demons would fly up at him, with the intention of negating his distinct aerial advantage. They hardly got airborne before he would let fly a burst of arrows that sent them hurtling back to earth. And throughout, he would dart and pivot as nimble as a dragon-fly, constantly changing his position in the air, so that when one or two demons managed to throw a knife or sword at him he had long since vacated the space and the projectile would collide harmlessly into the rock behind.

Antonin, standing at the back, with Ashtenaz, Riphthal, Tograman and Hazarm and the other demons, soon began to realise that things were not going as planned. Despite the demons' much greater numbers Gilchrist and his unit's skills and agility were far superior to their meagre fighting abilities. He watched with increasing concern as Cadman flew down. He strolled amongst those demons he had nailed to the ground, systematically smashing their heads with a heel or a fist. Their wailing was silenced as they were rendered unconscious. Soon, those demons who had jumped over the walls to join Antonin's initial force all lay motionless on the ground.

Cadman joined Joram, Ebin and Caleb as they formed a line, with Gilchrist behind them. The lesser demons flew at the warrior angels, their weapons drawn. Surmising that killing the leader would weaken the resolve of his subordinates, they targeted Gilchrist. Hitherto, the warriors had shunned their swords but now, they drew them from their sheaths using them to parry strikes and thrusts sending sparks into the air as the weapons clashed. This left the demons open to attack. Calmly, and methodically, Cadman, Joram, Ebin and Caleb used their free hands to twist fists and wrists, rotate elbows, dislocate shoulders and snap kneecaps. Screams of pain were abruptly cut short by quick, short jabs to the heads from angel fists.

Gilchrist stood still, his eyes seared on Antonin. It was obvious to the latter his demons were coming off second best. Then, he saw one of them flying at Gilchrist, his arm outstretched, a dagger in his hand. He began to hope that maybe this one had got through the defences.

Gilchrist was only too aware of the incoming danger and could sense that the tip of the dagger was aiming for his eye. In that instant, time seemed to stand still as first, he watched Joram evade a demon's sword thrust by side-stepping to the right and then grabbing hold of his hand. He swivelled round until his back was lodged against his opponent's front and struck the point of his elbow sharply in his left eye. Joram wasn't done with him yet. Stepping quickly behind the demon he took hold of his snake-infested hair. The vipers writhed and screamed in agony as Joram twisted them mercilessly one way and then the other. The demon itself was tossed hither and thither losing all sense of awareness just as Joram stretched forward and brutally cracked the butt end of the hilt of his sword against the back of his neck. Instantly, he fell to the ground. Then, through the corner of his eye Gilchrist watched another demon attack Ebin. As he came within touching distance, he flashed his sword deftly and severed one of his hands. He was beginning to register the pain from having lost his hand, when Ebin held him by the throat with his free hand and squeezed. He couldn't breathe. With the one hand he had left, the he tried to pull Ebin's arm away, but to no avail. The combination of the intense pain from his sliced hand and breathlessness became too much for him. He collapsed in the dirt.

Just as the demon still aiming for Gilchrist's eye thought he had managed to break through, the warrior made his move. He gripped the hand wielding the dagger. Instantly, the demon stopped his forward motion and his feet landed on the ground. The warrior squeezed the hand mercilessly and the demon dropped the dagger. Gilchrist caught it by its hilt as it fell. He brought it back up and buried its short, sharp blade deep into his adversary's shoulder and twisted it ninety degrees. Conscious of his own command regarding the necessity for silence, Gilchrist then smacked his fist against the demon's temple that sent it crashing to the floor.

Within a matter of a few short seconds since the fighting began, of the demons' force, only Antonin, Ashtenaz, Riphthal, Tograman and Hazarm were still standing. Without waiting for their captain's say-so Cadman, Joram,

Ebin and Caleb tore into them. Cadman sharply forearm-smashed Tograman in the face. Joram drove the hilt of his sword straight up under the Riphthal's chin, thrusting him backwards on to the ground behind. Tograman fell nearby and both demons lay insensate on the sandy soil, foul smelling-pus oozing from their heads.

Ebin quickly slashed his sword several times across Ashtenaz' torso. As he fell, howling with pain, Ebin held him up with one hand. Then, leaning forward, as if he was giving him some friendly advice, he whispered in his ear threateningly.

'I didn't like you making fun of my friend earlier on.'

Then he threw the demon away to his right.

Simultaneously, Caleb had made his move. He smiled coldly at Hazarm, tilting his head slightly to the side. He was a few inches shorter than his adversary, so, in order to bring him down to his size, he quickly swung his right foot and kicked Hazarm on the outer side of his left knee, dislocating it. As Hazarm's leg gave way, he crumpled forward. Caleb's fist, which was in an upward motion met the demon's chin on the way down. Hazarm abruptly pitched backwards landing in an inanimate heap on the ground, a stringless marionette.

Unfortunately for Caleb, as he looked down at Hazarm, Ashtenaz smashed into his hip from having been thrown by Ebin. Caleb was sent sprawling. He and Ashtenaz flew through the air, entangled with each other landing some twenty paces away, rolling and billowing dust. When they eventually stopped they lay side by side, facing each other, their noses no more than a few inches apart. Caleb was the first to react. He snapped his head back and butted Ashtenaz on the nose. Then, he shot to his feet. He looked at Ashtenaz, lying unconscious on the floor.

'Ugly brute,' he said, before walking back to the others. However, he became aware of a sharp pain in the leg Ashtenaz had smashed into. It hindered his stride. By the time he came near to his comrades he was limping badly.

'Why are you limping?' asked Joram.

'Coz someone chucked Ashtenaz at me and hit me in my leg,' he answered.

'You sure?' asked Ebin innocently.

Caleb glared at him.

Gilchrist walked up to Antonin and stood a mere arm's length away.

'Go away, Antonin. There's nothing here for you, now.'

'Oh, I don't know. What about you and me?' he smiled provocatively.

'This isn't about us.'

'But we have unfinished business.'

'I don't think so.'

'Don't you want to know?'

'Know what?'

'Which one of us is the better fighter. No one else, just us two,' invited Antonin.

The warrior angel was astounded. Was he still spoiling for a fight? He looked at him steadily, seeing again his sneering eyes and the snakes writhing on his head.

'Forget it, Antonin. I'm already on the winning side.'

He turned to look at the other warrior angels. Seeing his opportunity, Antonin began to whip his sword out of its sheath. Gilchrist, aware of this snapped his head round. Eyeing his target, he swivelled on the ball of his right foot. Raising his other leg he kicked Antonin sharply on the side of his throat with his instep. Antonin staggered as he spluttered and gasped for air. The vipers on his head squirmed and thrashed about desperately trying to breathe.

Slowly, he regained his composure and stood erect once again.

'You know we'll be back,' he whispered, his voice rasping from the blow. 'There are others in our pockets, ready to do our bidding, from Herod right down to the lowest Pharisee.'

Without warning, and using hardly any back lift, Gilchrist punched his nose. The force of the blow sent shock waves down to his feet. He collapsed in a heap and lay semi-conscious for a while. Eventually, he woke and staggered to his feet, glaring at Gilchrist. It was time to leave. Nothing could be gained from trying to provoke Gilchrist any more. He and some of the demons who had woken went around to shake the others from their stupor. They failed to stir a number of them.

'Don't forget this,' Ebin reminded them, kicking the hand he had cut off earlier in the skirmish.

Antonin stepped forward and stabbed the point of his sword in the severed hand. It was a slow and painful operation rounding up everyone since serious damage had been inflicted on all of them. Eventually, tottering, and with faltering steps, without so much as a backward glance they took off, seeming to limp in the night air, leaving those they could not wake behind.

Gilchrist looked at those demons Antonin couldn't wake.

'Ebin, chuck 'em,' he ordered.

Ebin proceeded to do as he was told, careful to throw them in the opposite direction towards the hills where the angels had just been singing.

For the first time since the encounter began, Dylan relaxed and breathed easily.

The choir's celebrations continued, unabated. Michael and Gabriel walked up to Axa.

'Congratulations,' Michael said.

The angels were making so much noise it was a convenient excuse for Axa to feign that he couldn't make out what he had said. He wanted to hear Michael congratulate him again.

'Sorry?' he said, holding a cupped hand behind his ear.

Michael shouted a 'Congratulations' into it.

'Thank you,' he mouthed graciously.

There was no stopping the celebrations.

'It was very good indeed,' added Gabriel in a loud voice.

Axa nodded his head appreciatively. Pride filled his whole being.

Dylan came out of his hiding place and paced over towards Gilchrist and his unit.

'I've never seen anyone move so fast! Where did you all learn how to do that? They didn't stand a chance.'

Dylan then realised that none of his angel comrades were sharing in his elation. They remained where they were when Antonin and his demons had left. Dylan quietened. Why were they silent? They formed a circle, closing ranks. For the first time since he had arrived, Dylan had the uncomfortable feeling he was intruding on intimacies, borne from long shared past battles in the name of their Lord. Indeed, he somehow felt he was violating the sanctity of a devoted band of warriors. Cadman looked at Gilchrist.

'You okay?'

'Okay?'

Cadman chose his words carefully.

'You know, coming face to face with Antonin again.'

Gilchrist took his time to answer.

'Yes, but I hadn't seen him since the rebel...'

His voice trailed off. He gathered himself.

'But why should it be any different for the rest of you? We all lost friends who were special to us.'

'I know, but you and he were very close,' Cadman persisted.

'Every angel in heaven knew you were like brothers,' added Ebin, 'not that that's possible for angels, but you know what I mean.'

Gilchrist nodded his head slightly and smiled wanly.

'We were.'

'Inseparable, from what everyone remembers,' Joram chipped in.

They were silent for a few seconds. They all knew what the next question was, but not one of the four wanted to ask it out of respect for their leader. Inevitably, Caleb was the one who couldn't wait.

'Did you really not have any idea what he had in mind?'

'Not a clue,' Gilchrist replied, shaking his head. 'One moment he was at my side, a radiant expression of God's beautiful creative power, and the next, he was at Satan's shoulder, hideous and repulsive, smiling grotesquely at me, enjoying every minute of his deception. I just could not believe what he'd been doing behind my back.'

'To this day, I can't understand why they would exchange the way they were for what they are now,' opined Caleb.

'Pride, they thought themselves better than their Creator.'

Caleb looked up at the hills at the Angel Choir.

'You know, I've been thinking...'

'Waw! Again!' interrupted Ebin. 'Twice in less than a year!'

'You're on a roll!' added Joram.

Caleb gave them a contemptuous look through the corner of his eyes and carried on.

'In years to come no one on earth will know about what we've done here, yet everybody will fuss about the Angel Choir: they'll get all the attention. They'll probably get a silent ovation in the rehearsal room, even.'

The others gave him short shrift.

'Go and join them, then,' Joram encouraged.

'I might just do that. They'll be better company.'

'Yeah,' responded Joram. 'Axa will be really pleased to have you there. We've all heard you sing, mind.'

'You can take over from Dylan as the angel who's out of tune, now that his cover's blown,' added Ebin.

'I heard that,' said the little angel.

'Come here,' said Ebin, stretching his arm out to him.

Dylan sidled up and stood before them.

'Are you okay, now?' asked Joram. 'He was scared earlier on. He even offered to help us fight Antonin and his demons.'

'I thought you were going to have some trouble.'

'No fears,' insisted Gilchrist. 'And do you know why?'

He had a ready answer.

'Because you had Melon He... I mean Caleb on your side?'

Gilchrist, Cadman and Ebin stared at him quizzically.

'No,' replied Gilchrist. 'Because right was on our side.'

Dylan gave Joram a questioning look. He smiled innocently at him whilst Caleb warmed even more to the little angel.

Chapter 47

Ashtenaz slowly flew through the night air back towards Bethlehem. The painful sword slashes he had suffered at the hands of Ebin hurt him like nothing he'd endured before. Not only that, he had a throbbing headache from Caleb's headbutt. He was in a sorry state, and none too happy now that he had been ordered back to speak to Lord Kandar.

As Antonin led his defeated force from Bethlehem, promising to himself he would someday avenge Gilchrist and his unit for what they had done to them, he suddenly remembered that Kandar was still waiting for them at that Pharisee's house. He dispatched Ashtenaz to inform him that they had left.

The streets were empty, the city's inhabitants asleep in their beds. As he approached the Pharisee's house he saw Kandar, still in his Shobal guise, waiting outside. Ashtenaz braced himself. Gingerly, he landed beside him ensuring that he stood more than an arm's length away. Kandar surveyed the swollen nose and flashing wounds.

'Well?' Kandar enquired.

'A message from Lord Antonin, my Lord. We were too late. She had already given birth.'

Kandar didn't respond. Uncomfortable with the silence, Ashtenaz added,

'There was no reason to stay any longer, so Lord Antonin gave the order to leave.'

Kandar looked away. He was deep in thought. After a few seconds he asked,

'And Gilchrist and the others?'

'We found them, but as I said, we were too late.'

Kandar raised his hand to his chin. Ashtenaz instinctively moved away a little.

Kandar smiled at him benignly. Ashtenaz hadn't shied far enough away, for in an instant Kandar swung the back of his raised hand towards him. As it flew through the air Kandar made a fist of it, smashing it into Ashtenaz' face. Maximum damage was inflicted as Kandar tilted his fist on point of contact so that the knuckle of his index finger drove into the demon's eyeball. Ashtenaz had no chance, since Kandar had moved so quickly. He fell to the ground and lay motionless. Kandar bent down and spoke to him in his harsh, grating voice.

'So, what are all these cuts and bruises, Ashtenaz? Do you think I'm stu-pid?'

Kandar turned to look away. He was fuming.

It was time to leave. His purpose here, in Bethlehem had come to an end. He walked into the darkness at the side of the house. There, he turned himself back into his monstrous demon form. He felt an exhilarating release. He had been bound by his human guise far too long. As a parting gesture, he banged the door to Philip's house a number of times. He smiled. That would have frightened the entrails out of him. A scant recompense for what might have been, he knew, but he still enjoyed doing it. He took off in the air. He would find somewhere else in Israel to work his demonic charm as a human, either as Shobal or maybe as someone else.

Chapter 48

Meanwhile, the Angel Choir was getting ready for their return journey to heaven. Meshek, the leader of the warrior angels who had escorted them to the hills, approached Michael.

'We're good to go, boss.'

'Thank you, Meshek. Take care of them: they gave of their all tonight.'

'Boss,' Meshek replied. Then, greeting the chief messenger with a short but courteous, 'Gabriel,' he strode back to his warriors.

Michael waited a few more seconds. Then, he raised his hand. The heavenly host quietened and gazed expectantly at him.

'My fellow angels,' he began. 'You have announced Jesus's arrival on earth in a fitting, appropriate and above all, most spectacular fashion. You should all be very pleased.'

They responded with loud cheers and clapping. This continued for a few seconds more. Michael raised his hand again for silence.

'May I take this opportunity, on your behalf, to thank Axa for his thorough preparation.'

There was more shouting and hollering. Again, Michael had to raise his hand.

'Now, as you can no doubt see behind me, those who have received your message are discussing what they should do next. Before long, they will leave these hills and go down to Bethlehem, to see the new-born Saviour of the world.'

At this, there were more prolonged whistles and cheering.

He raised his hand again.

'Please, my arm is getting tired.'

Everyone laughed a politely. Michael had said something funny. They didn't want to disappoint him.

'There is no more for you to do here tonight...'

'Aww,' they all uttered loudly.

'You will have to return to heaven shortly. You may speak amongst yourselves in the meantime.'

By now Tiras had joined the three angels. Michael turned to Axa.

'I meant every word Axa. That was a stupendous display of joy and exuberance and the announcement was just what was needed.'

Axa did not respond immediately, not that he did not like the praise Michael had just given him: who wouldn't? Rather, he had other things on his mind.

'Archangel Michael, you told the angels, "You must return to heaven shortly". Aren't you coming back with us?'

'No.'

'And you, Gabriel?'

'We have important things to attend to.'

'They err… wouldn't entail going down to Bethlehem and seeing the Lord Jesus, would they?'

The archangel looked at the musical director with a wry smile on his face.

'Not only can you prepare the Angel Choir to sing delightfully, you are quite perceptive too.'

'So, you *are* going to see Him.'

'Not to see Him, so much as to speak to Gilchrist.'

'Is he down there?' asked Axa, the flash of urgency in his voice fuelled by a deep envy.

'Yes, so are Joram, Ebin, Cadman and Caleb.'

Indignation began to swell inside Axa. Why should they be down there, attending to their Lord, when he could do so much more? What baby Jesus needed was tenderness, compassion and thoughtfulness, and he, as musical director of the Angelic Choir with his enormous resources of creative talent possessed those virtues in abundance. What could a bunch of battle-hardened warrior angels possibly have to offer? Besides, he would very much like to see the baby Jesus. The baby Jesus! Who'd have thought that the Prince of Peace would have come to earth as a baby, helpless and vulnerable? Axa was still having trouble getting his head round the notion. Not wishing to sound selfish, he said,

'I would very much appreciate if I and Tiras, as well as a small contingent of the leading voices in the choir were given the opportunity to go with you, to see Jesus.'

Michael pondered for a few seconds.

'How many were you thinking of?'

'Say… twelve,' ventured Axa.

'The three leaders from the four singing parts, as in, The Twelve?'

'Exactly,' Axa answered expectantly. 'A reward for their leading the singing so well,' he added in his most persuasive voice.

Michael thought for an instant and then glanced at Gabriel.

'I can't see why not?'

Axa was elated, as was Tiras beside him.

'You organise your singers. We'll need to leave very soon. We have to arrive way before the shepherds.'

'No sooner said than done,' Axa replied. Turning to Tiras, he said, 'You arrange things. I'm exhausted from the performance. I've expended a lot of nervous energy tonight and I need to lie down.'

Michael and Gabriel looked at each other long and hard. They walked a short distance and when they were out of earshot, Michael said,

'Creative talent brings with it a lot of emotional baggage, Gabriel.'

'And I thought we had come here to praise and worship Jesus, not to put on a performance.'

Tiras dutifully hurried off. He called the twelve leading angels in the choir to him and explained that whilst the rest of the choir was headed back to heaven, they were to stay behind. They had been given special dispensation to go down to Bethlehem to see baby Jesus.

A ripple of excitement spread through them. Sabta, Gether and Dumah were beside themselves hardly able to contain the thrill they felt. Before they had left heaven along with the rest of the choir, they had frantically searched for Dylan. Unable to find him, they had pleaded with Axa to wait for him. Their musical director had emphatically rejected their request. He could not possibly postpone their departure: they had a strict timetable to adhere to. They had even approached Michael but he had told them they had to leave and they were not to worry about Dylan: he would be fine. Although the three were overjoyed at how well the celebration had gone, they did feel uncomfortable that Dylan had missed the whole thing and that they were now getting to see baby Jesus as well.

Tiras returned to Michael and Gabriel and informed them that everything was ready. No sooner had Michael and Gabriel been briefed than they could see the massive throng begin to leave the sky above Bethlehem for heaven, escorted by Meshek and his detachment of warrior angels.

'Everything seems to be going to plan so far,' Gabriel whispered.

'Never in any doubt,' the archangel smiled.

The vast Angel Choir was still leaving when Michael turned to face the twelve angels who had been invited to stay and see Jesus. He stressed that time was of the essence.

‘We’ll get going then. Axa!’ he called, ‘you’d better get up if you’re coming with us.’

‘A minute earlier he couldn’t praise me enough, and here he is ordering me about as if I was an apprentice angel,’ he thought to himself.

‘Coming,’ he said and wearily got to his feet.

Chapter 49

The five guardians watched as fifteen angels, led by Michael, landed in the clearing in front of the rock. Dylan was in the cave, sitting on the floor, gazing at Jesus in amazement. A warm, golden glow was flooding the sky from the east heralding the arrival of the coming sun on this first Christmas Day morning. Gilchrist had been expecting them and strode over to greet Michael and Gabriel. He nodded an acknowledgement to the other twelve angel choristers and finally, he turned to Axa and Tiras. He addressed the former.

'Well, it all looked and sounded magnificent from here. You must be very proud.'

'Thank you, Gilchrist. Coming from you, that is very gratifying,' Axa responded.

Gilchrist detected a slight disregard for him from the choir master, evident from the fact that he was looking past him to the cave. Gilchrist looked at Michael.

'They were superb and utterly outstanding,' Michael said. 'All of them are on their way back to heaven now, but Axa asked if he and some of the select choristers could come down here and see our Lord.'

'Of course,' replied Gilchrist.

Gabriel looked at him and lowered his voice.

'How have things gone?'

'Fine, other than a visit from Antonin and some unsavoury clowns.'

Michael looked at him with some concern.

'No worries,' he reassured him. 'We dealt with them. They're long gone.'

'Are you okay?'

'Yeah.'

Turning to the chorister angels he announced,

'Our Lord was born some four hours ago.'

They all gasped.

'Mary, His mother is well but very tired, and Joseph, her husband, is a little flabbergasted by it all. He still can't quite believe that this baby is Jesus, the Messiah. He'll get over it though, with Mary's help. She's an incredible woman.'

Gabriel nodded his head.

The small contingent of choral angels were on tenterhooks.

'May we see Him, Michael?' asked Axa.

'I can't see why not. Lead the way, Gilchrist,' ordered Michael.

Just as Gilchrist was about to pace forward, there was movement in the entrance to the cave. He stopped abruptly, as Joseph appeared, carrying Mary in his arms who was carrying baby Jesus in her arms.

Spontaneously, all the angels, including the guarding angels fell on their knees in worshipful posture. As Gilchrist and Dylan had done a few hours earlier, the angels who had just arrived recognised Jesus immediately and did what any other angel would have done. On bended knees and with bowed heads they paid homage to their Lord.

A minute earlier, Joseph and Mary, on seeing that the sun was rising had decided that they wanted to show the dawn to Jesus. Or was it that they wanted to show Jesus to the dawn? Whatever? Mary, still lying on the straw, was too weak to walk after her exertions whilst giving birth. She had held Jesus out to Joseph and told him to take the baby out. Joseph, whose idea of family was the unit doing things together would have none of it. There was to be no exclusivity. Thus, his big powerful carpenter's arms used to carrying heavy lintels, and planting thick wooden posts in the ground, made light work of sweeping Mary up, while she cradled the Saviour of the world.

Slowly, the angels lifted their heads and got to their feet. The new arrivals amongst them gazed in curiosity, but most of all in adoration. Even though He was a mere baby, only a few hours old, they still recognised Him as the Loveliness and Comeliness of Heaven. Here though, as the Word made flesh and so, the image of the invisible God.

Joseph, oblivious to the celestial admirers, turned to face the east, to show the new born babe to the dawn and as he did so, the sun seemed to blaze a brighter light than it had ever done. The glare dazzled the baby's eyes and made Him start. Soon, He began to whimper and the whimper escalated into cries, which seemed all the more intense since the whole of Bethlehem and the surrounding district was so peaceful, in this, the first light of day. Mary started to rock Him gently in her arms. Seeing this, Joseph started rocking Mary vigorously. She put a hand on his chest.

'Joseph, Joseph,' she smiled gently. 'You'll make Him sick. I'll rock Him. Just hold us.'

The big carpenter did as he was told. Mary continued to rock, but the baby cried louder.

The newly arrived angels were distressed at His crying. Axa looked over to the five warrior angels. He was a little startled to see that they did not seem unduly mindful of their Lord's evident discomfort, merely standing round some with their hands resting on the hilts of their sheathed swords.

'Typical warriors,' he thought to himself. 'They could never know anything of sympathy and empathy.'

Then, Axa had a brainwave. The more he thought of it, the more he knew the idea was ingenious and yet so simple, making the best use of the talents that were available to them, there and then. As an afterthought, there was the added advantage that it would mean he, as Choral Director and the other the choral angels present would be held in high regard, indeed, would become legendary in heavenly circles for evermore.

'Archangel Michael, I've just thought of a way to soothe Jesus's crying: we choral angels could sing to our Lord.'

Michael was about to answer him, but Axa continued.

'Think about it, we could sing Him a lullaby!'

'All in hand, Axa,' replied the archangel, 'all in hand.'

Axa was so excited he did not hear Michael's answer, or else he chose to ignore him. This was going to be a much more important event than announcing Jesus's arrival to the shepherds; a mere trifling affair compared to the privilege of singing directly to Jesus. He rushed to tell the choral angels to prepare to sing.

Michael tried to remonstrate with him.

'But Axa...'

'What?' he asked, not really paying attention to what the archangel had to say. Michael raised his voice a little.

'Axa, it's already taken care...'

His voice trailed off, for in that very instant, a song broke out from deep in the cave. A song so sweet, that it left him speechless. Voluntarily, he had made himself mute for here was something so heavenly and blissful, to speak over it would be both obscene and profane. Axa, who was by now at the back of the angels, suddenly stopped his arranging. For an instant, he stood stock still, statuesque. Shaking himself he shot a sudden glance at his choir members. Had any of them decided to sing before his say so? No, none of them was singing. They looked at each other dumbfounded, as mystified as he was. Anyway, Axa knew every one of them and even though they were the very best singers in the angelic choir, the elite of the elite, he knew that not one of them possessed a voice so pure and clear, as gentle as the falling snow, yet so dynamic and powerful. He could hardly breathe such was the joyous intensity of the voice serenading him and every angel present. He was brought to tears. He looked around and every other angel including Michael, Gabriel and even the warrior angels were reacting just as he was. He glanced at Tiras and he was lost in joyful wonderment.

He noticed that Jesus, by now was sound asleep once more. As the singing continued, Axa looked around again, trying to see where it was coming from and more to the point, trying to satisfy his curiosity as to who on earth possessed such a voice. This was no mortal, for no human would be able to sing so many melodies and different harmonies, all at the same time. Whoever it was, Axa would have to have him in the choir of angels. By virtue of his position as Choral Director he would insist. He would even be given solo parts. But who was it? Axa looked around again, but in vain. Then, he noticed a slight movement at the entrance to the cave. When he saw who walked out it almost bowled him over. It was... Dylan! Axa was open-mouthed as was Tiras and the other choir angels. Sabta, Gether and Dumah couldn't believe their eyes... nor their ears. The choir director looked intently at Dylan to make sure that he was the one whose dulcet tones were enchanting them all. Yes, it was Dylan. No one else, just Dylan!

The little angel had heard Jesus's crying and had begun singing from inside the cave. As he stepped outside the bright morning sun had blinded him. He had closed his eyes, and kept them shut as he continued to sing to Jesus. Consequently, he did not see the new arrivals standing in the clearing outside.

Michael and Gabriel were enthralled. Having only heard about this little angel's singing prowess from Gilchrist, they were captivated on hearing his voice for the first time. They felt as if they had been struck by a force of such gentleness and tenderness, they were transfixed, their eyes brimming with tears. Michael thought back to the time in his hall when Gilchrist had reported to Gabriel and himself after following Dylan on his journey to Egypt. He had been a little disconcerted when Gilchrist had told them that he had cried profuse tears of joy when he heard Dylan sing. Gilchrist, the mighty warrior, centuries old, crying! And here he was, doing exactly the same thing: he couldn't help himself.

Just as Dylan's voice was soaring to a glorious finale, he opened his eyes and saw that he had an audience of more than just the five warrior angels. Taken aback, he suddenly stopped singing, though the gently textured melodies that he left hanging in the air still surrounded them. He looked at his audience more intently. There was Sabta, Gether and Dumah and the other nine leaders of the four parts in the Angel Choir. He looked across and there was none other than the Archangel Michael and Gabriel standing beside Gilchrist, Joram, Ebin, Cadman and Caleb. Then he saw Tiras! Well, if Tiras was there, Axa couldn't be far.

Just then, Axa, who was still standing at the back of the group of angel singers, strode out and came into view. He looked at Dylan.

Dylan, for some strange reason, was struck with fear. Why was he so fearful? He'd done nothing wrong. Somehow though, seeing what some would consider his nemesis walking towards him and knowing that he had just heard him sing, made Dylan shudder with fear.

Axa walked right up to him, and stood before him, the little angel's head just about managing to come level with his chest.

'He's invading a lot of my personal space. He's going to do something,' Dylan warned himself, silently.

He stared long and hard at Dylan. Then he walked round him. Dylan had never felt so nervous. Not daring to move, he swivelled his eyes it seemed the whole way around his head following Axa's every move.

Michael knew what Axa was doing.

'There's no one there Axa, just Dylan,' he said, strolling up to them.

Axa finished circling Dylan and stood before him again.

'But it can't be,' he muttered to himself.

'Why not?' asked the archangel.

Dylan was glad Michael was there for he wouldn't have had a clue what to say to his musical director.

Axa continued to stare, transfixed by the little angel.

'But... it's... Dylan.'

He bent down and looked him in the eye. Dylan, with some trepidation, returned the favour. He could sense the confusion in Axa's mind.

'I don't understand.'

'What don't you understand?' asked Michael.

'Well,' responded Axa, 'he's always out of tune.'

'That's what you thought, Axa.'

The choir master was perplexed as he turned to look at Michael.

'Did you ever wonder where Dylan would go to when he would leave heaven on his own, and more importantly, why? To my shame, I had never given it a second's thought.'

Dylan felt a jolt inside him. He was astonished though at what he heard next.

'At the orders of our Lord, the Ancient of Days, Gilchrist here followed him when he went on one of his missions, nearly nine months ago.'

Dylan looked at Gilchrist. He nodded his head to confirm what Michael had just said. The archangel continued.

'He saw Dylan comfort a sad, miserable, little boy, but what he heard was much more important, for Dylan sang to that boy, a joyous song of beauty and radiance, that made Gilchrist cry, much as we all did now, but also eased the boy's pain and soothed his troubled heart. You see, Dylan connected with the boy's hurt, sensed it from far away in heaven and responded with compassion and what's more, hastened to comfort him: something that none of us here, or any other angel in heaven has ever done. And he does that through song, a song that comes from the love and innocence that is deep inside him. God loves the downtrodden of this world; Dylan has always known that – more than any other angel.'

Dylan felt uneasy as all the angels present turned to look at him in awe. Michael continued.

'Axa, God specifically asked for Dylan, to come here to sing a lullaby to Jesus, His Son.'

Once again, Axa was nearly bowled over. God had asked specifically for Dylan!

Then Michael added his final comment with precise and deliberate emphasis that went piercing like a sharpened arrow far into the depths of Axa's whole being.

'He wasn't, and never has been, the angel who was out of tune.'

Axa turned to look at Michael. He was speechless. He understood Michael's meaning, as did every other angel standing in the clearing. He stood, silent for a while. Then, he sensed a movement beside him. Joseph and Mary had decided it was best that they return Jesus to the cave and Joseph carried them both carefully inside. Mary shivered from the cold of the early morning as if the day had shed its night cloak too soon.

The choir master bent down and looked at Dylan again. The little angel looked deep into Axa's eyes. They seemed confused, having difficulty processing what had just happened. It was as plain as day to him that Axa couldn't quite comprehend how such a heavenly sound had emanated from Dylan's lips. Dylan, whose tuneless singing had scaled such heights it had left Axa at his wits' end. How many times had he wondered at his ability to cause such musical mayhem? And why hadn't he, as conductor of the heavenly choir recognised that all the while, he possessed such a wondrous voice.

Dylan watched as he raised his hand and placed it on his shoulder. He then whispered hoarsely,

'I'm sorry. Sorry, for having doubted you. Sorry for not wanting you to sing in the choir. But sorry most of all for not realising you had such a beautiful, wondrous voice. I have done you great harm.'

Dylan was flabbergasted. He looked Axa in the eye. He was speechless for a second or two. Then, he found his tongue, and breezily, he said,

'No worries, Axa.'

Then he punched him playfully on the arm and waited a few short seconds before adding,

'Just, don't do it again.'

At this, the five warrior angels burst out laughing. Michael and Gabriel followed suit as did the choral angels. Dylan smiled and laughed. Axa laughed with him. Sabta, Gether and Dumah raced over to him. They couldn't believe that Dylan could have sung so beautifully, so purely. Axa left to speak to Michael and Gabriel.

'Why didn't you tell us?' asked Dumah.

'I did, more than once,' he answered, a little indignantly.

'When?' they asked as one voice.

'The last time was when we lay by the stream in heaven's garden, remember? You offered to help me learn to sing?'

'Yes, but...' started Sabta.

There was an awkward silence, eventually broken by Dylan.

'Well, you know now.'

'Yes, we *do* know,' confirmed Gether.

'Anyway,' said Sabta, 'where were you when we all left heaven last night? We tried to get Axa to wait for you. We begged him.'

Dylan was already elated at being honoured by his peers it didn't seem possible that he could be happier. But on hearing that his friends had not forgotten him his spirits soared.

Dumah lowered his voice to a whisper: Axa was still around.

'He would have none of it. We begged him, coz we knew how much the party to welcome Jesus meant to you, but he wouldn't listen.' He mimicked Axa's voice. 'No, we have a strict timetable and we can't hang about.'

They all laughed out loud. Axa and the other angels looked over at them.

'We're sorry you missed the party,' said Gether.

'Yes,' agreed Sabta and Dumah.

'It's okay, honest.'

'So, did you really get to sing a lullaby to our Lord?' asked Sabta, looking in awe at Dylan.

'Yeah,' he nodded. 'I've done it a few times now.'

'And you've been here all the while with Gilchrist and his warriors?' asked Gether.

'Well, most of the time, since just after Jesus was born.'

'Wow! What are they like?' asked Dumah.

'Great, they've told me I'm part of their gang now.'

The three angels were wide eyed and open-mouthed.

'Don't worry,' Dylan reassured them. 'I told them I had a better gang of friends already.'

They all smiled at each other.

Chapter 50

'Right, we haven't much time,' announced Michael. 'The shepherds will be here soon. We need to be gone before they arrive.'

He turned to face Gilchrist and the other warriors who were standing behind him.

'These aren't the only visitors who will come to see Him. Others will come: wise men, in fact, from the East. Each will be accompanied by warrior angels, and three will be carrying a personal gift for our Lord. One will bring gold, another, myrrh, and the last, guarded by Mibsam and his troop, will bring... frankincense. That was what Abdallah brought with him when you were escorting him from Petra to Memphis.'

The other four warriors looked at each other. Gilchrist kept his eyes fixed on Michael.

'So, we weren't escorting Abdallah, but the frankincense.'

'Correct.'

'So *that's* what it was all about,' Caleb gasped.

Michael continued.

'Final orders, Gilchrist. You and your warriors are to stay here, and guard Jesus and Mary and Joseph. They will stay here for over a year or so. Then they will leave, or else the...' He looked over to the cave. In a grave voice he informed them '... the boy Jesus will be killed by King Herod's men.'

All the gathered angels were horrified.

'Every baby boy under two years old in the vicinity will be killed.'

Gilchrist looked him hard in the eye. They both remembered what had happened in Egypt during Moses' time when the Pharaoh had ordered that all male Jewish babies be killed.

'Again,' said Gilchrist quietly.

'Yes,' whispered Michael.

For a few seconds they were all silent, then Gilchrist spoke.

'Is that why Antonin told me earlier on that Herod was in Satan's pocket?'

'Probably,' answered Michael.

'But, Michael,' said Joram, 'back in heaven, when you first told us about this mission you said that once He was born, Jesus would be safe.'

'I know, but I couldn't tell you everything at the time.'

'Where will they go? Back to Nazareth?' asked Gilchrist.

'No, they'll be sent to Egypt, but only for a while.'

Gilchrist sighed and nodded his head. There would be another slaughter of the innocents, but not in Egypt. This time, it would provide a refuge for Jesus and his parents.

'How will they know to leave?' asked Joram.

'Gabriel will appear to Joseph and tell him what to do.'

Caleb was standing next to Gabriel.

'Nice one, Gabe,' he responded, slapping him a little too hard on the back making him cough.

All the choral angels looked at him. His fellow warriors shook their heads, muttering under their breaths. Sensing everyone was looking at him he looked round.

'What?'

Michael and Gabriel looked at each other. The latter shook his head and waved his hand back and forth in front of him as if to say, 'Don't bother; best say nothing'.

Michael continued.

'Eventually, they will go back home to Nazareth. Until then, you stay with them. Your orders are the same as before.'

'Wherever they go, we go,' explained Ebin.

'Exactly.'

Axa interjected.

'Archangel, if Jesus is in such mortal danger, then – and I'm not trying to disparage Gilchrist and his fine combatants, far from it – don't you think more warrior angels should be here? After all, there's only five of them.'

'Good point, Axa,' replied Michael. He thought for a few seconds. 'Gilchrist, show him.'

'What? Break their cover?' Gilchrist questioned.

'There are no demons around now, since you and your warriors dealt with Antonin. Call them.'

At that, Gilchrist uttered a short, 'Come,' seemingly more to himself than anyone else.

Instantly, warrior angels began to appear as if from thin air. Lorcan, Abida, Jonathon, Peleg and Sabteka stood in front of the cave. Then, a group of thirty arrived. Dylan took a sharp intake of breath. They were wearing ordinary men's and women's clothes, dull and colourless, worn and ragged, the males' head-dresses wrapped carelessly around their heads. Dylan recognised them as the group of people Gilchrist had hovered above when they had arrived in Bethlehem earlier on. He looked at Gilchrist, who smiled back at him. Others came, he hadn't seen before, also dressed in human clothes. Tens of undisguised warrior angels then thronged the air. Last of all, a group of city down-and-outs who had been hanging around the well near the gates when Joseph and Mary had arrived appeared. Their leader, Jedah, still looking as sullen and intimidating as when he had looked threateningly at Ebin and Caleb as they sat on the city well disguised as the old married couple the night before.

Ebin and Caleb walked up to them with broad smiles on their faces. They shook hands with Jedah and the others.

'Don't ever do that again,' said Ebin.

'What? This?'

Jedah sneered at them as he'd done the previous night.

'We had to look away or else we'd have burst out laughing,' said Caleb.

'Your fault,' responded Jedah. 'You shouldn't have looked at me.'

Ebin and Caleb smiled at him.

'What's with the limp, then?' Jedah asked.

'Don't ask,' advised Ebin. 'He got in the way when I chucked Ashtenaz to one side. He lay on the floor then, having a rest.'

Caleb ignored his friend.

'Anyway, what have you been doing these last nine months?' he asked.

Jedah was never one to glamourize his work.

'This and that; keepin' an eye on things.'

Just then, Lorcan walked up to them.

'Oh, and saving this one's bacon.'

'Not the right thing to say,' advised Caleb,' considering no one round around here eats pig meat.'

'Okay, "We saved his skin,".'

'Can't say that either. We've got no skin: none of us has.'

'Is he always like this?' Jedah asked Ebin, plainly irritated.

The latter nodded his head resignedly, raising one eyebrow as he did so.

'Yeah, but we're friends,' responded Caleb, 'we like each other.'

Ebin gave him a hard, disdainful look. He turned to look at Jedah.

'What happened, then?'

'They were about to be rumbled by Sandon until Nidab and I stepped in and took a beating from the captain of the guards while Kandar was looking on, enjoying himself.'

Caleb and Ebin were astonished.

Lorcan offered his hand to Jedah.

'Thanks. We owe you one.'

'When was this?' asked Ebin.

'The night Abida arrived in Nazareth to tell you we'd seen Antonin here,' Lorcan explained.

'Why didn't Abida tell us?'

'Didn't want to bother you, especially since he was the cause of the problem, in the first place.'

Lorcan quickly described what had happened. Ebin and Caleb whistled quietly wondering to themselves how close the whole mission had come to failure that night.

'Nathanael gave you a bit of a going over, didn't he,' said Lorcan.

Jedah shrugged his shoulders.

'And Kandar had no idea it was you and Nidab?'

They smiled.

'Not a clue,' replied Nidab. 'Mind, if it hadn't been for him, Nathanael wouldn't have taken a blind bit of notice.'

'We'll catch up with him someday,' promised Jedah.

'We saw Gilchrist arrive on his reconnaissance trip, too,' added Nidab.

'Don't tell him that. He won't be happy he was seen,' warned Ebin.

Then Michael looked at Axa.

'Do you think there's enough there?'

Axa gave a resigned smile.

'I think so.'

Gilchrist acknowledged all the warrior angels, and then gave them the command to return to their positions. In an instant, they disappeared.

He looked at Michael.

'Archangel,' he said, 'what happens to Jesus after we get back to Nazareth?'

Michael shifted his feet uncomfortably: he'd been dreading this.

Well, our Lord will grow as a boy and become an adult.'

'I'd gathered that much, but what happens then?'

Slowly, Michael answered him.

'He will travel through Palestine and put God on display, show what He's like – really like – to all the people of Israel. He will shatter everybody's preconceived ideas of what He's like. Some will accept Him as God and Saviour. On the other hand, the religious heavies – the Sanhedrin, the Jewish council, those in power – won't like it, won't like Him and they'll reject Him. So...'

At this, Michael lowered his head, and breathed a long sigh. How was he to explain the next part?

'... they will act.'

'Act? What do you mean, "act"?' asked Gilchrist, a nervous smile twitching his lips.

Michael was tense, as was Gabriel. The archangel gave out another long sigh, wiping his brow.

'They will kill Him.'

It seemed Michael had confessed to a long-held guilt that he had concealed in the depths of his being for a long time.

Gilchrist looked at the other four warrior angels, the distress and disquiet he felt mirrored in their eyes. He took a step forward, a mere arm's length away from Michael.

'Kill Him!' said Gilchrist, his voice laced with threat. 'And who's going to kill Him?'

Joram, Ebin, Cadman and Caleb strode forward and stood in a small semi-circle behind their captain. They looked threateningly at Michael. Jesus was to be killed?!

'The Sanhedrin will fix it, and the Romans will do it.'

Gilchrist looked at Gabriel.

'Did you know about this?'

He nodded his head slowly, his eyes looking into the distance.

The other angels were all listening intently. They could feel the tension in the air. They sensed a huge, violent storm approaching. Strangely, it felt like an inverted hurricane for the eye of the storm, where they stood, was about to feel the full brunt of the gale, whilst Bethlehem itself and the surrounding area lay peaceful, bathed in the early morning sunshine. Trepidation gripped them.

Gilchrist was doing his utmost to control himself, but he could feel fury surging like torrents inside him. An appalling thought came to him.

'Wait a minute. Did you say the Romans would kill Him?'

Michael was silent. He ran his hand along the back of his neck. This was the most difficult part. He could only nod in affirmation. Gilchrist looked at him in absolute horror.

'That means...' he started, unable to finish. He gathered himself to continue. 'That means, He's going to be...'

'... crucified,' finished Joram, whispering the word.

Gilchrist was deep in thought. Many a time he had had the misfortune of witnessing a crucifixion. It was the most barbaric method of killing he had ever seen, little more than a license to maim, torture and humiliate as part of a process of prolonged execution. The condemned would be nailed through his hands and feet to a cross and left to hang, enduring agonies beyond imagination, while the breath was slowly sucked from his lungs. Gilchrist could think of no more insidious way to die. The degradation and shame let alone the anguish and torture Jesus would suffer was too much for him. It repelled him, disgusted him even. In his mind he recoiled like a human pulling back from some nauseous stench. Then rage consumed him; a righteous anger devoured him. He turned his head to look at his four comrades, again. Caleb was already fidgeting, tugging at his tunic, touching the hilt of his sword, whilst Cadman was staring at Michael through narrowed eyes and Ebin was breathing heavily. They were with him; they too were devoted to Jesus, and just like Gilchrist, had witnessed their fair share of despicable crucifixions. They could not stand idly by and let Jesus be crucified, much less be killed.

And so, Gilchrist, the legendary warrior angel, whom all angels in heaven, warriors, messengers and singers revered, and his four warriors, drew their swords and blazed a brilliant blinding light. The light shone with coruscating intensity sending shafts of lightning bolts, like shards of broken glass, shooting through the air. A searing heat, fierce in its intensity and severity blew what seemed like a thermal gale. Dylan and the other angels crouched on the ground raising their arms to protect themselves from the storm of light. It was an onslaught the like of which they had never experienced as sheltered angel choristers. All around they could feel the real threat of dangerous angelic violence and they were fearful and afraid. Even Gabriel, standing beside Michael, had to raise his hand to protect his eyes, but the archangel stood undaunted and unafraid, his face impassive, although his eyes evinced care and concern for these great warrior angels. In the midst of the blinding light, he looked them in the eye and spoke in a still, calm voice.

'Gilchrist.'

'This isn't right,' replied Gilchrist vociferously.

'Calm yourselves,' he appealed to them.

'Calm ourselves?! How can we be calm when our Lord is to be crucified?' replied Gilchrist.

The other warriors chipped in.

'What was the point in sending us here to guard Him?' asked Ebin.

'We needn't have bothered escorting her from Nazareth if that's what's going to happen to Him,' argued Joram.

'I know, I understand, but He will be resurr...'

He didn't get to finish what he had to say.

'Do you understand, Michael? Because it isn't right,' argued Caleb.

Shafts of light – dagger-like pieces – pierced the air: the choral angels remained on the ground.

'We cannot let this happen, Michael,' declared Gilchrist. 'He is our Lord and Creator. Everything that is exists because of Him. He holds everything together. We are duty bound, sworn to defend and safeguard Him. And anyway, we were commissioned by God to watch over Him. How can we stand by and let Him be killed? We would be disregarding a direct order from the Lord of the Angel Armies.'

'But it will please Him.'

'Please Him?!'

More lightning sparked from deep within the five warriors.

'What do you mean, "please Him"? Will it please Him to see His Son hanging and dying on a cross?'

'No,' replied Michael shrugging his shoulders a little, 'but that's what He wants. Besides, it is Jesus's great desire as well.'

'His great desire?!' Gilchrist retorted in horror.

He and the other four warriors were incredulous, at the same time ablaze with indignation and fury. Still Michael would not yield. In a quiet voice he informed them,

'You all must understand this: if you do not accept our Lord's bidding in this matter, then there is no place for you in the Angel Armies.'

The five angels in their smouldering glory were stunned.

'This is what Jesus wants. Indeed, He yearns for it.' Then Michael steeled himself to convey the ultimate threat: 'If you are not for Him... then you are against Him.'

Gilchrist visibly quaked, as did the angels standing behind him. They all trembled. Not one of them had the least desire to be God's enemy. They all knew that it was a fearful thing to fall into the hands of the living God. They all wanted to be on His side. In that short instant they all glimpsed the devastation that was Antonin's and every demon's existence. Gilchrist pondered what Michael had just said. Could it possibly be that it was Jesus's will and His Father's, that He should die on a cross, reduced to ignominy and public derision, in indescribable pain? Why would He do that? Gilchrist looked Michael in the eye. If he continued to resist, he would be no better than any of the fallen angels and would be outcast from the presence of God. He would become like Antonin whose whole endeavours were geared to oppose and defy the Lord of the Angel Armies. Gilchrist felt trapped: the only options on offer were either to become what he despised or agree to the unimaginable.

Then, he thought of Joseph and Mary. Hadn't Joseph been in the same situation? Either he would go through with his threat to divorce Mary, probably living the rest of his life a lonely man, becoming that which he did not want, or accept the unexplainable, with all that that entailed. He had been between a rock and a hard place, just as Gilchrist was now. But he had faith, and trusted in God, just as Mary had done. They had put everything on the line, their reputations and their well-being, since who had heard of such an astounding and unbelievable thing: a baby born of the seed of a woman. Yet, they both believed and showed it by coming to Bethlehem, giving birth to Jesus in a dark, nondescript cave, with only animals in attendance. No one had witnessed this other than themselves. Such a momentous event and although they had been on their own, they still possessed a wild and ferocious trust in God and the baby. It challenged Gilchrist and in those few short minutes he realised, just as Joseph and Mary had so willingly done, he had to trust his Lord and believe.

He looked behind him, at his comrades. How many times had he fought shoulder to shoulder with these brave warriors over the centuries? Not once had they been vanquished. Yet, he knew, and from the look in their eyes, they also knew, there was no way they were going to win this battle.

He brought his sword down by his side and extinguished his fierce light. The other four warriors followed his lead and smothered their brilliant radiance, holding their swords to the side, pointing downwards. Realising the blinding lustre had faded to nothing the choral angels gradually raised their heads and slowly got to their feet.

Facing Michael and Gabriel, the five warriors looked vanquished. They all breathed heavily, gasping for air, their energy utterly spent. Joram and Ebin leaning on their swords, pressing their tips in the ground, stumbled, and fell on the sandy earth; Caleb was already on his knees, then he keeled over, on to his back, utterly exhausted, while Cadman and Gilchrist could hardly stand up in their own strength. Their great might had been expended in their immense desire to ensure that no harm would come to their Lord. With their heads bowed they were in a pitiful state.

Michael turned to the choral angels.

'Look away, every one of you, look away,' he ordered sharply.

All, including Axa, turned their backs.

Michael did not want anyone seeing these noble warriors like this: crushed by despair at the thought of Jesus dying on the cross, their strength dissipated. They did not deserve that. He chose his words carefully and spoke gently to them.

'When Gabriel and I were first told that Jesus was coming to earth to die, our reaction was much like yours. We told him we couldn't allow Him to do this. We pleaded with Him, through our tears, to let us take His place even. He would have none of it. He explained that this was what He and His Father wanted. Ever since Adam had eaten the forbidden fruit, He had longed to bridge the chasm between people and God. The only way to do that was for Him to come to earth, become God in human form, take the sins of the world on Himself and die on the cross. Only He could do this. He repeated to us, "Only I can do this". God required a sacrifice that was perfection in order that forgiveness of sin could happen and so, enable peace and reconciliation between the Father and the people of the world. You and your warriors are the finest in the Angel Armies, Gilchrist, but He is the Warrior above all warriors. He will take the fight to Satan on behalf of all peoples, in a way neither you nor I can do, for he is their Captain. He will sacrifice himself, and in so doing – I don't know how – he will be triumphant. He will die, yet, will live: the Ultimate Warrior.'

The five angels were shell shocked, as were the choral angels. Dylan was beside himself. They had not envisaged Jesus's coming to earth ending like this. They had all expected a triumphant visitation, whereby Jesus would usher in the kingdom of heaven through might. But this! This was unimaginable. Gilchrist was dumbstruck as was every other angel. Words failed them all. Caleb raised himself on to his knees.

'But crucifixion, Michael,' he pleaded, 'why that death of all deaths?'

At this, Michael became solemn. He took a few seconds to compose himself.

'It has to be a shameful and painful death, for sin is shameful and painful. Complete wrong must be fully righted. Everything has to be corrected.'

Then, Michael looked at the choral angels who still had their backs turned to him.

'Dylan!'

The little angel turned his head to look at the archangel.

'Remember when Gilchrist brought you to see Gabriel and I and you said only our Lord would be able to take people's pain away, but you didn't know what He could do? Well, here it is, Dylan, but first, blood must be shed...'. He paused, took a deep breath and turned to look towards the cave, '... the blood of the innocent Lamb, the Lamb of God.'

Each angel was lost in his own thoughts. For the choral angels, the joy and delight of the celebrations they had rejoiced in an hour earlier had been extinguished by the stark reality of what lay ahead of their Lord.

'Gilchrist,' said Michael.

The warrior lifted his eyes to look at his superior.

'You have done well, guarding Mary, as have your comrades. I have one other charge for you. When He will be crucified I want you standing beside me, in the sky above, with your four warriors as well as twelve legions of the Angel Armies. We shall all be there at the behest of God, our Lord. We will witness Jesus's suffering and death and should He call, should He utter one word in our direction, then, we will be at hand, ready to respond. You would do me a great honour if you would accede to my request, as I said and stand at my shoulder.'

Everyone looked at Gilchrist.

'As you wish, I am at your command,' he replied, bowing his head, with his hand on the hilt of his sword.

'I can think of no other angel I would rather have at my side.'

Gabriel, who had been silent throughout these exchanges spoke up.

'Michael, the shepherds are nearly here. I can see them coming.'

They all swung round to look.

'Indeed,' Michael agreed. 'We must make haste. They have things to do and Gabriel and I and the choral angels need to get out of the way. Gilchrist, Cadman, Joram, Ebin and Caleb, I don't expect to see you back in heaven until your...' here he gestured to the cave, 'and their return from Egypt.'

Their strength partially returned, all five stood on their feet and nodded their readiness to obey. Michael addressed the choral angels.

'Come, we must leave. Our Lord awaits us.'

The twelve choral angels took off silently, with Axa and Tiras behind. Dylan took his usual staccato hop, skip and jump before take-off, but just as he was getting into his jump, Michael strode forward and grabbed him by the shoulder.

'Where do you think you're going?'

Dylan was still in awe of Michael, especially after having caught a glimpse of him calmly standing resolute in the middle of the earlier hurricane of light that Gilchrist and the others had unleashed.

'Well... going back to heaven.'

'No, you're not. Have you ever been to Egypt?

'I dunno.'

'Yes, he has – several times – that's where Kamal, the little boy I heard him sing to lives,' said Gilchrist.

Michael spoke to Dylan.

'You're job down here hasn't finished. You're to stay and go with Gilchrist and his warriors to Egypt when Joseph and Mary take Jesus there. Who else is going to sing lullabies to Him? Not any of these five, I can tell you, now. They may be the best warriors in heaven, but we certainly don't want them singing to baby Jesus.'

Dylan snorted a laugh. The other five stared at him.

Michael then looked at them all in earnest, including Dylan.

'Never ever forget, that each of you was appointed by God and Jesus to carry out this mission.'

He heard the shepherds' excited jabbering getting louder.

'I'll see you after you come back from Egypt. No more for us to do here, Gabriel. Let's go home.'

With that, they swiftly took off and within seconds they were out of sight.

Dylan walked over to Gilchrist.

'One thing I don't understand, Gilchrist.'

'What's that?'

'Well, if we had so many warrior angels about the place, why didn't you get them to help you when all those demons came after Antonin called them?'

'We didn't have a choice. We knew Antonin probably had more demons here. At the same time, we wanted him to think there were only five of us. If he had thought there were more than just us he would have brought a much bigger force. We had to try and make sure the fighting – if it was to happen – would be as low key as possible. We didn't want a huge battle happening here tonight, or else Bethlehem would have been destroyed. That's why having you around helped us in that respect.'

Dylan was surprised to hear that.

'How do you mean?'

'Well, I don't want hurt your feelings, but when he saw that you were the only back-up we had, it convinced him that we really were on our own.'

'So, you used me.'

'Yeah, kind of,' admitted Gilchrist, shrugging his shoulders.

'Thanks!'

Gilchrist smiled at him.

'But I saw you're faces,' Dylan continued, 'when the other demons came over those walls. You all looked shocked, worried even.'

'We *looked* shocked and worried, but that was all part of the act,' explained Caleb.

'But what about Cadman?'

'What about him?' asked Ebin.

Cadman looked at Dylan indignantly.

'Well, he didn't look shocked or worried at all. He still kept his sword to Tograman's throat.'

Caleb chuckled.

'We tried to persuade him to act worried – concerned even – nothing doing. He hates them so much.'

Dylan was quiet for a while, but he hadn't finished.

'Did you really follow me that night when I sang to Kamal?' he asked Gilchrist.

'Yes.'

'But I didn't see you.'

'No, but remember, you stumbled over that rock at the back of the house? That was me.'

'What?!'

'Yeah, and you kicked me in the head.'

Dylan was amazed, remembering the incident. He had kicked Gilchrist in the head! He felt slightly uneasy.

'Don't worry,' Joram assured him. 'He needed to have some sense knocked into him.'

'I don't think he would have felt it anyway,' added Caleb. 'You need a brain to feel pain.'

Gilchrist gave him a disdainful look.

They heard the shuffle of steps at the entrance to the cave. Joseph was standing there, as he and Mary had heard some people approaching.

'Four shepherds, Mary,' he said, sounding slightly puzzled. 'They're coming this way. Why on earth would four shepherds be coming to see us?'

Joseph walked out to meet them, a little suspicious, for he, like everyone else, knew that shepherds were not the most desirable of well-wishers to come and visit a new born baby. They explained to him what had happened in the hills in the distance. Joseph relaxed and led them towards the cave. The angels made way as the shepherds followed Joseph to see the Saviour of the world. Dylan and the warriors stood outside, but could hear them excitedly relate the strange celestial visitation they had had and its wondrous sounds and visions. Most importantly, they spoke of the announcement of a Saviour who had just been born in David's city: a Saviour who was Messiah and Master.

Chapter 51

Back in Nazareth, well over two years later, Ben, Mary's father was pottering around in the house. Outside, the streets were deserted; workshops were silent. Every sane person had stopped working and had fled indoors to escape the sun's scorching mid-afternoon heat. He surmised that most of the villagers were asleep, as was Abigail. She lay on cushions against the side wall, breathing softly. Seeing her there reminded Ben of the time Joseph and Mary had told them that she was pregnant. He smiled to himself as he remembered Abigail's reaction and how he himself had responded. Not a day had gone by since they had left for Bethlehem when he had not spent hours thinking of them and the baby that Mary had been carrying. He knew Abigail had done the same, for they spoke about it constantly.

He sighed.

Where were they now? After they had left Nazareth he and Abigail had presumed that they would be away for a few weeks, maybe two months at most, not two years! Six months earlier news came to the village of the terrible atrocities committed by Herod's soldiers massacring the baby boys in Bethlehem – the slaughter of the innocents. They were nearly driven out of their minds with worry for the baby and Joseph and Mary. What if Herod had caught them and thrown them in prison? What if he'd had them executed? What if he had got hold of the baby Jesus? What if...? A few times they seriously contemplated going down to Bethlehem to look for them, but decided it would be better to stay at home. If Joseph and Mary were to return with the baby while they were away they would not be able to forgive themselves. They decided to stay put. Even so, frustration at having to wait gnawed at them.

Ben opened the wooden shutters of the small back window of the house. The place needed some fresh air. It was stiflingly hot in there. He walked over to open the door to the house to get a through draft. An empty earthenware pitcher was leaning on its side against the door post. He bent down to pick it up and opened the door. He stood up and looked outside. Instantly, he let go of the pitcher. It fell on one of the few flagstones in the house and shattered noisily on the floor. Abigail stirred and opened her eyes slowly. She looked around, not knowing what had woken her. Then she saw her husband, standing stock still in the doorway. What was he doing?

'Ben!' she called.

No answer.

She leant on her elbow.

'Ben, what's the matter?'

Still no reaction.

Then, she felt as if she had been hit by a thunderbolt as she first heard the rush of hurried footsteps on the compacted soil outside and then saw her daughter Mary fling herself into her father's arms as they lovingly embraced each other.

Ben had dropped the pitcher and had been unable to move due to the relief and elation he felt at what he had seen a mere ten paces away from him. Mary, his lovely daughter, was smiling at him and beside her stood Joseph. Then he saw the toddler Jesus standing between them holding tight to his father's hand, looking shyly at him. If he could, he would also have seen five dishevelled warrior angels standing in a semi-circle behind them along with a short, rotund angel.

Mary had run up to him and they held each other tightly. Abigail, realising that her daughter had returned then shot up and raced towards them. She had never moved so quickly. Ben disengaged himself and let her put her arms around Mary.

The two women held each other for a while, crying tears of joy.

'Where have you been all this time?' asked Abigail.

'Egypt,' replied Mary.

'Egypt!?'

'It's a long story. We'll tell you later.'

Abigail noticed that Mary's face was aglow. She gave her daughter a knowing smile. Mary nodded and took hold of her mother's hand and placed it on her small bump.

'And this time, Joseph is the father,' she grinned.

Abigail's eyes sparkled.

'I always knew he had it in him.'

Both women giggled.

Ben was oblivious to their amusement. He stood rigid, with his back to them, unable to move. Breathing heavily, he slowly stepped forward, nervously aware that he was now approaching the God Child, the One all the prophets had foretold would come, and all Israel had eagerly awaited. It felt to him like he was approaching a lion. He nodded a welcome home to Joseph. He thought it odd when he glimpsed some gold jutting out of a sack slung over his back. He bent down and gazed in wonderment into Jesus's face, God's face. For well over two years he had prepared himself for this moment; recited what his first words would be to the Messiah. All of that went out the window, though. The seconds passed by. Lost in wonderment, he stared into the Saviour's eyes. Presently, he swallowed hard, and introduced himself.

'Hello. I'm your grandpa,' he said, his voice trembling. 'Would you like to come with me to meet your grandma?'

The five warrior angels watched intently. They had spoken of this moment many a time on their journey back from Egypt. They felt this was Ben's reward for taking Mary's side when Abigail had been so unbelieving when she had first told them that she was pregnant.

Dylan had tears in his eyes, as Ben tenderly took hold of the Messiah's hand. The toddler let go of His father's hand and let His grandfather lead him to the house. Ben did not think it odd that he was leading God by the hand, showing Him the way. As they approached the door of the house, Ben had an irresistible urge to sweep the young child up in his arms. Jesus felt a sudden, short rush of wind pass by His face and He giggled joyously as His grandfather swept Him up. He held Jesus tightly as he embraced Him. Then, he pulled his head back and looked at His beautiful olive face and bright, vibrant eyes. Wet tears of joy glistened down Ben's cheeks. Without saying a word, Jesus followed one trickle with His finger and then wiped it away with the palm of His hand.

Abigail, who had been standing patiently in front of the open door, could wait no longer.

'Ben,' she interrupted. 'Could you please share Him with me?'

Slowly, he turned to look at her.

'This is your grandma.'

Abigail held her hands out to hold Him and Jesus leant forward. She was loving that He was so trusting even though this was the first time they had met. She smiled, not quite believing that she was holding the Saviour of the world in her arms. Joseph joined them, and they all went into the house closing the door behind them, the occasion calling for some serious family time.

The angels stared at the closed door.

'That's that then,' remarked Ebin.

'Job done,' sighed Joram.

'I guess so,' agreed Gilchrist.

They were all silent for a while, until it was broken – as usual – by Caleb.

'You know, I'm always a little sad when we come to the end of a mission. I'm feeling it more so now – never felt sadder, in fact.'

'Me too,' agreed Ebin.

Cadman and Joram nodded their heads.

'I know,' said Gilchrist. 'We'll never do a job quite like this again.'

Dylan wiped his tears away.

'What happens now?' he asked.

'You go back to heaven for a well-earned break,' answered a gruff voice from behind them.

They spun round and saw Keenan and his unit of warrior angels.

'Keenan!' smiled Gilchrist, proffering his outstretched hand.

The warrior angels greeted each other warmly.

'Since when have you been here?' asked Gilchrist.

'Arrived last night, ready to take over.'

'And we're to go back to heaven?'

'Yeah. No 'angin' around either. God's waitin' for you.'

Gilchrist and his four warriors looked apprehensively at each other.

'We'd better get going then,' he said.

Gilchrist was in a magnanimous mood.

'Dylan! You can have the honour of leading the way.'

The other four warriors looked at their commander doubtfully.

'You *do* know the way?' Ebin asked Dylan.

'Don't you trust me?'

'You know I do,' he replied, not sounding very convincing.

'Right, I'll be flying at a searing pace,' Dylan announced, 'so try and keep up coz I won't be slowing down or stopping for anyone, especially you, G.'

Gilchrist looked at him in bemusement.

Keenan and his angels were intrigued as they watched him perform his hop, skip and jump before taking off.

'Is that *the* Dylan?' Keenan enquired, as he watched him swaying from side to side in the air, trying to gain speed.

'The one and only,' answered Cadman.

'Thank goodness,' added Caleb.

'He can't fight and he flies so slowly it seems he's in reverse,' said Ebin.

'But he can sing,' said Gilchrist, 'and for that we'll be eternally grateful to him.'

'Best get after him, then,' advised Joram. 'Don't want to be left behind.'

'Well, I'll be seeing you all,' said Gilchrist before he and the others took off to race after Dylan, mindful of his earlier warning.

Chapter 52

Once back in heaven they proceeded to Michael's Hall to meet with the archangel. He welcomed them warmly, but once Dylan left after being given permission to see Sabta, Gether a Dumah, he looked gravely at the five warriors.

'Right, then,' said Michael, curtly. 'De-brief, now, in the Eternal Throne Room.'

They had been expecting this: an audience with God probably to discuss the little matter of their indignation at the idea of Jesus being crucified. To say 'indignation' would be putting it mildly, for it verged on outright rebellion: open resistance to God, and Jesus's will. They had walked too close to the cliff edge. They followed Michael as he led them into God's presence.

To their surprise and dismay all the other angels who had worked with them to ensure Jesus's safe arrival in Bethlehem were there as well. Their spirits sank. This was going to be a public dressing down. The five nodded at Lorcan, Abida, Jonathon and Peleg as well as Candrell who had brought the mule and cart along the Jordan Valley. The group of thirty travellers camped outside the city and many other warrior angels were present, as were Jedah – still as gruff looking as ever – and Nidab and the other layabouts in his unit. All those who had contributed to the mission in Bethlehem were there, save for Sabteka, for he was already embedded somewhere in Samaria on a mission. Every one was radiant in his angelic finery, in stark contrast with Gilchrist and his warriors' rumpled and unkempt garb. All in all, they numbered over a hundred warrior angels.

Struck by the splendour and grandeur of the room and the cherubim encircled in flight around God, they approached nervously. Once in front of the throne, they knelt, bowing their heads, as did Michael. God smiled at how untidy the five looked. Only they, of all of heaven's angels would dream of coming into His presence looking so dirty and bedraggled. He liked them.

He ordered them to stand. Then He smiled at all the angels gathered before he addressed them.

'Archangel Michael has brought you all here for Me to thank you for all you did for My Son.'

They all stiffened their posture.

'Lorcan! Abida! Jonathon! Peleg! You spent nine months in the dirt and dust of Bethlehem. You will never know how important it was for the angel army to have your intelligence. I thank you.'

The four warriors bowed their heads. God turned to Jedah.

'Jedah! You and your angels' service was appreciated just as much. I know you got kicked a few times.'

Jedah flashed his Lord a brilliant, joyous smile.

'It's true we got a few kickings.'

He shrugged his shoulders before adding,

'It was nothing, my Lord. Me and the boys are 'ard.'

God chuckled quietly to himself. The other warriors rolled their eyes. They had heard this so many times before.

'You smiled, Jedah,' remarked Caleb in fake surprise.

Jedah turned towards him, swiftly wiping the smile away and looked at him straight faced. All the warriors present burst out laughing, including Caleb.

God then looked intently at Gilchrist and his warriors.

'As for you, my loyal and faithful warriors...'

That surprised them.

'... I asked a lot of you when you guarded Mary and My Son when He arrived on earth, but I must say...'

Ebin and Caleb gulped. 'Here we go,' they thought.

'... I was very pleased with how you carried out your orders. Things went very well, and I have you to thank for that.'

All five were a little baffled. They looked at Michael. God must have known what had happened. He knew everything. Why wasn't He admonishing them, upbraiding them for their act of defiance? Gilchrist thought that he had to clear the air, for his own peace of mind, as well as his comrades'. He had to say something, even if it had to be said in front of the other warriors. He took a deep breath.

'My Lord, I'm sure I speak for the five of us, but there's one thing we don't understand.'

'What don't you understand?' asked God.

'Well...' Gilchrist faltered.

He looked at the other four. They could feel his awkwardness. All five had had many a conversation during their sojourn to Egypt, foreseeing this very moment when they had to face God to account for their near rebellion.

'What happened in Bethlehem.'

'What happened there?' asked God calmly.

'When we stood up to Michael, and said we wouldn't allow Jesus to go to the cross,' he replied. Then, lowering his head, he whispered, 'What we did was bordering on open rebellion.'

The other four warriors bowed their heads. All warriors present were stunned into silence. They hadn't heard anything of this. They looked at each other. Later on, they swore they could hear the stars in the cosmos sparkle, like thin sprigs of wood breaking, or the early morning frost, crunching under foot.

Presently, God spoke.

'Gilchrist! Joram! Cadman! Ebin! Caleb! Lift up your heads. I told you I couldn't have been happier with the way you accomplished that particular assignment I entrusted you with. What you did, when you stood up to Michael in all your angelic glory, showed me that what I had given you to do – to guard my only begotten Son – you took very seriously. It was misguided, but it also showed your great love for Him.' His voice registered a trace of sorrow as he added, 'He has to die: there is no other way.'

'So, everything's right between us?' ventured Caleb, trying hard to suppress an elated smile that was beginning to spread all over his face.

'There wasn't, and never has been, anything wrong between us.'

All five slapped each other – hard – on the back, grabbing each other's shoulders, shaking them vigorously and laughing uncontrollably. God laughed out loud with them and Michael joined in as well, as did the other warriors.

As the laughter died down, God looked at the five in earnest.

'Furthermore, let it be known that you aren't, and never have been a ragtag bag of inconsequential warrior angels.'

Their Lord let the truth of what he had just said seep into them. Then He announced,

'Michael!'

The archangel looked at the five warrior angels.

'Come with me. I need to speak to you, in private.'

They all bowed in adoration of their Lord and then left.

Once outside the Throne Room, Gilchrist asked Michael,

'Where are we going?'

'You'll see.'

They dutifully followed Michael, not knowing where he was taking them. Ebin was the first to realise where they were headed.

'He's taking us to the rehearsal room,' he whispered to Caleb.

'The rehearsal room? Why?'

'You know why.'

'No.'

'An audition for you to join the choir.'

Caleb looked at him.

'This is your big chance,' added Ebin.

'Don't be so dull!'

'They may even give you a harp.'

'What, with these sausage fingers?' responded Caleb, holding them up.

'You said you fancied joining the choir.'

Caleb was starting to get a little concerned.

'No way will Axa want me in the choir. Anyway, what would you do without me?'

'The possibilities are endless,' answered Ebin wistfully.

'Be quiet,' Caleb said derisively.

Just as Ebin had surmised Michael led them into the rehearsal room, but not to any kind of audition. He took them on to the stage. A powerful white light shone on them rendering the rest of the room completely dark.

'Why have you brought us here, Michael?' asked Joram.

'Yeah, we can sing, but nothing like the choir,' added Caleb.

Ebin stared at him. The archangel looked at them in earnest.

'God has one more task for you and knowing you all as I do, it will be the most irksome one you've ever undertaken.'

All five looked at each other expectantly. What did Michael have in store for them? Whatever it was, they were ready to rise to the challenge.

'And what exactly is this mission?' asked Gilchrist.

'I don't really know how to put this. It's all a bit awkward.'

'Michael, tell us,' pleaded Ebin.

The archangel breathed heavily and looked at them in all seriousness. The warrior angels had not seen him like this before.

'You'll all have to take credit,' he said.

'Credit?' asked Joram.

'Credit for what?' asked Cadman, narrowing his eyes.

'Credit and thanks for what you did for our Lord.'

Whilst still looking at them intently, in a loud voice that resonated through all of heaven, he proclaimed,

'Warriors! Bear arms!'

At that, the whole room was bathed in a blazing light making visible a multitude of warrior angels standing shoulder to shoulder, in front of them. As one, they unsheathed their swords, held them high above their heads, and loudly stamped the floor, sounding like a sharp thunderclap. All five jumped backwards from the shock, their hands instinctively straying towards their swords. Then, there was silence. The warriors were honouring them, making plain their admiration for diligently and faithfully taking care of Mary, thereby ensuring Jesus's safety. The five comrades froze. For a few seconds they stared in wonderment, not quite believing that this great Angel Army was paying them respect. Those angels who had been present in the Eternal Throne Room barely minutes earlier were also there. Jedah, holding his sword higher than most, winked at Caleb.

Then, the Angel Choir and messenger angels suddenly appeared. Deafening applause, like a raging torrent, filled the space, as the huge throng loudly and passionately made plain their admiration. Thanks to Dylan, who had already received a joyous welcome when he had met up with Axa and the Angel Choir, word had spread about how they had confronted Antonin and his demons and the mesmeric way they had defeated them and sent them packing.

Dylan was now standing in front of the whole host, alternately clapping his hands gleefully and then rubbing them vigorously against the sides of his sumptuous stomach. His nostrils were wide open, the broadest smile imaginable across his lips whilst his rosy cheeks shone brightly. The ovation the five received went on and on. They looked around, starry eyed, amazed at the reception they were given. Gilchrist felt a little uncomfortable, if truth be told. With bashful eyes, he looked round and saw Mibsam and Meshek and other warrior captains. He satisfied himself with nodding his head at them and many of the other warrior angels who were assembled. Cadman, Joram and Ebin reflected their commander's discomfort, unused to standing in the limelight in front of their fellow angels. They were like fish out of water. Caleb, on the other hand, was relaxed, feeling quite at home, like a dolphin swooping and diving in the deep blue ocean. He basked in the adulation, lifting his hand to accept the acclamation, trying for all his worth, to tell everyone, by his facial reactions that it really was nothing.

Gilchrist and Dylan happened to catch each other's eye. The warrior angel, knowing that he had contributed as much as anyone to the success of the mission, motioned him to come and join them. Dylan shook his head. No way was he going to steal their limelight. Then he saw Gilchrist speak to Ebin.

The powerful warrior turned to look at the little angel and nodded his head. Dylan watched, as Ebin walked purposefully across the stage and after stepping off it came right up to him.

'Gilchrist wants you on stage, with us,' he said above the noise.

'There's no way you're getting me up... Whoa! Whoa!'

He didn't get to finish his protestations for Ebin, with only one hand, got a hold of him by his shoulder and carried him on to the stage.

'Don't! Don't! Put me down,' he pleaded, his short legs cycling frantically, trying in vain to find something solid to stand on rather than thin air.

'Sorry, Dylan, boss wants you up there.'

'You're not sorry, at all.'

Ebin lifted Dylan up, and looked him in the eye, their noses mere inches away from each other.

'You're right. I'm not!'

To the wild cheers of his fellow choristers, Ebin put Dylan to stand in front of Gilchrist as the other four warriors joined the applause given to him. He straightened his tunic now that Ebin had released him from his iron grip. He raised his eyes to look at Gilchrist. The warrior smiled at him before turning him round to face the gathered throng now chanting his name. Breathless, and not believing his own eyes, he saw the banks of angels before him. He saw Sabta, Gether and Dumah and even Axa, all shouting their admiration for him. The ovation seemed never ending.

Michael stepped forward, and spoke to the five warriors in a loud voice, doing his best to be heard amongst the clamour, the broadest smile imaginable on his face.

'I'm sorry, I couldn't resist winding you up just now.'

The applause continued for some time until eventually, it subsided. Michael then ordered the gathered angels to return to their various duties. In a matter of seconds, only he, Dylan and the five warriors were left. The six angels were elated, incredulous at the reception they had been given by their peers. Michael turned to look at them. The sadness in his eyes and sombre expression muted their euphoria in an instant. He breathed heavily.

'I meant what I said in Bethlehem,' he said, his voice faltering. 'You would all do me a great honour if you were to stand by me when our Lord is crucified.'

They solemnly nodded their heads and were all struck by the feeling that whereas they had completed their mission on earth, Jesus's had only just begun.

Acknowledgements

Much like Gilchrist, I have had a small but dependable band of people who have helped me prepare this book for publication. Ann Morgan worked unstintingly to improve the quality of writing and I am deeply indebted to her. She is a good and long-time friend – diolch i ti. Gareth Morgan designed the cover and Gruffydd Morgan did the necessaries on the graphic side of things – I am deeply indebted to these two, as well. Ken McDermott contributed immensely to the formatting. One of the advantages of such a project as this is meeting new friends who are so ready to help and give of their best. Such has been my experience with Ken. Neither can I fail to mention Sonia Davies, whose assistance was timely. Thanks go to Ffion and Anwen for their unique contributions. A clutch of family and friends read initial drafts and their thoughts and insights were invaluable. *The Bodyguards* would have been all the poorer without the contributions of every one of these fine people. Lastly, I would like to mention Rachel, my wife and our four daughters, Sioned, Lowri, Ffion and Anwen, for just being there.

Printed in Great Britain
by Amazon

31364908R00134